Lucy was halfway out the door when someone gripped her by the arm.

"Hang on a second," Dylan said, letting her go the moment she stopped moving. "I just want to be clear about something." His jaw was tense but his eyes were soft. "I don't know why you dislike me so much, but this isn't about us."

The way he said *us* made Lucy's stomach flip. There hadn't been an "us" in a very long time. There would never be an "us" again.

"I know. It's about Open Arms and Safe Haven. Two things I care about. Two things that I won't give up."

He leaned in close and seemed to be trying hard to keep his voice calm as he said, "Well, I want you to know that I'm not giving up, either. Maybe it's your turn to find out what it's like to lose something you care about."

Dear Reader,

It was bittersweet to write the final book in the Chicago Sisters series. When you write characters for three books, you become more attached than I thought possible. At the same time, it seemed perfect to go out with Lucy's story in *The Hardest Fight*.

Lucy is the oldest sister in the Everhart clan. She feels responsible for changing the world for the better. She also feels as if she has to do it quickly because her time on this earth is limited, more limited than most. Lucy has battled breast cancer once but can't stop thinking about the very real possibility she could get it again. That's why she shut the door on Dylan Hunt five years ago. He was the only man she ever loved, and Lucy was sure it was best for both of them to let him go without telling him she was sick.

Lucy reminds us that even the bravest people are still afraid. For Lucy, it's the fear that helps her keep fighting. But she needs to learn that there's no weakness in asking for help or letting others be there to support her. Lucy is excellent at being there for everyone else but not so good at letting people take care of her.

I love a happy ending, and as the Chicago Sisters series comes to an end, I hope you are glad you came along for the ride! Feel free to visit me on Facebook (AmyVastineAuthor), on Twitter (@vastine7), or on my website, amyvastine.com. I love hearing from you.

xoxo,

Amy Vastine

HEARTWARMING

The Hardest Fight

——

Amy Vastine

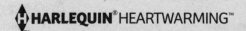

Recycling programs
for this product may
not exist in your area.

ISBN-13: 978-0-373-36731-3

The Hardest Fight

Copyright © 2015 by Amy Vastine

Printed in U.S.A.

Amy Vastine has been plotting stories in her head for as long as she can remember. An eternal optimist, she studied social work, hoping to teach others how to find their silver lining. Now she enjoys creating happily-ever-afters for all to read. Amy lives outside Chicago with her high-school sweetheart turned husband, three fun-loving children and their sweet but mischievous puppy. Visit her at amyvastine.com.

Books by Amy Vastine

Harlequin Heartwarming

The Weather Girl
The Better Man
The Best Laid Plans

To my uncle, Tom Kuhn.
Sometimes we don't know how strong we are
until we have no choice but to be strong.
Be strong and know we are here beside you.

CHAPTER ONE

"YOU'RE NOT GOING to believe this." Paige Clayton tossed an innocuous-looking envelope on top of the piles of paper on her cluttered desk. As the executive director of Open Arms Women's Advocacy Center, she had more on her plate than all the overpaid CEOs in the Windy City.

An unwelcomed feeling of dread hit Lucy Everhart as she reached for the letter.

"We've had an anonymous donor offer to pay all our bills and pledge an extra million dollars to our cause?" She knew better, but a girl could dream. As Paige's second in command, Lucy wore many hats. Her official title was Director of Legal Affairs, but Lucy also worked as one of the counselors at Safe Haven, Open Arms's temporary shelter for women and their children. She gave much of her time to outreach and fund-raising as well, which was most likely why Paige had called her in today.

Paige let out a heavy sigh. "I wish."

Times were tough, and Open Arms was suffering the consequences of the country's economic downturn. Government funding had been cut drastically over the past couple of years, and private donations were at their lowest in the center's history. Less money came in while more women knocked down the door. It wasn't surprising that abuse increased as a result of rising unemployment rates. Money troubles triggered tempers like nothing else.

Lucy slid the letter out of the envelope. It didn't take long for her face to flush red with anger. "Are they serious?"

"These people want to meet to discuss our 'bottom line.'"

This was all part of a conspiracy to run Open Arms out of the up-and-coming Logan Square neighborhood, where Safe Haven was located. The gentrification of that area had pushed out many who had lived there. Older places were being torn down in favor of fancy new condominiums and expensive single family homes. The new neighbors weren't happy about having a women's shelter on their block. Someone had bent the ear of a certain alderman; Lucy was sure of it.

Two months ago, the City of Chicago cut its funding to Open Arms. That money had been going to pay the mortgage on the seven-bedroom house they had acquired before the neighborhood had become such a hot spot. Lucy had projected that they'd have to give up the house or make some drastic cuts elsewhere if they didn't get more money soon.

"We can convince the board that we'll be able to cover the mortgage through the winter for sure. We'll need to get creative around March." Lucy began to pace. She thought better—clearer—when she was on the move. "We'll promote the heck out of this year's Hope and Healing fund-raiser."

"We know what to expect from the Hope and Healing fund-raiser. It won't be enough," Paige lamented.

"We'll come up with ways to make it bigger and better. Plus, the holidays always bring in lots of donations. People feel the most charitable between Thanksgiving and Christmas."

"Most of those donations aren't monetary. We get blankets and shampoo. People clean out their closets and give us their clothes and toys."

"We won't let anyone take what's ours." Lucy threw the letter back on Paige's desk.

"They don't want to take it. They want to *buy* it." Paige held her head in her hands.

"Maybe we call an appraiser and see what the house is worth."

"Don't even go there," Lucy warned. "We are not going to think the worst before we even attempt to fight. Let's meet with the board, light a fire under them to appeal to their connections and find donations. I'm not giving up. If there's one thing I know how to do, it's fight to win."

When Lucy took up a cause, she did so with the intention of seeing it through. She had shut down puppy mills and rallied to give workers their fair pay. She'd helped clean up neighborhoods and build playgrounds.

Life was short. People had a limited amount of time on the planet. Their objective should be to leave the world a better place than they found it. Lucy worried she had less time than most, so she dedicated her time and energy to any cause she found worthwhile. Open Arms was her favorite. She wasn't going to let it fail.

"You're right," Paige said, sitting up and squaring her shoulders. She tucked her black, pin-straight hair behind her ears. In her midfifties, Paige resembled Isabella Rossellini with her dark hair and hazel eyes. She was dedicated to Open Arms, forgoing any kind of personal life. Lucy knew she wouldn't go down without a fight. "That's why I called you. You're my rock."

Lucy smiled. Her sisters, Kendall and Emma, referred to her as that, as well. Whenever they were on the verge of some sort of emotional breakdown, it was Lucy's clear head they sought out.

A knock on the door interrupted them. Hannah, Paige's assistant, poked her head in. "I've got a woman here who needs to speak to someone in our legal department."

It really wasn't much of a department. Lucy was the only staff member with a law degree. She was the one who would help women obtain orders of protection or act as a legal advocate when needed.

"We're going to figure this out," she said to Paige before following Hannah out. "I promise."

"I know better than to argue with you. You always win."

Lucy winked. "Exactly."

A woman fidgeted in the chair outside Paige's office. Her designer clothes weren't part of the usual wardrobe of an Open Arms's client. Wealth didn't make anyone immune from abuse, but it could keep some women from accepting aid. The woman sported rings on several fingers, except the ring finger on her left hand. That one was empty, and the woman kept staring at it as if something was missing. Her face lifted at the sound of Paige's opening door.

Lucy recognized her as soon as their eyes met. Nora had been here a few months back, spent no more than a week at Safe Haven before disappearing. The angry red mark on her cheek spoke volumes about where she'd been since she left.

"Nora, right?"

Nora's gaze fell to her feet, as if she was ashamed of being recognized. "I'm really sorry to bother you."

"You're not bothering me. Come on, let's go talk in my office." Lucy often amazed herself with how calm she could sound at moments like this, even though all she wanted to do was find the man who had put his hands on this woman and give him a taste of his own medicine.

Lucy's office was really more like a glorified closet with one small window that provided an excellent view of a parking lot. The cramped space left little room for more than a desk and two chairs, but it had a door and provided them with some needed privacy. She invited Nora to sit and took her own seat behind the desk. Unlike Paige, Lucy had an almost obsessive need to keep her things orderly.

"As sorry as I am that you've found yourself in need of our assistance, I'm happy you're allowing us to be here for you. How can I help?"

Nora bit her bottom lip and lifted her purse into her lap. "I'm not sure anyone can help me." She began to dig through the seemingly bottomless bag. "I wasn't going to come, but there was nowhere else to go."

"I hear that a lot, actually." Most of the women who came to Open Arms had a million reasons why they shouldn't be there. They had lived with the shame and the fear so long, it prevented them from believing they could escape. "I'm more helpful than people think."

The woman set a manila folder on Lucy's desk. "I'm pretty sure my husband has something in these files that can get me in trouble, but I don't know what it is."

Lucy often helped women obtain an order of protection or explained the confusing language lawyers and courts loved to throw at the layman. This was the first time someone had come to her about something a bit more complicated.

The folder was filled with bank statements, spreadsheets, invoices and other financial documents. As Lucy perused the paperwork, Nora told her story. She and her husband had met at work when she was hired as his personal assistant seven years ago. He had climbed the corporate ladder quickly. The more money he made, the bigger his ego—and temper—grew. They had still just been dating the first time he hit her, but she'd believed him when he remorsefully pleaded for her forgiveness and promised it would never happen again.

He had lied.

Instead of breaking things off, Nora had believed she could change Wade by proving her love and married him six months into their relationship. The only one who changed, however, was Nora. Wade quickly had her cut ties with everyone in her life. She'd been "encouraged" to stop talking to her parents, her brother and her friends. Wade had told her they didn't care about her the way he did, weren't responsible for her the way he was.

As she became more isolated, he became more controlling. He picked out all her clothes, told her when to get her hair cut, had rules about how she should clean the house. When she didn't comply, she was punished. If he left marks, he made her stay home, and since he was her boss, no one questioned it.

Wade soon left his job to start his own wealth management corporation with a couple of other guys, taking Nora with him. It had been his way of removing all her social connections outside of him.

Alone and unable to meet her husband's unreasonable standards, Nora had considered several means of escape. Some were more desperate than others. There was no telling what she would have done if she hadn't seen a flyer for Open Arms tacked on a bulletin board at the coffee shop where she bought Wade's morning latte.

"I'm grateful for everything Open Arms did for me, but when I left him the first time, he sent me a warning via my mother. He said if I didn't come home, he would have no choice but to tell the world about what I had done. I hadn't done anything, but that didn't mean he had nothing to tell. Wade doesn't make idle threats."

"I see you have several accounts in your name—that was smart," Lucy said, paging through the other files. It would take time to make sense of all this.

"I thought about opening up an account a couple of years ago. I figured if I ever wanted to leave, I was going to need some cash. The only problem was Wade watched every penny and nickel I spent—my checks from work were deposited directly into our joint account. There was no way for me to funnel money into anything."

Lucy was confused. The statements in the folder were for three separate bank accounts, all in Nora's name. "You didn't open these?"

Nora shook her head. "I came across all that by accident. He was hiding it in a drawer in his office at home." She pulled out a flash drive. "This, too. I don't know what's on it, but I have a feeling it's all connected."

"You need a lawyer." Lucy had heard some crazy things working here, but this was the wildest of them all.

"That's why I'm here. You're a lawyer, right?"

"Yes, but—"

"I have no credit cards, no access to the money in our joint account, nothing. All I have is this." She pulled out an envelope with several hundred-dollar bills in it. "I pawned my wedding ring this morning. You can have it all if you'll help me."

Lucy knew better than to take this case. It had trouble written all over it. Yet, if there was one thing Lucy couldn't resist, it was putting someone in their place.

"That's your money. My services are free."

Nora sighed with relief. "Thank you." Her teeth dug into her bottom lip again. "One more thing—he's going to kill me when he finds out I took all of these files."

"Not if I can help it," Lucy said with a sure smile. She wasn't afraid of anyone.

PAIGE HAD SET UP a meeting with the board a few days later, and with Lucy's help she'd convinced them to hold off on accepting any offers before they put forth their best efforts to save Safe Haven. However, the board also thought it was important to meet with the prospective buyers to hear them out, at least.

Lucy had appealed to her two allies on the board. They seemed to be in agreement with her about the necessity of keeping possession of both the shelter house in Logan Square and the office space in Lincoln Park. They promised to make some calls and find some money. There were two other board members who were less opposed to selling the house. Their contacts were tapped out. The fifth and deciding member always voted however Paige wanted her to vote. She trusted Paige's judgment unequivocally.

In order to prove to Paige that Safe Haven

could be saved, Lucy had spent countless hours during the week brainstorming ways to raise the money to keep up with the payments. She had even enlisted the help of her sisters. Emma came up with the idea of having a live auction at the fund-raiser this year in addition to the small silent one they usually did. Kendall agreed to donate her time and talents to the cause.

Lucy was confident they could find a way to keep things going through the new year. That was why she wore an easy smile the morning of the meeting with the developers. They were going to show these people that the women who spent time in Safe Haven had been pushed around enough; they certainly weren't going to be pushed out of a neighborhood that provided them with much-needed security.

"You look like you don't have a care in the world. How do you do that?" Paige asked, appearing quite the opposite. Her hair was slipping out of its barrette and the worry lines on her forehead seemed almost permanent.

"They can offer us any amount they want. The board will side with us."

"What if it's a lot of money?" Paige wrung her hands as she paced around the reception area of Open Arms.

"We don't need their money."

Paige nodded and repeated Lucy's words a bit less confidently. "We don't need their money."

The front door to the office opened and a parade of people waltzed in. Lucy hadn't expected the buyer to bring an army. Perhaps they really were at war. She put on her game face until the last man stepped over the threshold. Her breath caught and her face fell. She hadn't seen him since she'd told him to stay away from her almost five years ago.

Dylan Hunt had always been a golden boy. Blond hair, blue eyes, broad shoulders and a brilliant mind. He had also broken Lucy's heart. It didn't matter that she was the one who'd ended the relationship. He hadn't fought for her, hadn't cared enough to ask why. She'd been so easy to let go of, he had done it without a second thought.

"Ms. Clayton?" The only woman in the developer's group approached Paige first. She was all glamour and gold. She wore her wealth like a shield, clearly separating herself from the underclass.

Paige ushered them into the conference room, where the board members were already waiting. At the same time, Lucy wrestled with the emotions threatening to destroy her nerves of steel. Her skin prickled with each step Dylan took in her direction. All the memories came rushing back. The warmth of his hand against her cheek, the smell of his skin after a shower, the sound of his heart when she rested her head against his chest.

His gaze was fixed on her, locking her in place. Dylan was ice-cold. He had that fake smile plastered on his face, the one that even he used to hate. He stopped in front of her and sank his hands into his pockets.

"Lucy Everhart, what a surprise to see you here." There was no way he was as surprised to see her as she was him. If he was working for this buyer, he had done his homework on Open Arms and would have known the part she played.

Her heart pounded so hard the sound of it seemed to echo off the walls. If Lucy believed in things like fate and karma, she might have wondered what she had done to deserve this kind of punishment, but she was too rational for that. Bad things happened all the time; it was just the way the world worked. Except when bad things happened to Lucy, they often bordered on life-threatening.

"You're as beautiful as ever," he said. He

flashed her another one of his award-winning smiles, complete with the dimple on his right cheek. Her looks had been what drew him to her the first time they'd met, and they were probably why he'd stayed with her for so long. That was the only reason Lucy could come up with for why he had walked away so easily. He had only cared about the wrapping, not the gift she had inside.

If he only knew how flawed she really was, he wouldn't be so generous with his compliments today. Lucy was damaged goods, someone who wasn't perfect enough to be Dylan Hunt's significant other.

"You see the beauty, but you forget about the beast," Lucy said, finally finding her voice. "Welcome to my jungle." She gestured for him to lead the way into the conference room.

Dylan leaned forward, his lips so close she almost put her fingers on them so her own mouth wouldn't be tempted. "You're wrong, Lulu. That's the part of you I'll never forget."

CHAPTER TWO

DYLAN HAD PRACTICED what he was going to say when he laid eyes on Lucy Everhart for the first time in almost five years, but nothing came out the way he had planned. As much as he wanted to play it cool and not give away the scar he still had on his heart, she provoked the truth right out of him. He'd always loved her tenacity, but today he could have done without it.

"I appreciate you agreeing to meet with us." Elizabeth Kerrington was the epitome of a wolf in sheep's clothing. She dialed up her perfect manners and lovely pleasantries right before she went in for the kill. Today's hunt was for the piece of prime real estate that Open Arms owned in Logan Square. Elizabeth's company had already purchased the two properties on either side of it and all she needed to begin building her luxury condominiums was Safe Haven.

"I didn't realize you would be bringing so

many people with you." The executive director of Open Arms was more than rattled. She called out to her assistant to bring some extra chairs before turning and accidentally knocking a stack of papers off the table. Dylan was concerned she might have a nervous breakdown at any moment.

Elizabeth had already taken a seat. "No worries, Ms. Clayton. My associates can stand if need be. I don't want to take up too much of your time. I'm sure there's plenty of do-gooding for you to get back to."

Lucy arched a brow and crossed her arms over her chest. "Us do-gooders are part of an impressive network. We called up all the local superheroes and asked them to watch the streets for us while we conducted our business with you, Mrs. Kerrington."

Elizabeth scowled while Dylan restrained himself from chuckling. Lucy was sassy as ever. The assistant dragged in a couple of chairs and apologized as she shoved them into the already cramped space.

"Let's just get right to it, shall we?" Elizabeth asked.

"Let's," Lucy answered, taking a seat on Ms. Clayton's side of the table.

"Obviously, we're interested in purchasing

the property you own on Western," Elizabeth said with a wave of her hand.

Lucy's expression gave nothing away, but her counterpart swallowed hard and began to fidget. Ms. Clayton was the key to the success of this deal. Dylan had done his research. The board was split. There was one vote to win over and that member would be swayed only by the executive director.

She was nervous, possibly anxious to get to the bottom line. How much was Prime Developments willing to pay? Open Arms couldn't deny they needed the money. There were signs of financial trouble everywhere Dylan looked. From the broken door when they walked in, to the duct tape holding one of the chairs together, it was clear there weren't extra funds for the little things.

"Are you making an offer?" Lucy asked.

As Prime's legal counsel, Dylan had been invited to this meeting to help with negotiations. He saw it as a chance to show off his ability to read people. It was a talent, really. A skill that came in very handy when interviewing witnesses or figuring out how hard to push someone with relevant information. Not only could Dylan tell when someone was lying, his powers of observation allowed him to appear as if he was able to read their minds. It was the same tactic that so-called psychics used to convince people they were talking to their dead relatives. These tricks had served him well in his career and helped him dodge a few bullets in his personal life. That girlfriend in college who was cheating on him only got to cheat once before she wasn't his girlfriend anymore.

Dylan could read everyone. Everyone except for Lucy. The woman was a complete mystery. He never knew what was going on in that pretty head of hers, which was what had drawn him to her in the first place. Her mind was a fascinating place when she let him in. Lucy was smarter than most people assumed.

Lucy wasn't going to stop him from making a good impression. If Dylan could help Prime get this property, he would prove himself to everyone at his firm, especially his boss, who just happened to be his mother. Their familial relation didn't give him any advantage in pleasing her. Results were all that mattered to Clarissa Stevens-Hunt. So, whatever it was that Lucy thought, it wouldn't keep the board from taking Prime's offer if Dylan had anything to say about it.

Elizabeth held out her manicured hand,

waiting for Dylan to place the offer he had drafted in it. "I think you will find our offer more than generous."

Dylan wouldn't call it generous. It wasn't nearly what the property was worth, but it was surely enough to entice a needy organization such as this one. He watched as Elizabeth's assistant slid copies of the offer across the table. Ms. Clayton passed hers off to Lucy without even looking at it. Obviously, it was too tempting. Lucy was the one who would do the negotiating, of course, because she was the tough one.

She had been Dylan's biggest competition in law school. He had thought she hated him when they met. Turned out she had been more interested than she'd let on. They had dated the last year of law school and for two years after that. Dylan had believed she was the One, and everything she had said and done told him she felt the same way. That was how he had learned about the tiny glitch in his superpower. She had broken his heart without any notice. Actually, she'd ripped it out, stomped on it and driven over it with a steamroller just to be sure she'd done the job thoroughly. She was tough, all right.

"Generous?" Lucy questioned with a tilt of

her head after reading the offer. "I'm guessing you assumed we were too busy 'do-gooding' to have done our homework." She folded the piece of paper in half and set it in front of her. Ms. Clayton glanced at it but didn't pick it up. "The members of the board are educated businesswomen. This is insulting."

Elizabeth uncrossed and recrossed her legs. She ran her tongue over her teeth, a sure sign that Lucy had struck a nerve. She took a breath before replying. "We aren't looking to offend anyone. What would it take to get your interest?"

"We aren't interested in selling," Lucy answered, but Ms. Clayton bit her lip. The director clearly wasn't as sure as the legal advisor.

"Well, not all of us are interested," Tanya Robbards, one of the board members, corrected. *"Yet."*

It was Dylan's turn to negotiate. "We aren't here pretending we don't know the predicament Open Arms has found itself in. Surely, you understand that if we wanted, we could wait a few months until the house goes into foreclosure. What we're offering you—" he pointed at the folded paper, hoping Ms. Clayton would simply look at it "—is a chance to continue to do your work in this city."

"We don't need your money to continue our

work," Lucy cut in. The cold, level gaze she gave him did nothing to cool the heat that had crept up his neck. He hated that she could get under his skin so easily yet be so unaffected herself.

"You don't, or Open Arms doesn't?" he challenged. "If you foreclose on the house, you gain nothing. If you sell, you have enough equity to keep the rest of the organization running smoothly." He sought to prey on Ms. Clayton's fears. "You wouldn't have to worry about losing this place, as well. So many women and children would still benefit from what you do."

Ms. Clayton's gaze drifted back down to the paper and the offer she hadn't even seen yet. Her fingers tightened around the arms of her chair. She needed one more tiny push. He gave Elizabeth the sign she had been waiting for, and she went for Ms. Clayton's jugular.

"Add another five thousand to that number," Elizabeth said. "I'm sure that will help Open Arms purchase a new house in another neighborhood."

With wide eyes, Ms. Clayton glanced over at Lucy. Her lip had to be bleeding given how hard she was biting it. She was just about to break and glance at the number when Lucy stood up, snatched the paper off the table and crumpled it up.

"We appreciate that you're so concerned about keeping Open Arms's doors open. Perhaps you'll consider donating. We accept all major credit cards and love it when corporations match an employee's gift." She opened the door and waited for them to leave the room.

"I suggest you carefully consider what we're offering," Elizabeth warned.

"Safe Haven is very important to this agency," Sharon Langston, another board member, replied. "We'll be in touch if we're interested."

"We promise," Lucy added.

"Ah, you say that, but do you really mean it?" Dylan asked. She had made promises to him in the past, like she would love him forever and wanted to change the world with him. She hadn't meant *that*, now had she?

She didn't answer. Her expression was pained. Again, he couldn't tell what that meant. Did she realize how badly she had hurt him five years ago? Did she feel any remorse?

"Well, you have thirty days," Elizabeth said. "After that, the offer will be off the table for good. Then, like Mr. Hunt explained, we will simply wait for it to foreclose."

Elizabeth and her team all stood and exited

the office. Lucy seemed to be holding her breath as Dylan approached her. He, on the other hand, took her all in. She still smelled like lilacs. The lilac bushes that edged the front gate of his greystone always made him think of her in the springtime.

"Say hello to your family for me," he said as he walked by. The Everharts were some of the nicest people Dylan had ever met. The first time Lucy had invited him to spend Thanksgiving at their house, he had wanted to be adopted by them. Her dad was so down-to-earth and her mom made everyone feel at home under her roof. Dylan had prayed for her every day when they found out Maureen had been diagnosed with breast cancer.

Even though Lucy had been so brave, she had broken down more than once in his arms over the possibility of losing her mom. He had been so grateful she had survived. When Lucy left him, he had mourned not only the loss of her but of the whole Everhart family.

Lucy didn't respond to his request. She probably wouldn't do as he asked. She didn't care about him or his feelings. She never had.

BACK AT THE OFFICE, Dylan did everything he could to avoid his mother. Open Arms hadn't signed on the dotted line and Elizabeth was less than pleased. That meant the same would go for his mother.

Clarissa Stevens-Hunt was one of Chicago's top corporate lawyers. Stevens and Ellis had been the city's most prestigious law firm since Dylan's great-grandfather founded it back in 1924 with his partner, Roger Ellis. Great-grandpa Stevens passed it on to his son, who passed it on to his daughter, who couldn't wait to bring her son into the fold.

Since the day Dylan was born, it was his destiny to work at Stevens and Ellis whether that was what he wanted or not. Clarissa had never allowed Dylan to consider any other possibilities. The only thing he was supposed to worry about was meeting her high expectations. He'd spent the past seven years trying to prove to everyone, especially his mother, that he deserved his position at the firm and wasn't just there because of his heritage.

He stared at the stack of case files on his desk. This was Dylan's reality—a lifetime of business law, white-collar criminal defense and sometimes a little real estate. There had been a time when he thought he might actually do something worthwhile, maybe convince his mother to let him dabble in some environmental law so he could advise corporate clients on sustainability issues and green standards. He had to get in her good graces before he dared to approach her about it. Securing this deal for Prime was about the only thing that could do that.

Clarissa Stevens-Hunt was the exact opposite of someone like Maureen Everhart. Warm and fuzzy were not character traits anyone would use to describe his mother. Dylan rarely saw her while he was growing up. She worked day and night, weekends and holidays. The woman had a smartphone before anyone else in the world knew what a smartphone was. Her phone was the last thing she checked before she went to bed and the first thing she looked at when she woke up. She'd missed family events, birthdays, vacations, even Dylan's high school graduation. Her job was always the most important thing in her life, and that was how Dylan was supposed to think, too.

Only, Dylan had vowed he'd never put work above the people in his life. He was going to come home for dinner every night, ask his kids about their day, maybe even coach little league baseball. Dylan didn't have a family of his own; but today, he needed to get out of work by five if he was going to make it to his neighbor Jeremy's basketball game by six. Missing the game was not an option.

Jeremy was eight years old. His father had never been a part of his life and his mother's addiction had led her to relinquish her parental rights. His maternal grandparents had taken him in and raised him as their own since the boy was three. Eugene and Gwen lived below Dylan and had sought his legal advice when they were trying to take custody of Jeremy. A year later, Gwen had been diagnosed with ALS and was told she had only three years to live. She survived for two.

It was during those two years that Dylan had bonded with Jeremy. They each filled an empty spot in the other's life. Dylan had dreamed of having a family with Lucy. When she left him, that dream went with her. Being there for Jeremy while Eugene had been taking care of his wife had meant fewer hours at work and disappointing his mother, but it had been the most worthwhile period of Dylan's life.

"If anyone calls, I'm unavailable until tomorrow," Dylan told his assistant. He'd be up all night finishing some briefs, but seeing Jeremy play would be worth it.

"And if your mother calls?"

"My mother will call my cell if she wants to reach me, so you won't have to worry about that." *He* would have to worry about that, but Bridgette would be off the hook.

"How did your Prime meeting go?" Bridgette asked as Dylan shut down his computer.

Other than seeing the love of his life looking better than ever, it had gone the way he thought it would. Part of him had hoped Lucy would be a disheveled mess. The other part knew she would have thrived without him. She had definitely blossomed into a strong and independent woman.

"They didn't sign. No one wants to accept a loss, but they're smart women, they'll take the money and start over somewhere else, I'm sure."

Bridgette smiled. Her hair was a different shade of red than it had been the day before. She must have gotten it colored, but since she hadn't mentioned a hair appointment yesterday, Dylan knew not to say anything. She was one of those women who told people she had never seen a gray hair on her head.

"Well, if anyone could tell what they were thinking, it's you," she said, picking up his coffee cup from earlier this morning. She was always taking care of little things like that for him. "Have a good night and don't forget that tomorrow your eight-thirty got moved to seven-thirty and your eleven is now three-thirty."

He couldn't thank her enough for the reminder. Bridgette was excellent at her job. It often made him wonder if she had been assigned to him because his mother thought he needed someone like Bridgette or if he had worked hard enough to deserve her. Some people in the firm thought he was treated differently because he was the boss's son, but Dylan had never considered that a good thing. Being treated differently didn't always mean being treated *better*.

Dylan managed to make it out of the building and all the way home without crossing paths with his mother. By six o'clock, he was dressed in jeans and a T-shirt, sitting next to Eugene in the bleachers of Whitman Elementary's gymnasium.

Eugene leaned forward, his elbows on his knees. He was in his sixties and one of the gentlest souls to walk the earth. The man had been to hell and back, between losing his daughter to a world of drugs and his wife to disease, but somehow he'd maintained his positive spirit.

He was a true inspiration and Dylan's only real friend over the age of eight.

Eugene gave Jeremy a thumbs-up when the little boy scanned the crowd for his two biggest fans. With his hands cupped around his mouth, Dylan cheered loud enough for the entire gymnasium to hear. "Let's go, Big J!"

"He's nervous even though I told him all he had to do was have fun out there," Eugene said.

"He'll have fun once they get started."

Jeremy was a bit of an anxious kid. He could be shy around new people, but once he got to know somebody, his true personality would shine through. The other kids on his team were joking around during warm-ups while Jeremy and another boy passed the ball back and forth.

A man in a suit and tie entered the gym, eliciting the biggest smile from Jeremy's new friend. The guy climbed the bleachers and joined a woman holding a baby girl a couple of rows down from where Dylan and Eugene were sitting. He kissed the woman and promptly stole the infant away from her, planting more kisses on the chubby baby's cheeks. Dylan felt a tinge of jealousy at the sight of the happy family. As much as he wanted that life, the possibility of ever getting it seemed slim to none. There weren't many opportunities to date when he worked eighty hours a week, and no one he had dated held a candle to the woman he had wanted to be the mother of his children.

The buzzer sounded, cueing the teams to get ready to play. Jeremy gave them one more quick glance before paying closer attention to his coach's last words of advice. Dylan had never bothered to look in the stands when he was a kid. He knew no one would be there. His dad had been a trader at the Chicago Stock Exchange, while his mother billed her hundred hours a week for Stevens and Ellis. The nanny dropped Dylan off and picked him up but never stayed for the game. That was why he swore he'd do things differently when he had kids. Jeremy wasn't his but close enough.

"How's work going?" Eugene asked as the boys ran up and down the court, no one able to get the ball through the hoop.

"Same as always," Dylan replied. His phone rang and the caller ID told him it was his mother. He rejected the call and slipped the phone back into his pocket. If he didn't answer, she might think he was busy with something work-related.

Eugene chuckled. "That's what I get for mentioning work, right?"

"Yeah, knock that off."

"Maybe if I ask if you've met any pretty ladies lately, one will call you and ask you to dinner."

It was Dylan's turn to laugh. "I wish."

Jeremy got the ball under the basket, but instead of taking a shot, he passed it off. The other boy scored and everyone cheered. The family with the baby screamed the loudest.

"Good assist, Jer!" Dylan shouted.

"So, met any pretty ladies lately?" Eugene asked.

Dylan was about to answer when none other than Lucy Everhart slipped through the gym door. He pulled his baseball cap down to hide his face as she scanned the crowd.

His chest tightened and his mouth went dry. *What in the world was she doing here?*

CHAPTER THREE

LUCY WAS LATE for Simon's game and had no one to blame but herself. She'd spent the better part of the day talking Paige out of calling Mrs. Kerrington and taking her pathetic offer. Today's meeting had planted dangerous seeds in Paige's head and made all of the board members question if selling Safe Haven was the right choice or not.

The thought of Dylan and his sparkling blue eyes, pleading with Paige to think of all the good she could do with the money from the sale, was enough to make Lucy scream. As if he had any idea what it took to make a difference in the world working at Stevens and Ellis. Years ago, he had sworn he'd find a way to fight for those without a voice instead of selling his soul to his mother's affluent and avaricious clients, but it appeared he had done just that.

Kendall waved to get her sister's attention. Lucy smiled and began trudging up the bleachers. Kendall's husband, Max, bounced their daughter on his knee. The man was completely smitten. Five-month-old Darcy had her father wrapped around her little finger already. Kendall was in for trouble when that one got big enough to ask for things.

"Sorry I'm late," she said, taking the spot next to Max and holding out her hands for her turn with the baby.

"I just got here," he protested. Darcy loved new attention more than anything and lunged for her aunt, so Max reluctantly let her go.

The baby girl's screech was earsplitting. It was her way of saying hello. Lucy made a funny noise in return and Darcy giggled, showing off the two cute baby teeth in her mouth. Her adorable laugh always made Lucy smile. Kendall made amazing babies. The tiny, delusional part of Lucy's heart that wasn't completely convinced she didn't have a family in her future ached a bit more than usual.

"Simon scored a basket." Kendall reached across Max to give Darcy a toy. "Just before you walked in."

Of course he had. Keeping Safe Haven from going into foreclosure wasn't going to be easy, and every minute Lucy spent working was a minute she wouldn't get to spend with her family. Lucy's anger toward Prime Developments and Dylan Hunt resurged.

"Your little one dropped her toy," someone said behind her.

Max snatched up the elephant rattle and shook it in front of Darcy, much to her delight. Lucy tried to push the negativity she felt aside. She was here to watch Simon and enjoy her time with Kendall.

"Thanks," she said to the older gentleman behind them. The hair at his temples was gray and his beard was more white than brown. He gave her a nod and a gentle smile. Just as she was about to turn back around, Lucy made eye contact with the man sitting beside him and her temper flared. "Are you following me?"

Dylan sighed and readjusted the brim of his hat. "No, I'm not following you." He dared to sound indignant. "Are *you* following *me*?"

Lucy handed Darcy back to Max. She wasn't going to dignify his question with an answer. "What are you doing here, then?"

"I'm here to watch a basketball game. What are *you* doing here?"

She faced forward and tried to pretend he wasn't sitting back there. If she ignored him, it would be as if he didn't exist. Kendall made

Max switch seats so she could be next to Lucy. She hooked arms with her sister.

"Is that who I think it is?" Kendall whispered, glancing over her shoulder.

"Don't look at him," Lucy demanded. She wasn't surprised by her sister's uncertainty. Kendall had lived out east when Lucy and Dylan were together. "And don't let me look at him."

"Well, aren't you the queen of the cold shoulder? No one does it better than you, Lulu."

How dare he use that name not once, but twice, today. As much as she wanted to keep her cool, exhaustion was making it impossible. She swung her head around to find Dylan glaring back at her.

"I've had just about enough from you," she snapped.

"I'm sorry, but what exactly did I do that offended you so much?"

"Oh, like you didn't know I was going to be there today! Just like you probably knew I was going to be here tonight. No one does more research than the almighty Dylan Hunt."

His eyes narrowed into angry slits. "Hate to burst your self-absorbed bubble, but the world does not revolve around you. I had no idea you were going to be here."

"Oh, that's right. Your world revolves around your family's money and power." Lucy could feel her skin tingling with her own indignation. "I hope you know I'm not going to let the board sell Safe Haven today, tomorrow or ever. Whatever your big plan is, you can forget it because we're not interested. You can leave me alone now."

"I'm already done with you," he sneered. Those words stung more than she expected. "You don't really have a say. Your role at Open Arms doesn't give you the power to decide what you do with that house on Western. Your board will realize Prime is offering them an easy out. There was more than one person at that table today ready to accept our offer even before Elizabeth sweetened the deal. I could tell."

It burned her to know he was right. She hated that he could read people so well. Some of their fellow students in law school had actually believed he was psychic. Lucy knew better than to buy into that baloney. He was observant, that was all. Too observant.

"They'll never sell, and if by some miracle they do, it won't be to anyone associated with you. I'll make sure of that."

Kendall tugged on her arm. Hard. "Lucy, stop."

It was unclear how many times Kendall had already said that before it finally registered. The quarter had ended and the referee walked up the bleachers, stopping before he got to Lucy's row.

"I'm going to have to ask you both to leave. This isn't the place for whatever is going on between the two of you. You need to take it out of the gymnasium, please."

"You're kicking me out?" Lucy's embarrassment heated her cheeks.

"I'm asking you to leave the gym, yes." The ref glanced up at Dylan, as well.

"Fantastic," Dylan mumbled under his breath, which for some reason struck another nerve.

"Don't act like this is my fault. You're the stalker."

"Get over yourself," he said, rising to his feet and shaking hands with the man next to him. "Tell Jeremy I'm sorry I couldn't watch him play. I'll be at the next one—as long as we sit as far away from certain crazy people as possible."

Lucy huffed and grabbed her purse. "I'll be outside," she said to Kendall.

The referee followed them out, waiting until

the door closed before returning to the game. Lucy peered through the narrow window that offered her a partial view of the court. She could feel Dylan staring a hole in the back of her head.

"Don't think seeing you again was easy for me just because I knew it was coming," he said. His voice was soft, as it often sounded in her memory. "You left me, remember?"

She hadn't forgotten, although it was more like she had left him before he got the chance to leave her. He would have left. Eventually.

Lucy swallowed down the emotion lodged in her throat. Her feelings for him had never really gone away, and they demanded to be felt right now. There had been a vulnerable side to Dylan that made her protective of him. A side that longed to break free from his mother's expectations and demands. He had wanted to make a difference, to work beside Lucy as she made a difference, too. They were going to change the world…together.

She could deny it all she wanted, but part of her still loved the man who once climbed up onto the bar at their favorite restaurant and announced to everyone that he was madly in love with her. She still thought about the guy who had fallen asleep more times than she could count on her couch, surrounded by law books after a long night of studying.

Lucy searched for some courage and turned around, only to find the corridor empty. He was already gone. It shouldn't have been such a shock. She already knew that the man she had fallen in love with didn't exist anymore.

"I'M SORRY," LUCY mouthed to Kendall when they finally emerged from the gym after the game. Lucy had been able to see everything that happened on one end of the court but not the other. The final score was still a mystery.

Her younger sister gave her "the look," the one that said she forgave her but wasn't the least bit happy.

"So, how'd you do?" she asked Simon.

The smile on his face spoke a million words. "We won by four points!"

Lucy held up her hand for a high five and he didn't hold back. She shook her hand out to ease the sting. The kid was growing up too fast. Lucy could remember when he was as small as his baby sister. At eight, Simon was too heavy to carry and had feet that were almost as big as his mom's.

"I think that means I need to take you out for ice cream to celebrate."

"Yes!"

Max side-hugged Simon. "I have to head back to the restaurant, but you did awesome, buddy."

Kendall had lucked out in the kid and the husband department, at least the second time around. Max wasn't Simon's father, but no one would ever know by watching the two of them interact. When Simon's father died, so did the light inside of him. But then Max came into their lives, and he lit him back up and helped him shine even brighter than before.

As Kendall and Simon said goodbye to Max, Lucy watched as the older gentleman who had been sitting with Dylan walked by hand in hand with another kid on the team.

"Are you sure Dylan wasn't mad at me for not making a basket?" the boy asked the man.

"No, no, no! He would never be mad at you for that. He'll be at the next game, I promise."

The guilt was like a stab straight through the heart. Dylan really had been there to watch the game. Not only was she embarrassed for the attention she had drawn to herself, but now she had to live with the fact that she had made a little boy doubt himself.

"Can we go to the Triple C, Aunt Lulu?" Simon asked, grabbing Lucy's hand. Lulu was the name Simon had called her when he was just learning to talk. Dylan had thought it was cute, so he took to calling her Lulu, as well. The nickname always left her with mixed emotions.

She forced herself to smile for Simon's sake. "Where else would we go?"

The Chi-Town Chilly Cow was an Everhart family favorite. Lucy remembered going there as a kid and wanting to order everything. Her dad would only let them get a one-scoop cone, so she would order a different flavor every time they went. Now she could get whatever she wanted, but ice cream was not part of her diet. Given the studies on dairy, there was no way she was giving her body any more ammunition to do her in.

Lucy let Simon order the craziest sundae on the menu. Something with chunks of brownies and chocolate chip cookies in it, topped with gummy bears and more chocolate. The girl behind the counter began to ring it up, when Lucy stopped her.

"There should be a note back there saying Lucy Everhart gets free ice cream for life." Thanks to her idea that the Triple C go all organic, the owners had experienced an explosion in sales. They'd offered her a lifetime supply of ice cream as a thank-you. She rarely took advantage of the perk unless she was treating her favorite nephew.

"There is, but you're not Lucy Everhart," the girl said.

Lucy's forehead wrinkled. "I'm not?"

"No, you aren't. I've been working here for almost a year. Lucy Everhart comes in here all the time. She's a really tall brunette. Comes in with this supercute guy. I *know* Lucy Everhart."

"Emma," Lucy said with a growl.

Kendall nodded. "I told her it was going to catch up to her one of these days, but you know Emma. She thought she could get away with it forever."

Lucy pulled out her driver's license. "I am Lucy Everhart. The woman you've been giving free ice cream to is my sister. Do me a favor and add an extra note back there that warns your coworkers not to be fooled by tall brunette frauds."

The girl inspected the ID as if she was a bouncer at a college bar. She even tried to scratch the picture off to no avail. Once she finally agreed she'd been duped by the most conniving of the Everhart sisters, she gave Lucy Simon's sundae for free.

Simon and Kendall took turns devouring

the frozen treat while Lucy kept Darcy entertained. It didn't take those two more than a few minutes to put the whole thing in their bellies.

"So...Dylan Hunt," Kendall said, wiping her mouth with a napkin.

"Don't start."

"I don't remember him being so incredibly hot."

"Don't. Start." Lucy didn't want to think about how good-looking Dylan was or wasn't. Of course, he *was* incredibly hot, just as Kendall had said. He was the most attractive guy Lucy had ever dated.

"You got kicked out of my son's basketball game because you made a ridiculous scene. I get to start."

"Fine," Lucy huffed. "Dylan showed up at Open Arms today with his client—the developer that wants to buy the house we use as a shelter in Logan Square. I spent all day trying to convince Paige we don't have to sell yet."

"Yet? I thought that was why you were adding the auction to the fund-raiser."

Lucy wanted more than anyone to believe that was true. "Right. The fund-raiser should bring in a lot of money."

"Enough to pay off the house?" Kendall

asked. Her hopefulness was almost too much to bear.

"No, but enough to get us by until I come up with another plan." What that plan would be was beyond her.

"Things will work out the way they're supposed to. So, back to incredibly hot Dylan—is he married? Did he ask if you were married? What's he been doing the past five years?"

Kendall was obviously trying to punish her for embarrassing them all at the game today. This was some cruel payback. "I don't know, no and I don't care. There really is nothing to tell. He's probably trying to think of a plan to convince Paige to beg the board to sell. He'll fail. He'll move on. I'll never see him again."

"And I thought I'd never have to see Max once I finished remodeling Sato's," Kendall reminded her. "And look how that turned out."

"Fine, never say never. But it doesn't matter."

"Really?" Kendall could always tell when Lucy was hiding something.

"Really." Even if Dylan wasn't working for the enemy, she couldn't let herself forget that she'd sent him away and he'd gone willingly. "Running into him twice in one day? Maybe the universe is trying to tell you something,"

Kendall said although she knew Lucy didn't believe in that kind of stuff.

"The universe doesn't communicate with anyone."

Kendall threw up her hands. "I don't know what happened five years ago. You didn't want to talk about it then, and I'm sure I won't get it out of you now. But he was the only guy I ever thought had a real chance with you. You two seemed so perfect together."

Lucy wasn't perfect for anyone. She had been guilted into this conversation, and now it was over. Lucy didn't let any man have a chance with her because what was the point? She was a ticking time bomb.

Cancer was always lurking around the corner. It was sinister, biding its time, waiting for Lucy to drop her guard and believe she was safe from its clutches. She'd beaten it once, but how long would it really be before it put her to the test again? She certainly wasn't going to ask someone to commit to her when their lives might have very different expiration dates.

CHAPTER FOUR

DYLAN DROVE HOME and sulked on his couch for a few minutes before the urge to do something with his hands overtook him. Fixing and fiddling with things were the best stress relievers. Dylan had installed all the crown molding in his apartment with Eugene's help. A former carpenter, Eugene often spent hours teaching Dylan how to do things right the first time. Together, they had refurbished the fireplace in Dylan's place and updated all the trim work in Eugene's.

The building they lived in was an older greystone that was split into two residences. Eugene had the downstairs two-bedroom unit and Dylan owned the two-story loft above it. Moving here had been the best decision he'd made after Lucy broke up with him. He could have easily afforded a fancy rehab in the neighborhood, with all the modern conveniences, but Dylan found he enjoyed taking something that was a little rough around the edges and sprucing it up on his own.

His latest project was the kitchen. Since he rarely cooked, it wasn't a big deal for him to take his time updating it. Dylan had stained the cabinets a dark, warm gray. With the stainless steel appliances and marble backsplash he'd picked out, it was going to be ultrastylish. He needed Eugene's help to hang the uppers, but he figured he could put the door pulls on the lower cabinets tonight.

It was a mindless task, which wasn't good. It allowed his thoughts to wander back to Lucy. The woman had a way of making him want to run away and never leave her side at the same time. In the end, he had decided that if she didn't want him around, he wasn't going to force someone to care about him.

He had no idea where he had gone wrong with Lucy and often wondered what his life would have been like if they had stayed together. Would they be married right now? Would they have kids? Would they be happy, or would she be miserable?

Dylan wasn't sure he could make her happy. It was too difficult to tell how she really felt about anything. Whenever he thought he had her figured out, she made sure he knew he'd been wrong. He still couldn't believe he had misread her feelings for him so completely. He had never hidden his feelings from her. He loved her so much he worried he would love her forever. Unrequited love was a horrible cross to bear.

His phone rang. It was his mother. He couldn't avoid her at this time of night. In her opinion, if he was working this late, it was work that could be interrupted by a call.

"Dylan Hunt," he answered as if he didn't know it was her.

"How did it go today? I didn't hear anything from Elizabeth. Does that mean the deal went through?"

Did she micromanage everyone this way? He was sure she didn't. It felt as if she never trusted him to be competent enough. He'd felt that his entire life. He was determined to prove he was capable, which was why he'd taken on this particular case.

"The board is still considering its options. If they vote to sell, they'll hopefully sell to Prime Developments. Not much more I can do at this point but wait."

"I see Lucy Everhart works there. Is that the same woman who stole the Wigmore Key from you?"

Dylan rubbed his temples. The Wigmore Key wasn't something that could be stolen. His mother still resented the fact that Lucy had won the prestigious award from Northwestern Law instead of Dylan. What she failed to realize— or maybe just wouldn't admit—was that Lucy had earned it.

"She's the same woman who won the award."

"Well, there you go. You need to use your relationship with her to move things along. What more do you need than an alumni connection?"

Dylan couldn't stand how his mother saw relationships only in terms of what two people could do to advance each other's plans. He also hated that she refused to acknowledge that Lucy was more than a rival from school.

It didn't seem to matter to her that Lucy and Dylan had dated for years. Or that she was the woman he'd wanted to marry and the one who obliterated his heart. To Clarissa, they had graduated from the same law school and Lucy should give Dylan what he wanted out of respect for that connection.

"I don't think Lucy views our shared past as a reason to work with Prime Developments." He didn't want to tell her how Lucy had sworn not to let the board deal with anyone associated with him personally. "I'm going to keep my distance and let the board think things over."

His mom sighed. "That sounds like the exact opposite of what you should do, Dylan. If that house goes into foreclosure, there will be plenty of people vying to snatch it up in an attempt to force Prime to buy it from them for a killing. You need to use every advantage you've got to get this done quickly."

He had nothing except one very angry ex-girlfriend. "I have it under control. The executive director is still on the fence about selling. If I lean on her a little and she supports the sale, the deal will go through for sure. The board trusts her and her judgment."

"Then do it. Do whatever you need to do to gain her trust. What does she need? Give it to her in exchange for the deal." She pulled the phone away to talk to someone else for a moment. It was no surprise that she was still at the office so late into the night. The woman never stopped. If she could find a way to sleep and work at the same time, she would do it. "I have a case to get back to. We'll do lunch next week. I'll have my assistant set something up with yours."

She'd never offered to get together for lunch before. Dylan was so caught off guard he didn't get a chance to accept the invitation before his mother hung up. There had to be some ulterior motive. She was probably displeased about something and needed to scold him in person to make her point. Maybe he wasn't billing enough. He definitely wasn't working as many hours as she'd like. Maybe she had caught wind of the rumor that he'd been asking about doing some pro bono work. That wasn't really a rumor. He was seeking something a little more spiritually satisfying than what he'd spent the past few years doing.

Scrubbing his face, he wondered how much more of this he could take before he broke. This job, this life—none of it was what he'd dreamed of. There was more than enough money in the bank, but money couldn't buy him anything he really wanted.

What he wanted was a blonde fireball with dreams bigger than both of them. He wanted her to smile when she saw him and put her hand in his whenever she was near. He wanted to kiss her lips anytime they were close enough and to feel her heart beat in rhythm with his.

Dylan had lived a charmed life, for sure. He had been born with a silver spoon in his mouth. He grew up in the lap of luxury, wore designer clothes, drove the fanciest cars and went to the best schools. But what Dylan wanted had nothing to do with money and material things. He wanted a family of his own. He had wanted that family to begin with Lucy, but he could never deny her anything.

So, if she wanted a fight, he'd give her one.

GIVING PAIGE CLAYTON what she wanted was fairly easy once he thought about what she really needed. Dylan entered Open Arms with a few helpers in tow.

"Can I help you?" her assistant asked, standing up to see why they were invading.

"Is Ms. Clayton in?"

Ms. Clayton came out of her office and stopped short when she saw Dylan. "Mr. Hunt, how can I help you?"

Lucy came flying out of her office, apparently at the sound of Dylan's name. She was in jeans and a T-shirt today. Casual never looked so good. "Seriously? What are you doing here?"

"I noticed your office furniture has seen better days. You said you'd love any donations, and we had some chairs and such sitting in storage. I was hoping you could use them."

He motioned for them to join him by the door so they could see the chairs and other goodies he had brought with him. Ms. Clayton's mouth dropped open and he could practically hear her internal squeal at the thought of getting a real desk chair. Lucy didn't appear as excited, not that his perception meant anything. She could be just as thrilled, but she wouldn't show it.

"We don't need hand-me-downs from Stevens and Ellis," she said, stepping back toward her office.

"Uh, yeah, we do," Ms. Clayton said, giving Dylan a pat on the shoulder. "This is really kind of you."

Lucy let out a harsh, derisive laugh. "He's trying to bribe us, Paige! We don't take bribes, Dylan. It's unethical for your firm to give us anything."

"This is a personal donation. I bought them from Stevens and Ellis with my own money, and I want you to have them. Would you like to see the receipt?" He pulled a sheet of paper from his back pocket.

"Personal donations are completely ethical. We accept, Mr. Hunt," Ms. Clayton said. "Bring those babies in here."

Dylan's guys brought in all the new office furniture and helped remove all the broken, worn-out stuff. Ms. Clayton smiled ear to ear while Lucy stood with arms crossed and a scowl on her face. This had to mean she was unhappy, but Dylan noticed she swapped her desk chair for a new one. She never did what he expected; at least that much was predictable about her.

Once everything was in place, he sent his hired hands away and made Ms. Clayton one more offer she couldn't possibly refuse.

"I noticed there are a couple of things that could use fixing around here." Dylan pointed to the hole in the wall by the entrance and the broken light fixture above Ms. Clayton's assistant's desk. "I have a friend who could help me get these things patched up for you in no time."

"We don't have a budget for repairs right now," Ms. Clayton said, embarrassment coloring her cheeks. "Thank you for offering, though."

"Oh, no, it would be another donation," Dylan clarified. "I would take care of all the materials. Eugene and I would do the work ourselves."

"*You* would do the handiwork?" Lucy leaned against her doorjamb.

He tried not to be offended. His Mr. Fix-It side hadn't shown itself until after she left him. She didn't have to act so surprised by it, though.

"Is that really so hard to believe?"

She shrugged as if it didn't matter any way. Lucy didn't care about what he could or couldn't do. She simply wanted him gone. He needed to make this deal for Prime Developments and then he would leave her alone.

Ms. Clayton was pretty much putty in his hands. Her smile was large and grateful. "Sometimes I feel like this place is falling apart around me and there's nothing I can do about it."

"Well, it wouldn't be a big deal for me to help out. I'm one of those guys who sees a need and likes to fill it."

Lucy let out another sarcastic guffaw and turned to her boss. "Please tell me you see what 'need' he's trying to fill here. Or maybe I should say *whose* need he's trying to fill, because it isn't ours."

"Good to know your trust issues are still holding you back." Even though she was right for questioning his motives, he couldn't stop himself from going on the attack.

Her arms fell to her sides and Lucy stood straight and tall. "Don't you dare claim that my not trusting your intentions is a personality flaw."

Ms. Clayton had been watching the exchange nervously. "Why do I feel like you two know one another?"

It was another blow to Dylan's ego that Lucy hadn't mentioned their history to Ms. Clayton. He really must not have meant that much to her back then. "She didn't tell you we knew each other in law school?" Dylan decided he'd let Lucy be the one to acknowledge their romantic connection.

"She did not." Ms. Clayton glared at Lucy, who was rolling her eyes.

"Let me guess, this isn't the first time Lucy has left out some details. I bet that drives you nuts, but you let it slide because picking a fight with her is pointless. She never loses, which also drives you nuts but also makes you glad she's on your side."

"Whoa." Ms. Clayton was impressed. "Get out of my head."

"Dylan fancies himself one of those people who can read other people's minds. What he really does is make you believe you want to buy what he's selling. Of course, in our case, he's going to try to convince you to sell what he's buying."

"I've never claimed to be a mind reader. I simply notice things others ignore."

Lucy shook her head. "And ignore the things people are trying to get through your thick skull." She slipped back into her office and shut the door.

Little did she know she was making herself crystal clear. She hated him. He didn't need to be a mind reader to figure that out. What he didn't understand was why.

Ms. Clayton stuck out her hand and Dylan shook it. "I accept your offer to help us out. I may not read minds, but my instincts about people are usually spot-on."

"Thank you," Dylan said sincerely. "I really do enjoy fixing things up."

This might be a way to get Open Arms to sell to Prime Developments, but it was also a chance for Dylan to do something good, something worthwhile. Lucy could doubt his intentions all she liked. He truly did want to help out. Couldn't he help both Prime Developments and Open Arms?

Paige smiled as if she believed him. "We have lots of things that need fixing."

"I promise not to discuss real estate while I'm here." He wouldn't need to. Once she believed he was one of the good guys, everything else would work itself out. Open Arms wasn't going to be able to afford their mortgage payments soon enough. They might not want to sell, but there would soon be no other reasonable option. They would eventually sell the house to someone. Why not to his client? Being a person Ms. Clayton trusted put Prime Developments in an excellent position and would give him the win he needed to confidently go to his mother with a new vision for his career at Stevens and Ellis.

"Good," she said. "And I promise not to ask how close you and Lucy were when you were in law school together." She closed her eyes and rubbed her temples. "I'm picking up on some very strong you-were-more-than-just-classmates vibes. Am I right?" She opened her eyes, the corners of her mouth upturned in a self-satisfied grin.

"And she thinks *I'm* the mind reader."

"She should know better than to underestimate me. So should you, Mr. Hunt," she said with a wink.

CHAPTER FIVE

LUCY HAD NEVER met a checkbook she couldn't balance. She might not have gone to school for accounting, but she had good number sense. The files Nora had given her were filled with a lot of numbers—numbers that were not adding up. Of course, the incessant hammering going on in the main office was not helping her concentration.

Paige was too smart to fall for Dylan's manipulation, so why was she being naive about his true intentions? He was so transparent, it was pathetic. He had to know no one was going to believe he was doing anything for Open Arms out of the goodness of his heart. He wanted their house. He also wanted to drive Lucy crazy.

She covered her ears and shut her tired eyes. It sounded as if an entire construction crew was out in the reception area. The banging and drilling and sawing were creating a sensory overload. If she had wanted to listen to this racket all day, she would have gone to work for her dad's construction company.

Pushing back her new chair from her desk, she practically flew the three steps to the door and yanked it open. She wasn't expecting to come face-to-chest with Dylan. His navy blue T-shirt was pulled tight across said chest, the muscles clearly defined under the cotton. His arms were raised up over his head and his focus was on something above her door.

The urge to wrap her arms around his waist and press her cheek against him nearly knocked her off her feet. Shocked by the impulse, Lucy stepped back and cleared her throat. There would be no comfort found in Dylan's arms ever again.

He lowered his chin and leveled his gaze with hers. "Sorry, are we too loud out here? The noise is bugging you, isn't it?"

She refused to let him know he was right. "No, you're just in my way."

Dylan took notice of the fact that he was blocking her path. He sighed and stepped aside. "Of course."

Lucy slid past him and she made her way into Paige's office, closing the door so their new handyman couldn't overhear.

"How can you work with your door open?"

"Did you see how quickly they got that hole patched up?" Paige was grinning from ear to ear as she leaned forward. "Eugene offered to give the whole place a fresh coat of paint. I'm thinking we should add a little color to this place. Maybe do everything in yellows and grays. That's in right now. What do you think?"

"What are you talking about?" Lucy felt as if she had stepped into another dimension. "Who's Eugene?"

"Dylan's friend. The guy helping him with the repairs." Apparently, they were all on a first-name basis now.

Lucy hadn't noticed anyone else once she got past Dylan and his too-tight T-shirt. "I came in because it's supposed to be quiet here on Saturdays. I can't get anything done with all this noise. Do you want to get some lunch with me before I head home?"

Paige sank back in her fancy leather chair. "Are you really going to make me get up?" She closed her eyes and swiveled the chair from side to side, something she could never do with her old one. "I love this office furniture. Have I mentioned that?"

"Only a hundred times. It's not annoying or anything. Oh, wait. Yes, it is. It's very annoying."

Paige opened one eye and then the other. "I'm not falling for anyone's tricks if that's what you think. There is no reason not to enjoy the gifts we are being given."

"He's making you like him," Lucy argued. "If the board is swayed to sell, you're going to feel like you owe it to him to sell to his client because he's been so nice to you."

"If the board votes to sell, why shouldn't we sell to his client? What's your deal with this guy? Give me a reason not to like him."

The real reason would only lead to more questions that Lucy didn't want to answer. "Just trust me on this one. Please."

Paige narrowed her eyes as if trying to read Lucy's mind. Seemingly giving up, she sighed. "Fine, but one of these days I'm getting the whole story. I'll bring the wine, you'll bring the details."

Not even Lucy's sisters knew the details. Dylan was an off-limits topic even with those closest to her. Opening those wounds any further could only result in disaster. Lucy wasn't going there—ever.

The pounding of a hammer brought Lucy out of her head. She stood up and motioned toward the reception area. "Can we please go get some lunch before I take all of their tools away and throw them out the window?"

Paige laughed and pulled herself up and out of her chair. "Can I like Eugene? He has nothing to do with Prime Developments *and* he wants to paint this place for free. Did I mention that he offered to do that?"

"You did. And I don't care who you like as long as it's not—" Lucy opened the door and was once again greeted by Dylan's blue shirt. Her eyes found his. "Why are you always in my way?"

"I was just coming to tell Paige that we're breaking for lunch."

"We were heading to lunch, too." Paige nudged Lucy aside. "Do you and Eugene want to join us?"

Had she completely forgotten everything they were just talking about? Lucy was going to lunch to get *away* from Dylan, not to socialize with him. "We're going to City Vegan. That's not really Dylan's style."

"We could go somewhere else," Paige suggested.

"No, don't change your plans for us." Dylan backed away from the door. Lucy's shoulders relaxed until he added, "We'll go to the vegan place."

"Since when do you eat vegan food?" she asked, frustrated by his air of nonchalance around her. If he had really cared about her five years ago, he should find it as hard to be around her as it was for her to be near him. She had broken up with him. Why did it feel as if she had been jilted?

"You're the only one who can change her diet? I remember you telling me that eating less meat could save my life. Maybe I listened to you."

She didn't believe him for a second. When her mother had gotten sick, Lucy changed several of her habits. What she ate became a matter of life or death. Dylan had been supportive but had not been a fan of a vegetarian or vegan lifestyle. Tofu burgers had never satisfied him the way the big, juicy ones made out of midwestern Angus beef had.

He was obviously trying to ruin her entire day. Maybe this was his way of punishing her for the breakup. Maybe he wasn't being as mature about it as she originally thought.

If getting under her skin was his plan, she would do everything she could not to show her irritation. He wasn't the only one who could act as if their past meant nothing. She took a breath and pasted on a smile. "Great."

"Great?" Dylan and Paige both echoed. Evidently, neither of them had been expecting that answer.

Lucy motioned for Dylan to step aside and exited Paige's office. "Come on, Eugene. Put down your hammer and let's get some lunch!"

Eugene stopped midswing. His eyes moved back and forth between Lucy and Dylan. That was when Lucy realized she had seen the older gentleman before. He was the man with the little boy at Simon's basketball game. The man who was sitting with Dylan and had heard her verbally blast him for being there. No wonder he could hardly believe they were going anywhere together.

"Well, you heard the lady," Dylan said. "We're going to lunch. With them. Let's go."

"I promise not to get us kicked out of anywhere this time," she added in an attempt to reassure Eugene. That seemed to do the trick. His shoulders relaxed and he slid his hammer into a loop on his tool belt.

"This time? Oh, that sounds like a story," Paige said, closing her office door.

Paige, and her need to know things. Some stories weren't worth being told. The endings were too depressing.

CITY VEGAN WAS one of Lucy's favorite restaurants. In her mind, there wasn't a bad thing on the menu, but she could tell Dylan and Eugene were having a hard time finding something they dared to try.

"What's soy chicken?" Eugene asked Paige. "I thought this place was vegetarian."

"It's fake chicken. It's soy made to look and taste like chicken," Dylan answered for her.

Eugene's nose scrunched up and he set down his menu. "If vegetarians don't like meat, why would they want to eat something that looks and tastes like chicken?"

Lucy was used to fielding this kind of question. The animal rights activist inside her pushed her to skip meat more often than not, but being a child raised on midwestern beef and Chicago hot dogs, she hadn't given it up completely.

"There are a lot of people out there who don't eat meat because they believe it's wrong. That doesn't mean they don't miss the taste and texture of it. Soy chicken allows them to pretend to eat meat without harming any animals in the process."

"Well, you learn something new every day," Eugene said, picking his menu back up.

"If you aren't used to eating this way, I suggest these noodles." Paige leaned in, reaching across Eugene to show him what she was talking about. Her hand brushed against his arm and he smiled at the contact.

Lucy cocked her head and stared at the two of them. Was Paige flirting with this guy? She giggled at something Eugene said and playfully pushed his shoulder.

Oh, she was definitely flirting.

It was still unclear how Dylan and Eugene knew one another. Theirs seemed an unlikely friendship. Lucy couldn't help but wonder if it had something to do with the boy, whom she deduced was Eugene's grandson. It sounded as if he lived with Eugene but was spending the weekend with an aunt and uncle. Perhaps Dylan had known the boy's parents. Why else would he attend the eight-year-old's basketball game?

They ordered lunch and Dylan joined in the conversation between Eugene and Paige. The three of them laughed and socialized while Lucy sat in silent objection to this ridiculous game Dylan was obviously playing. She fought an eye roll when he showed off his skill at reading people.

The waitress became his unwitting subject. He guessed she was newly engaged, a student at DePaul University and not originally from Chicago. Paige hung on every word but doubted he could have gathered that much information from the few interactions they had had with the young woman.

"If I'm right, lunch is on you. If I'm wrong, I'll buy," he offered.

"Don't make any bets with this man," Lucy warned. She had seen Dylan swindle too many people in the time they were together to let her friend become his next victim.

Paige wouldn't listen. "There's no way he's right about all of that. I'm in."

"You have to swear you don't know that girl, though," Eugene said. "Don't be cheating this nice lady. If you know her, fess up right now."

Dylan raised his hands. "I swear I have never seen her before in my life. Ask her when she comes back to the table. I don't have to cheat to win. I promise you that."

This was true. Dylan Hunt did not cheat and he almost always won. It used to drive Lucy crazy. Still did, apparently.

The waitress came back to refill their drinks, and she confirmed for Eugene that she had never met Dylan. She was surprised to be asked but happy to share that she actually was recently engaged, showing everyone her ring and gushing about how romantic the proposal had been. She also admitted to being a student at DePaul, studying library science. Spitefully, Lucy thought there was no way Dylan would have guessed the woman wanted to be a librarian. Last, the waitress informed Paige that she was originally from South Carolina. Lucy had picked up on her slight accent earlier and had known Dylan was right about that one.

"That totally freaks me out." Paige's eyes were wide and her mouth hung open. "How did you know all that?"

"My grandmother was a psychic," Dylan said straight-faced. "She taught me how to read minds."

"Seriously?" Eugene asked, his expression a mirror image of Paige's.

Lucy snorted. Dylan had a way of turning even the most intelligent people into naive nitwits. "He can't read minds."

"Well, not hers," Dylan said, jerking a thumb in Lucy's direction. "It's the metal plates in her skull. Blocks me out."

"You have metal plates in your skull?" Paige's jaw dropped farther.

Lucy sighed heavily. "No, I do not have metal plates in my skull. And no, he cannot read minds. He pays attention. That's it. He heard her Southern accent. He noticed her showing off her ring to someone else. He probably just guessed based on her age that she's a student. He can't read my mind or anyone else's."

"Actually, she has a DePaul lanyard sticking out of her back pocket. That's how I knew. I didn't guess. I rarely guess." The way he glared at her made Lucy's cheeks flush.

"Of course. I should have figured you got a good look at her backside."

"Excuse me?" Dylan's voice rose slightly.

"Oh, please. You always notice a beautiful woman's assets."

"I think all men appreciate a beautiful woman. You make me sound like some sort of creep."

The heat of her anger warmed Lucy's whole body. She didn't even care about his stupid mind tricks. Five years of built-up feelings were hitting her all at once. He had let her leave him. He would have left her when he found out she would be permanently scarred. He never would have wanted to be with someone whose curves weren't real.

She did her best to tamp her emotions back down. "If the shoe fits…"

Eugene cleared his throat and Lucy noticed

the other diners in their section of the restaurant were gaping at her.

"I was told no one was going to get us thrown out of here," Eugene said. "If you two can't be civil, that's exactly what will happen."

Lucy and Dylan each took a deep breath and kept their mouths shut so no more words could sneak out. This was a huge mistake. Thinking they could spend an amicable lunch together was laughable. Lucy was about to get up and leave when the food arrived. Eating would thankfully keep their mouths busy.

All conversation ceased at their small, square table. Eugene let Paige know her noodle recommendation was a good one, but that was pretty much all anyone said until it was time to go. Dylan pulled out his wallet to pay the bill.

"Put that away," Paige said, reaching for her purse. "I lost the bet. Lunch is on me."

"It's fine. I didn't really read her mind. It was all simple observation, like Lucy said."

"The bet wasn't about whether or not you could read minds, it was about whether or not you were right. You were definitely right. Lunch is on me," Paige insisted.

Dylan stole a glance in Lucy's direction. He was probably afraid of being verbally assaulted if he let Paige pay. With a full belly and some self-reflection, Lucy could admit she had been harder on him than he deserved. Eugene must think she was crazy.

"How about you all let me pay? I'm the one who ruined everyone's lunch." She had also made it clear to Dylan that he was affecting her more than she wanted him to know. She pulled out some cash and slipped it in the bill folder. "Tell our waitress to keep the change. I'm going to head home to finish some work."

Paige and Eugene thanked her and offered her a goodbye. Dylan said nothing. She was halfway out the door when she felt someone grip her arm.

"Hang on a second." Dylan let her go the moment she stopped moving. "I just want to be clear about something." His jaw was tense but his eyes were soft. "I don't know why you dislike me so much, but this isn't about us."

The way he said "us" made Lucy's stomach flip. There hadn't been an "us" in a very long time. There would never be an "us" again.

"I know. It's about Open Arms and Safe Haven. Two things I care about. Two things that I won't give up."

Dylan looked as though she had punched him in the gut. His hurt expression quickly changed to one full of nothing but exasperation. He leaned in close and seemed to be trying hard to keep his voice calm. "Well, I want you to know that I'm not giving up, either. Maybe it's your turn to find out what it's like to lose something you care about."

He disappeared back into the restaurant, leaving Lucy without an opportunity to have the last word. She knew better than anyone what it was like to lose. Where were his sense of passion and willingness to fight for what he wanted five years ago? He seemed to care more about this real estate deal than he'd ever cared about her.

CHAPTER SIX

IF DYLAN HAD to write a list of words that described Lucy Everhart, it would include every synonym for *infuriating*. Her nasty attitude toward him was beyond tiring. It was unbelievable that she could be so bitter when she was the one who had ended their relationship half a decade ago. If anyone had a right to be hateful, it was Dylan, not she.

He decided he needed to do whatever it took to get this deal promptly done for Prime Developments. Paige was the key and Dylan had her all figured out. The gifts of furniture and repairs opened the door exactly as he'd planned. What he hadn't expected was the way she'd taken to Eugene. It was an added bonus.

The good news was that Eugene seemed equally smitten. He was definitely disappointed when Paige didn't stick around on Sunday while they painted. She had business to attend to at Safe Haven and left them to work under the watchful eye of Hannah, her assistant.

Lucy was not around, which was a relief. He couldn't take any more of her wrath. She made him question everything about their shared past. The things she had said at lunch made him feel as if she'd doubted his fidelity when they were together, which was unbelievable. When she had been in his life, there had been no one else. No one caught his eye the way Lucy still did.

"I have to go," Eugene said, wiping his hands on a rag. "Jeremy gets home in an hour."

They had primed all the walls and trimmed everything in the light gray Paige had picked out. Dylan could finish the rest on his own fairly easily. "Thanks for your help this weekend. I owe you one."

"You always owe me one. I think we're up to somewhere around a hundred ones by now."

"You know I'm good for it, right?"

"Maybe if you give my number to Paige so she can call me, you know, whenever she needs a handyman, I'll call us even."

Dylan's eyebrows lifted. Good ol' Eugene was more than smitten. Taking care of Jeremy was all he ever focused on. It was good to see him doing something for himself. "Well, well,

well. I think someone hopes she calls for *more* than just a handyman."

Eugene fought a smile as his cheeks pinked up. "Don't forget to touch up the ceiling where we patched."

"I won't," Dylan promised, chuckling at his friend's attempt to change the subject.

Finishing the job alone wasn't difficult. Hannah was busy gossiping with someone on the phone, classic rock was playing on the radio Eugene left behind and rolling paint on the wall didn't take too much skill. Dylan let the music move him while he worked. His hips began to sway a little and his head bobbed to the beat. During a particular part of the song, he might have strummed a few chords of air guitar.

"What are you doing?"

Dylan's head snapped in the direction of her voice. Lucy was staring as if he was spray painting graffiti on the walls. He gave his work a quick once-over to make sure he hadn't messed something up while enjoying the music. When he was satisfied that everything was fine, his gaze landed back on her. "Painting."

"Painting?" She cocked a brow. "Not channeling Eric Clapton?"

Was she teasing him? When the corners of her mouth curled up the tiniest bit, he relaxed and shrugged. "You know how I feel about Eric Clapton. I can't resist when he's on."

She almost unleashed a grin but controlled herself and moved on to Hannah, who was more than eager to get out of there. Dylan tried not to eavesdrop on their conversation, but it was impossible. Lucy somewhat reluctantly agreed to stay until he was finished painting so Hannah could have the rest of her Sunday off.

No one wanted Lucy to babysit Dylan less than he did. Things had been going so smoothly, and now he was destined to walk on eggshells the rest of the afternoon. Luckily, she slipped into her office and shut the door. Maybe this way they could each pretend the other didn't exist.

Dylan went back to painting, ignoring the pull Lucy's presence had on him. What was she doing here on a Sunday? Did the woman ever take a day off? Had she known he was here and come to check on him? How long was it going to take her to inform him for the millionth time that he was unwelcome and she planned to do everything in her power to win this fight?

Lucy didn't come out or say anything to

incite another argument, but sounds coming from the other side of the wall made Dylan curious. Groans of frustration. Slamming of books. Obscenities shouted, perhaps at the computer. Dylan couldn't be sure.

Against his better judgment, he set his paint roller down and knocked on her door. "Do I need to call for help?"

The door swung open and a beautiful but frustrated Lucy had exasperation written all over her face. "You're a lawyer."

It was a strange statement and one Dylan wasn't sure what to do with. "I am. Do you need a lawyer? Did you kill someone in here?" He leaned forward and took a peek inside her office for a dead body.

Her shoulders sagged. "I need to consult with someone on a case. I can't figure out what's going on and I'm ready to pull my hair out."

She had pretty blond hair. The last thing he wanted was for her to yank it all out. Dylan's fingers itched to run through it as they used to when she hadn't been so opposed to his existence.

"You can consult with me," he offered. He quickly questioned whether that was the answer she was looking for. He could never be sure with her. "If that's what you need."

Lucy stepped back and waved him into her office. Warily, he crossed the threshold. Maybe this was some sort of trick. She might be luring him in only to take him out. He pulled on the collar of his T-shirt and sat down.

"I agreed to take this divorce case, but it's bigger than that. My client brought me all these files and said that she's afraid her husband set her up, possibly tricked her into committing a crime. I think he might have embezzled some money from his company and made it look like it was her doing. Do you have any idea what any of this means?"

She turned her laptop around, revealing a spreadsheet. Dylan pulled the computer closer and began scrolling through the information. He was no accountant, but he had analyzed enough similar documents in white-collar cases to know that Lucy had every reason to be concerned.

"It's called smurfing. You deposit small amounts of money into several accounts. The banks would have to report a fifty-thousand-dollar deposit but not five ten-thousand-dollar deposits. He just had to make sure he did them over a long enough period of time, since he was doing it all under her name. What else do you have that connects your client to this?"

Lucy shared the other files from the flash drive as well as hard copies of some documents, including bank statements in her client's name. Dylan examined everything carefully and asked questions as he scanned each piece of potential evidence.

What felt like minutes turned into hours. It was as if they were transported back in time, back to when they would work on mock cases in their criminal defense class or when they spent entire days studying for the bar exam. They had always collaborated so well, balancing out one another's strengths and weaknesses. Dylan realized it wasn't just working with Lucy but working on something meaningful that made him feel more alive than he had in a long time.

"Look at this," he said after scanning one of the PDFs with a list of financial transactions. "I think he's taken more than what he put in the accounts in her name. This company comes up multiple times but it's not on the list you showed me earlier." He dug through some papers until he found the right one. "Brick Industries must be something he set up to funnel money into."

"So he embezzles around fifty thousand dollars and dumps it into accounts in Nora's name. Then he takes more?" Lucy squinted as she examined the documents in front of her. It made little wrinkles appear in the corners of her eyes.

Dylan watched her, taking in every line and freckle. It had been so long since he had been this close. He wanted to lean in closer, press his lips against her collarbone and breathe in the smell of her lilac-scented skin. "He took a lot more," she said, snapping him out of his fantasy. "Oh, my gosh, this guy is *bad*."

"I'd say he took close to half a million. That money is somewhere. Doesn't look like it has Nora's name on it, though."

"She wasn't kidding when she said he would kill her when he found out she had this stuff. These files can put him away for a very long time."

Dylan wasn't aware that there were threats made. "He doesn't know yet?"

"We have no idea. She hasn't been in contact with him since she left and we placed her at Safe Haven. I filed the petition for the dissolution of the marriage and heard he was served on Friday. I'm sure all of this was what he planned to hold over her so she'd withdraw her petition, but we've yet to get a response from his counsel. Who knows what he'll do now that he doesn't have any of this evidence anymore."

"Something tells me this guy is going to be extremely angry."

"Everything makes a guy like this angry." Lucy sat back and gazed out the now-darkened window as if she just realized how serious this all was. "This has the potential to make him lethal."

None of this sat well with Dylan. "What precautions are you taking?"

"None."

"He knows you're her attorney. He could come after you to get to her."

Lucy shook her head and her expression changed. "I am *more* than capable of taking care of myself. Don't worry about me."

Tough as nails. She'd always been the one who wanted everyone to believe she was invincible. Maybe she was, but Dylan really didn't want to test the theory. "You need to be vigilant. This guy is going to be desperate. I know you think you're going to live forever, but desperate men are dangerous."

Lucy's jaw tightened and she averted her eyes. Once again, it was not the response

Dylan was expecting. He'd give anything to hear her thoughts. "Like I said, don't worry about me." She stood up and began gathering her files. "Thanks for your help. I assume I can count on you to keep all this confidential."

"Of course."

"Sorry for keeping you from finishing your paint job." She shoved the documents into her bag and shut down her computer. It was as if Dylan had become the bad guy and she couldn't get out of there fast enough. Obviously, the concern he'd shown was more than unwelcome. How could he forget he wasn't someone she wanted in her life?

"It's okay. I'm sure Eugene won't mind coming back to finish up. He enjoyed talking to Paige the other day."

"I noticed." Lucy eased up, slowing down her escape. "He seems like a decent person. I feel bad that I got you kicked out of his grandson's basketball game last week. It's been bugging me."

Another shocking confession. Dylan quickly closed his mouth after his jaw dropped. "I'm going this Wednesday. Hopefully we can be civil."

"I think I can handle that. I owe you that much for helping me out today." She was all packed up and had her bag slung over her shoulder. "I have to go. Do you need a few minutes to clean up out there so I can lock up?"

He needed more than a few minutes to process everything that had happened in the past few hours. He had to remind himself he was there for one reason and one reason only. His job was to convince Paige to support the sale of Safe Haven to Prime Developments. It wasn't to help Lucy even if that was what his heart wanted him to do.

"I'll be out of your hair in a few," he said, rising to his feet. Lucy might have called a truce for the basketball game, but their fight over Safe Haven was far from over.

THE NEXT FEW days were dreadful. Dylan's thoughts constantly drifted to Lucy's case while he was supposed to be working on his own. Instead of developing a strategy and an argument for a client who was trying to avoid paying off his debts by filing for bankruptcy, he was researching legal precedents for Lucy's client.

It was difficult not to jot down notes to share with her when he knew he was going to see her in a few short hours at Jeremy's game. At least he assumed she would be there. Assumptions were always a bad idea when it came to Lucy.

Bridgette knocked on his door and popped her head in. "Shouldn't you be wrapping things up? I thought you were leaving at five today."

It was already ten after. He'd been gathering up cases to share with Lucy for over an hour, sixty minutes he was supposed to be billing to a client. His mother would probably fire him if she knew what he was up to.

"I'm leaving. Can you make sure Calvin has drafted that buy-sell agreement for Highwood Industries? I have a meeting with them tomorrow, right?"

"Ten o'clock. I'll make sure he's ready," she promised. Calvin was one of the paralegals under Dylan's supervision. Things never seemed to get done in a timely matter when Calvin was in charge. Bridgette was more reliable than he would ever be.

Dylan decided to grab something to eat on the way to the game. He carefully folded his notes for Lucy and slipped them in his pocket. He wasn't sure if she'd appreciate the work he'd put into her case or not, but it felt good to work on something that could truly help someone who needed it.

Eugene was sitting in his usual spot in the bleachers when Dylan arrived. Kendall and a man he didn't recognize sat nearby, but not as close as the last time. No sign of Lucy. Maybe she wasn't coming.

"Jeremy said he's going to get a basket, but only if you promise to stay for the whole game."

Dylan scanned the court for his favorite player. Jeremy waved and looked relieved to find him in the crowd. "Lucy and I called a truce. I'm not going anywhere until the final buzzer."

Eugene patted him on the back. "Let's keep our fingers crossed. She seems happier today."

Smiling and linking arms with her youngest sister, Lucy stepped into the gym, shouting words of encouragement to her nephew. It was nice to see that the Everhart sisters were still so close. Following behind the two women were Lucy's parents. Dylan felt his heart tighten.

Maureen, Lucy's mom, was the only one who noticed Dylan in the stands. She nudged Lucy and whispered something. Lucy didn't have to search very hard to find him. She lifted her hand in a halfhearted wave before confirming for her mother that he was who she thought he was.

"Dylan Hunt, how are you?" Maureen marched right up and held her arms open for a hug.

"I'm good, Maureen. How are you doing?" he asked before accepting her warm embrace.

"We've never been better. Come down here and say hello to the family. You remember Kendall, right?" Maureen pulled him down the steps with her as she gave him a quick update on everyone in Lucy's family. "Honey, look. It's Dylan Hunt. Can you believe it?"

Mr. Everhart had always been a bit more reserved than his wife. He glanced at Lucy before acknowledging Dylan with a nod and a quiet hello.

Maureen demanded he sit with them and fill her in on what he'd been up to since she'd last seen him. Lucy appeared only slightly mortified, so he sat down after calling for Eugene to come join him. Introductions were made, and thankfully the game began, giving them all something else to focus on.

Sitting with the Everharts was another trip down memory lane that Dylan wasn't sure he was ready for. Everyone was friendly, but he could tell they were all on guard, watching Lucy's reaction to everything they said and did. Except for Maureen, of course. She treated

Dylan exactly as she had five years ago. It was as if he and Lucy had never broken up.

But they had. She had broken his heart and he would probably never be the same. He tried not to think about it as she sat in front of him, cheering for her nephew.

Kendall's son passed the ball to Jeremy, who shot it and made a basket with only a few minutes left, putting their team up by one. Jeremy beamed up at his grandpa and Dylan, who were both on their feet clapping like madmen.

"I think we're all going to have to celebrate with some ice cream after this game," Maureen said to Eugene.

"I think so."

Dylan made eye contact with Lucy, who must have been thinking the same thing he was. This happy little reunion was more than either of them could take.

"Simon got ice cream last week, Mom. That's what happens when you miss a game," Lucy said teasingly but clearly in hopes there would be no postgame socializing.

"Maybe two weeks in a row is a little overkill," Kendall added, coming to Lucy's aid. Their dad and Kendall's husband both nodded in agreement.

Maureen was not swayed. "You can never have too much ice cream. Right, Emma?"

Emma must have wanted to give Lucy a harder time than the others. "I missed ice cream last week. I'm all for hitting the Triple C on the way home."

Her boyfriend slung an arm around her shoulders. "Are there circumstances that would ever persuade you to pass up ice cream, Nightingale?"

"None that I can think of," she replied, smiling up at him and giving him a sweet peck on the lips. They looked happy and it created an ache inside Dylan that would not be ignored.

The two boys came running over after shaking hands with the other team. It wasn't going to be hard to convince them to go out for a treat.

"Did you see that shot?" Jeremy asked Dylan.

He mussed up the boy's hair. "That was awesome, dude."

Maureen was quick to incite a riot, bringing up ice cream before anything else could be said. Dylan hoped to sneak away, hoping Eugene wouldn't be mad for ditching him, but Jeremy had other plans.

"Can I ride with Dylan? Simon, want to ride in Dylan's Z28?"

Simon's eyeballs nearly popped out of his head. He must have known a thing or two about cars.

"You've got a Camaro Z28?" Kendall's husband perked up.

"What color?" Emma's boyfriend was equally interested.

"It's black," Jeremy answered. "It's *so* cool."

"Can I ride in it, Mom?" Simon asked, leaving no doubt in Dylan's mind that a quick getaway was out of the question.

Kendall didn't agree to a ride but suggested they all go check it out in the parking lot. Everyone left the gymnasium, the boys running ahead but followed closely by the other "boys" who wanted to see Dylan's car up close and personal.

Dylan and Lucy ended up walking together in the back of the crowd. "You have some car fanatics in your family, huh?" he asked.

"Simon is crazy about cars. Some kids can tell you everything you want to know about dinosaurs. My nephew can tell you which car has the most horsepower." She came to a stop, causing Dylan to do the same. "You don't have to get ice cream with us."

"I don't have to, or you don't want me to?" The latter seemed more likely.

"My mom is being pushy. You don't have to come. I'm sure this is all really—"

"Awkward?"

Her green eyes smiled back at him. "Yeah."

Dylan tried to appear unaffected by it all, even though those eyes had a way of making his heart beat hard against his rib cage. "It's not a big deal."

Outside, everyone was gathered in front of one particular parking space. Only, they weren't gawking at Dylan's car.

"What the heck?" Lucy pushed Emma's boyfriend out of the way.

Broken pieces of plastic lay scattered on the ground. It seemed someone had taken a bat to Lucy's car. The headlights were both smashed, the side mirrors were knocked off and there was a spiderweb crack in the windshield. None of that compared to the nasty word scratched into the hood.

"Why would someone do this?" Maureen asked as Lucy assessed the damage.

Dylan had no doubts about who had vandalized her car. He had been worried about her since learning the specifics of her new case. Now he was overwhelmed by dread.

"I guess you got a response to that petition."

CHAPTER SEVEN

BEING A TARGET was nothing new. Lucy had put herself in the line of fire a bunch of times over the years. Whenever someone fought against injustice or stood up for what was right, they tended to attract some attention from those who preferred the status quo. Nora's husband, like many abusers, liked the way things were going in his life, and he surely blamed Lucy for threatening to take that away.

The police car's blue and red lights spun around and around as the officer wrote down the last of the information for his report. "We'll follow up on this and get back to you as soon as we know anything," the officer said, handing Lucy a card with the report number for her insurance.

"That's it?" Dylan had chosen to stay behind while the rest of the Everhart family got the children out of there. "Don't you think you should escort her home and make sure this lunatic isn't waiting to do something to her?"

"I don't need the police to escort me home. I need a cab." Lucy wasn't afraid of Wade Young, despite the beating her car had taken tonight. She assured the officer she could take care of herself and sent him on his way.

"I am not letting you get in a cab and go home alone. Are you crazy?"

"He's not going to do anything else to me tonight. This was his warning to back off. What he doesn't realize is I'm in the business of putting people like him in their place. He doesn't scare me."

"Well, he scares me."

Dylan's fear seemed so sincere that it gave her pause. He wasn't supposed to care. He didn't *really* care, and she didn't need him to, anyway. She had proven that long ago.

"I'm going to be fine," she said firmly. She started to make her way toward the nearest main throughway. She wouldn't find a cab on the school's quiet street.

Dylan blocked her path. His eyes pleaded with her as well as his words. "Will you at least let me drive you home so I know you're safe and your mother doesn't think I'm a horrible person for letting you get in a cab after your car was destroyed by some psychopath?"

Lucy pushed aside her pride and agreed to

a lift. On the bright side, she could tell Simon what it was like to take a spin in the Z28. She sank back in her seat. Unfortunately, the tension in the car made every moment of the drive far from the joyride Simon would have had in her place.

"I put together some notes and found some legal precedents you might be interested in," Dylan said, gesturing to the file folder he had moved off her seat when she got in. "If they can't get this guy for damaging your car, maybe you can make sure he goes to jail for some of the other terrible stuff he's done."

Lucy switched on an interior light and opened the folder, surprised he had bothered with a case that wasn't his. Not only had he saved her some time, but he'd been as thorough as ever. His detailed notes were incredible.

"Thank you for doing this."

Dylan shrugged. "That woman doesn't deserve to go to jail, and she definitely can't spend the rest of her life looking over her shoulder for that jerk. Whatever I can do to make sure she's safe, I'll do it."

He made Lucy's heart skip a beat. This was the Dylan she had known and loved.

Once they made it to her condo, Dylan slipped into the only open parking spot on the crowded street. He turned off the engine and proceeded to get out of the car.

"What are you doing?" Lucy asked.

Dylan walked around and opened the passenger door before she was able to unlatch her seat belt. "I'm walking you in," he said innocently. "You didn't really expect me to drop you off and drive away, did you?"

Lucy jumped out and slammed the door shut. "I'm fine. You don't have to follow me around the rest of the night."

"Humor me, Lulu. I won't bother you again once I'm sure there's no one waiting for you inside."

That name tugged on the imaginary stitches holding her heart together. His Lulu didn't exist anymore. She had died the day she was diagnosed with cancer. This Lucy was all that was left. She was flawed and defective, but she was stronger and more tenacious than she'd ever thought possible.

As gutsy as she was, though, giving him what he wanted was probably the only way to get rid of him. Dylan could argue for hours, as she had learned from experience.

Without a word, she unlatched the gate and led the way up the stairs. Lucy lived in a modest two-bedroom condo in Lincoln Park, not far from her sisters, who were spread out around the neighborhood. All the doors to her second-floor unit were intact and needed unlocking, which served as another clue she was safe as safe could be.

Once inside, she flicked on the lights and tossed her keys on the table in the entryway. Dylan cautiously made his way through the living room to the kitchen. Just as he was about to head down the hall, the door to the second bedroom opened. A blur of smoky gray ran right through his legs, causing Dylan to shriek and jump back, nearly falling over. Lucy's cat, Elmer, leaped gracefully onto the couch and meowed hello to his owner.

"Boy, imagine if that had been some killer and not a nine-pound, declawed feline," Lucy teased. "But I'm sure the screaming would have scared the bad guy way more than it did the cat. Elmer is pretty fearless."

Dylan scowled as he held a hand over his heart. "You could have warned me that you own a silent ninja cat."

His refusal to admit he'd overreacted made her laugh. "I forgot to mention I had a watch-cat? I could have sworn I told you that when I was explaining why it was perfectly safe for me to come home."

Righting himself, Dylan ran a hand through his hair. "No, you forgot about that part."

Lucy decided to save him the trouble and check the other rooms of the condo herself. There were no bogeymen hiding in the closet, no reason for Dylan to stay a minute longer. Having him here again after all these years threatened to unravel her.

"See? No one's here. No one is going to kill me. My mother will appreciate that you looked after me. Now, I have some work to do, so if you don't mind…" She held the door open.

Dylan's feet seemed to have taken root; he didn't move and Lucy wasn't sure what she'd do or say if he didn't leave. Her feelings for him made her too vulnerable. He was the only man she'd truly let in—not just her home, but her heart.

"Your mom is exactly like I remember," he said, taking that first step toward her. "She looks well. Is she well?"

Hit by memories of running to his apartment after hearing her mother's diagnosis and banging on the door until he answered, Lucy tightened her grip on the doorknob. She remembered that day as if it was yesterday, falling into his arms as she gave in to the fear that her mother might die. Dylan was the only person who had seen her that way throughout the entire ordeal. Around her sisters, Lucy had been the strong one, the one who had promised to do whatever it took to help their mom fight.

"She's amazing. Cancer didn't stand a chance against Maureen Everhart."

He was close now. His blue-striped tie was slightly askew and the memory of how he had promised to be there to dry her tears ripped through her. Whose fault was it that he hadn't been?

"Guess we know where you got your fighting spirit from, don't we?" He took a deep breath and gently cupped her cheek. "Please be careful, okay?"

Lucy stared down at his fancy black leather shoes. She and Dylan were both different people from the two idealistic law students who thought they would change the world together. They were equally to blame for the distance that now existed between them.

"Nothing and no one stands a chance against me," she replied. Lifting her eyes to his, she feared he could see how much regret she carried. She was sorry she hadn't been enough. Sorry her body was damaged. Sorry she had to make him believe she didn't care.

Dylan dropped his hand and sighed. "I knew that. I won't forget again."

He slipped through the doorway with a polite good-night. It was always so easy for him to leave, which should have made pushing him away easier, too. Still, it cut to the quick every time he did.

A FEW DAYS LATER, Kendall called in need of a last-minute babysitter. She had parent-teacher conferences to attend and Max wasn't able to sneak out of work for another hour or so. He managed Gianna's Cucina, an Italian restaurant located on the other side of the city. Being part owner was a huge motivation to work extra hard to keep the fledgling eatery in business.

Lucy was happy to help out her sister. Spending time with her niece and nephew allowed her to indulge her maternal side. She'd never have her own children, so Simon and Darcy were as close as she was going to get.

She didn't knock when she arrived at Kendall's, which usually wasn't a big deal. Today, it almost got her run over. Simon and another little boy raced through the foyer, nearly colliding into her.

"Sorry, Aunt Lulu!" Simon shouted over his

shoulder as he climbed the stairs two at a time. His friend was hot on his heels. Lucy recognized the boy as Eugene's grandson.

Kendall stormed into the foyer and handed Lucy the baby she was carrying. "What did I tell you about running through the house?" she yelled up the stairs. The boys were too busy making car noises to respond. Exasperated, Kendall opened the closet and yanked her coat off the hanger. "Sorry about that. Eugene was supposed to pick up Jeremy ten minutes ago. He should be here any second. I swear."

Lucy wasn't sure how to feel about her family being connected to someone who had such close ties to Dylan, but she chose to keep her concerns to herself for the time being.

"Thanks for helping out. I should only be gone an hour, hour and a half tops. Darcy ate. I just changed her diaper. Max promised to bring home some food, so don't let Simon have any more snacks. Call me if you need me. Love you. And you." Kendall gave her daughter a kiss on the cheek and was out the door before Lucy had a chance to say anything at all.

Little Darcy stared blankly at her aunt. Her face had an orange tint to it, leaving Lucy to believe dinner had consisted of either carrots or sweet potatoes. Her big, brown eyes were surrounded by what had to be a hundred lashes.

"What's up, sweet pea?"

Drool fell from the baby's lips as she grabbed Lucy's nose and giggled. Sometimes that sound was enough to melt *and* break Lucy's heart. How different things could have been if the cancer had never invaded her cells, if she hadn't needed to push Dylan away, if they could have married and started a family like all the other healthy, capable and willing couples out there in the world.

If. If. If.

None of those ifs mattered because cancer *had* shown up to the party, and it took her breast with it when it left. The worst part was that there was no telling when the disease would return. Lucy couldn't bear to bring a child into the world when the possibility of leaving him or her motherless was so great.

Darcy was content to play with the dozen or so toys that were strewn across the living room floor. Simon's and Jeremy's footsteps thundered up above and somewhat quieted when they were once again reminded there was no running in the house.

The doorbell rang and Lucy lifted Darcy up to join her in answering it. She opened the door expecting Eugene but found Dylan instead. Her heart skipped a beat as it always did when he was around. He seemed just as surprised to see her.

"I swear I'm not following you," Dylan said, treating her as if she was some sort of wild animal that might attack when threatened. "Eugene asked me to pick up Jeremy. He's helping out one of our neighbors with a plumbing issue."

Lucy stepped aside and invited him in. "I didn't think you were following me," she mumbled, feeling defensive.

He was dressed in a perfectly tailored charcoal-gray suit with a red tie that made him look as if he was running for office on the Republican ticket. She wondered if his politics had changed just like everything else about him.

"Where's Kendall?" He glanced around with his hands in his pockets and his bottom lip caught between his teeth. He seemed to be trying hard not to let his gaze fall on her.

Lucy shifted Darcy to the other hip. "Not here. I'm babysitting."

Once his baby blues found her, they locked on with an intensity that forced her to look away. She called for the boys, who groaned when they heard it was time for Jeremy to go home. They stomped down the stairs with grumpy faces until they noticed it was Dylan who had come to get Jeremy.

"Can Simon see your car?"

"Can I go to Jeremy's house until Mom gets back?"

"Can we ride around the block?"

"How fast does it go?"

The questions were coming a mile a minute. They were both busy tugging their shoes on when Lucy found her voice.

"We can take a look at the car, but no rides today, Simon." She turned to Dylan. "Is that okay with you? If you need to get out of here, I understand."

"I've got nowhere better to be than here with you, Lulu."

"Hey, I thought I was the only one who could call you that name," Simon said with a knitted brow.

"No one else calls her that?" Dylan asked, finally breaking his stare. "I thought for sure it would catch on. I stole it from you when you were a little guy, I liked it so much."

"You knew me when I was little?"

"I knew you from the time you came out of your mom's belly until you were about three."

Simon's shock registered all over his face. It wasn't surprising that he didn't remember. The two of them had met only a few times over those three years. Kendall had lived out east back then. The sisters saw one another only every three or four months.

Dylan had tagged along on one of those visits right after Simon was born. It had been during that trip that he had confessed to wanting a big family because he hated being an only child. On the flight home, he had attempted to guess how many kids Lucy wanted, reading her mind on the first try. She had lied and pretended he had gotten it wrong. Once he had guessed all the numbers between one and fifty, he'd caught on to the fact that she wasn't playing fair. It quickly became a joke that she wanted fifty-one.

Who could have known even one would be too many? Lucy shook her head, hoping to shake the memories loose. Whenever she was around Dylan, it became abundantly clear how much she had lost.

"How come you stopped being my friend when I was three?" Simon asked.

Lucy readied herself for the accusations that were sure to fly. Big, bad Aunt Lucy had chased away the guy with the coolest car in the city. Poor Simon could have ridden in the Z28 a hundred times by now if only she hadn't kept them apart.

"Stop being your friend? I didn't stop being your friend. I thought you still lived in North Carolina. Thank God I ran into your aunt and found out you were right here."

"Aunt Lulu didn't tell you I moved to Chicago?" Simon shot Lucy a questioning glance.

Dylan shrugged. "Don't be mad. I was hiding from her." He lowered his voice. "She's not very good at finding people when she plays hide-and-seek."

Simon and Jeremy laughed as if his ridiculous story was true. It was sweet of him not to blame her, but he really shouldn't have thrown her hide-and-seek skills under the bus.

"Maybe I didn't want to find you," she quipped.

No harm was meant by the teasing gibe, but Dylan's grin slipped. Maybe he was more bothered by the breakup than she had thought.

Simon gave him a pat on the back. "I don't believe it. Mom says Aunt Lulu hates losing so much that sometimes she pretends to win. You don't have to pretend, Aunt Lulu. We like you no matter what, right, Jeremy?"

"Sure," the other boy replied as he put on his coat. "Right, Dylan?"

Lucy held her breath in anticipation of Dylan's answer. Not that it should matter. It didn't matter.

"Why don't we head out and see the car," he said, dodging the question altogether. The boys were easily convinced to move on and flew out the front door.

"It's okay if you don't like me," Lucy said when the two of them were left with no one other than the baby. "I totally get it."

Dylan paused before stepping across the threshold. "That would make it so much easier for you, wouldn't it?" he asked over his shoulder. "It's nice to know neither one of us gets what we want sometimes."

CHAPTER EIGHT

WHEN EUGENE HAD asked Dylan to pick up Jeremy from the boy's new friend's house, a little voice in his head had told him to make up an excuse to get out of it. Of course, he could never tell Eugene no because that wasn't a word Dylan ever heard when the tables were turned.

So, he'd agreed to get Jeremy from Kendall's house, knowing there was a possibility of crossing paths with Lucy. All these connections to her were becoming a complication. They were interfering with his work. They made it impossible to sleep. He was distracted and constantly doubting himself. Lucy messed with his head. Maybe it had something to do with the fact he still couldn't get inside hers.

Maybe he was reading her all wrong, but it sure seemed as if Lucy wanted to assuage her guilt for not liking him by believing he disliked her, as well. Too bad for her, because the sad truth was he still loved her. He loved her even though she hadn't loved him five years ago, either. At least not enough to want a life with him.

He needed to get over her. He thought he had, but it was clear that was a lie he had told himself. It had been a secret he could hide because she wasn't around to remind him. Until now. Now she was everywhere.

He tried to avoid looking her in the face, as if she was Medusa. But staring at her too long unfortunately didn't turn him to stone. That would have been a relief. Stone was cold and unfeeling. Gazing upon Lucy stirred up too many feelings within him.

Dylan's heart pounded as he stepped out of Kendall's house and into the cool autumn night. Fall was in full swing in Chicago. The days were shorter and the nights were colder. It wouldn't be long before the weathermen would be carrying on about things like windchill factors and possible snow accumulations.

"Did you know the Z28 has the Corvette's V-8 engine?" Simon asked Jeremy. "This car can go faster than a Porsche 911 or a Lamborghini!"

Dylan caught up to the two boys. Lucy wasn't lying about how much Simon knew about cars. He was a boy after his own heart.

Dylan, too, had fallen in love with sports cars when he was about Simon's age.

"It's lightning fast, but I'd have to get it on a track to show you. Chicago PD takes speeding very seriously."

"Something tells me you're speaking from experience." Lucy joined them, carrying Darcy wrapped up in a blanket.

Dylan let the boys climb in the car and check out the interior. Being near Lucy wasn't easy. Seeing her hold a baby was almost too much. The ache in his chest was thanks to all the what-could-have-beens. She would have made an excellent mother to their children.

"I imagined you'd be married by now, working on your fifty-one." He didn't know why he said it. Of course, reminiscing with Simon reminded him about those heart-to-heart conversations he and Lucy had had. They had both wanted big families; at least, that was what she let him believe.

"Fifty-one was just your last guess. I never said it was right."

"I guessed every number from one to fifty. If you want more than fifty-one, then you should probably get started."

"Maybe the correct answer isn't any number

bigger than fifty," she said, bouncing Darcy on her hip.

Dylan narrowed his eyes. "What are you saying?"

Lucy bent at the waist to peer into the car. "Come on, Simon. Let's go back inside so Dylan can get Jeremy home to his grandpa."

"You never wanted any kids?" There was no way that was true. Why wouldn't she want children?

As she straightened up, Lucy moved Darcy to the other hip. She met his stare and her green eyes were cold as ice. "Some of us are better at being aunts than moms. Let's go, Simon."

Reluctantly, Simon climbed out of the driver's seat. He thanked Dylan for letting him see the car and Dylan promised him a ride the next time. As he watched the three of them walk back to the house, Dylan couldn't help but wonder if he had ever really known Lucy at all.

EUGENE WAS WAITING for them when they got back to the greystone. He thanked Dylan by inviting him in and offering him a couple of the cookies Mrs. Granville had given him for fixing her sink. Jeremy was only too happy to indulge in the goodies, as well.

"Simon's stepbrother has a bed that looks like a race car and Simon has a million Hot Wheels," Jeremy shared in between bites.

"A million? Where does he keep them all?" Eugene asked as he poured three glasses of milk.

Jeremy went on to describe every room in Simon's house. The typically shy boy seemed to come to life as he recounted his playdate. As much as it hurt Dylan to spend time with Lucy, seeing Jeremy this way made it worth the heartache.

"Well, I hope you thanked Mrs. Jordan for having you over," Eugene said, handing his grandson a napkin.

"She wasn't there when I left. Simon's aunt Lulu was."

"His aunt was there, you say?" Eugene turned his attention to Dylan. "Did everyone play nice?"

"Everyone got along just fine. We didn't stay long."

Eugene's laughter was warm and hearty. He gathered himself and encouraged Jeremy to get ready for bed. Dylan snatched one more cookie out of the tin before Eugene could put the lid on it.

"When you were together with that woman, did you bicker constantly? Because I try to picture the two of you getting along and I just can't do it."

Dylan sighed. "We used to be on the same side of things. Now what I want is in direct conflict with what she wants, hence the bickering."

Eugene sat down across from his friend. He turned his wedding ring around and around on his finger. "What is it that you want, exactly?"

"I have a client who's trying to buy a house that Lucy's center owns."

"That's what your client wants. What do *you* want?"

Dylan's gaze was fixed on that wedding ring as Eugene turned it. The man knew more about loss than Dylan hopefully ever would. Eugene had lost his wife to illness and his daughter to addiction. He knew what loneliness felt like and how dreadful it was to close the door on someone he loved.

"I want a lot of things, Eugene. But we don't get everything we want—you know that."

"How does Miss Everhart fit into those things you want?"

Dylan shifted in his seat. Lucy seemed connected to all the things he wanted out of life. The family he had wanted was supposed to be her family, too. "She doesn't fit anywhere. She broke up with me five years ago because she didn't want a life with me."

"She broke up with you?" Eugene sat back in his chair and rubbed his jaw. "The way she heats up every time you're near, I was sure you must have broken that woman's heart."

"I know, right? She acts like I ruined things between us, but she was the heartbreaker in our relationship. Not me."

"I can't believe Paige was right. She said there was no way Lucy got dumped. She thinks the woman is so smart, she would have broken up with you before you got a chance to do it."

"You and Paige have been talking about me and Lucy, huh? When have you been having these little chats?"

Eugene's cheeks flushed red. "She may have called me a couple of nights ago with a handyman question and it ended up being an hour-long conversation about lots of things that we have in common."

Another connection that put Lucy in his orbit. As in the case of Jeremy and Simon, Dylan couldn't begrudge Eugene's happiness.

Eugene, more than anyone, deserved to smile, and just the thought of Paige Clayton seemed to have that effect.

"Well, I'm not sure how I feel about the two of you discussing my relationship, or lack thereof, but I am glad to hear you and Paige have hit it off. That's exciting."

Eugene fiddled with his wedding ring yet again. "I don't know. I mean, I have Jeremy. She's admittedly married to her work. I'm not sure what we're getting ourselves into."

"Maybe you're making a friend. A nice person to talk to on the phone when you need someone to listen. Maybe she'll be someone to grab lunch with or that person who will drop everything to catch a movie with you. You don't have to put a label on it. Just enjoy her company. You deserve it."

"That's good advice from someone so young and *so* single."

Dylan pushed back his chair and rose to his feet. "Yeah, well, I might be young and I'm definitely single, but I know your selflessness is infinite. It would be nice to see you do something for you for once."

Eugene stood up and put a hand on Dylan's shoulder. "I could say the same thing about you, young man."

THROUGHOUT THE NEXT WEEK, Eugene's words echoed through Dylan's mind. Why would Eugene be worried about him? Didn't Dylan do things for himself all the time? The more he thought about it, the more he realized maybe not.

Dylan did things for his clients, for his company, for the people he cared about. At the end of the day, there wasn't much time left to do things for himself. If he could get Lucy off his mind and out of his heart, maybe he could find a way to be happy with someone else. It seemed like an impossible task, so for now, he'd have to focus on convincing his mother to let him do a bit of environmental law. If he was doing something he was passionate about, maybe some of that passion would bleed into his personal life with someone new.

STEVENS AND ELLIS was housed on the seventieth floor of the AON Center. Dylan had unobstructed views of Lake Michigan from his office. He couldn't begin to guess how much the firm paid to lease the space. Enough to feed all the hungry people down on the streets below. It was better Dylan didn't know the exact number.

Stepping off the elevator with his phone

in his hand, he scrolled through the morning news. Real estate analysts were predicting a big turnaround in the coming year; houses in neighborhoods like Lincoln Park and Logan Square would be selling for more than they had in ten years. That was great for Chicago, but bad for Prime Developments until they got their hands on Safe Haven.

Bridgette's anxious expression stopped him before he could greet her good-morning. Someone else had read the news—probably as soon as the paper was available. He slipped his phone into his breast pocket.

"Your mother is waiting in your office," she said. "She took your coffee. I can get you another one, though."

Dylan shook his head. "Don't worry about it."

Clarissa was seated at his desk as if she owned the place. Well, she did own the place, but it was supposedly *his* office. Her hair perfectly matched the color of her light gray suit. Her skin was flawless. Her blue-eyed gaze followed Dylan as he removed his black overcoat and hung it on the rack.

"You're drinking my latte," he said as he sank into one of the guest chairs.

Clarissa wrinkled her nose. "I thought it

tasted funny. What's wrong with regular coffee? Black and full of caffeine. Nothing's simple with your generation."

It wasn't even eight in the morning and she was already criticizing him. That had to be a record. "What can I do for you this morning, Clarissa?"

"I want to know what you've accomplished in regard to the Prime deal. How close are you to getting this shelter to accept an offer?"

"I've gotten in good with the executive director, created some trust there. Once they really think about it, they'll see that selling is in their best interest, and they'll sell to Prime because she likes me."

"Your confidence is nice, but there must be more you can be doing to negotiate this deal. What about that Everhart woman? Have you tried working that angle?"

Negotiations statistically went more favorably when there was a connection between the two sides. However, negative feelings could derail the whole thing. Dylan's presence seemed to create nothing but negative feelings in Lucy.

"That is not a good angle," Dylan confessed. "The executive director is the route to go. The connection is very positive and I expect talks to open up again really soon."

"I don't remember things ending badly between you two. I assumed you simply decided to go your separate ways."

Dylan was shocked that she was acknowledging his relationship. "Lucy and I ended things as amicably as two people can when one of the people in the relationship simply pulls the rug out from under the other."

"Some women are so pathetic. So what if you broke her heart. I can't believe she'd hold a grudge this long," his mother said, waving a dismissive hand.

Dylan laughed at her assumption. It was so telling as to how well she paid attention to him. He had been devastated by his and Lucy's break up. It practically drove him into a deep depression. He had hidden in his apartment, stopped hanging out with mutual friends for fear of crossing paths with her, forgotten how to laugh. There had been nothing but dark days following the brush-off Lucy had given him.

"I wanted to marry her, be the father of her children, grow old with her. I never would have broken her heart."

Clarissa leaned forward with her elbows on his desk. Her blue eyes were warm like a summer sky instead of their usual blocks of ice. "I didn't realize."

There were a million things she didn't realize about her son. Dylan didn't have time to enlighten her about them all. He shrugged off her uncharacteristic concern. "It was a long time ago—I'm over it," he lied. "But whatever it was about me that made her end our relationship is still very fresh in her mind."

"Fine," she said, returning to business. "Then you'll keep focused on the executive director. You've ingratiated yourself with her, now you need her to see the property as a liability. You need to convince her selling is the only option. We can't wait for her to figure it out on her own."

"I don't think she'll respond well to pressure."

"The pressure needs to come from somewhere outside of you and Prime. You need to convince her you're here to rescue her by offering her this deal. Do you think you can do that, Dylan?"

Bridgette knocked on the door and Clarissa shouted for her to come in before Dylan had the chance. Bridgette did a double take when she spotted Clarissa behind the desk and not Dylan.

"There's a Ms. Lucy Everhart here to see you. She said it's not important, but if you had a few minutes, she would appreciate if you would give them to her."

"Send her in," Clarissa replied to Dylan's horror.

"No," he spat out as Bridgette headed for the door. "Let me finish with my mother first."

"Nonsense. Send her in," Clarissa said, overriding him.

Bridgette knew better than to question the head of the firm and silently apologized to Dylan with a look. He waved her off, understanding she had no other option.

Clarissa sat back in his chair. "See? Maybe she's had a change of heart." She paused before adding, "About her stance on selling, of course."

"I doubt it," Dylan said, trying to refrain from blowing his top. He stood up just as Bridgette led Lucy in.

She was dressed in black leggings and a winter-white wool coat. She had a messenger bag wrapped around her body and she was clutching some files. Her head was covered by a pink beanie that matched the color of her lips and the twist of ribbon on her lapel.

"Sorry. I should have called," she said with her gaze fixed on Dylan.

He cursed himself for being happy to see her. As his mom had insinuated, she certainly wasn't here to confess feelings that had never existed in the first place.

"Dylan's always happy to make time for a former Northwestern Law grad." Clarissa stepped out from behind the desk and extended a hand. "Clarissa Stevens-Hunt. It's been a while."

Lucy startled, then recovered nicely. "It has been quite a while. Nice to see you again."

Dylan stifled a laugh because the only time Lucy and his mother had been in the same room together was at their graduation. His mom had missed the three dinners, two lunches and Christmas party they had set up so Lucy could get to know his family. Maybe she broke up with him because she'd seen how dysfunctional the Hunts were.

"Well, I have work to get back to." Clarissa gave Dylan a hug as if it was something she always did. Dylan tried not to appear too thrown by the gesture. "You should bring Mindy to the house this weekend for dinner. We'd love to see her."

Dylan struggled to keep a straight face as his mother disappeared through the doorway. *Who in the world was Mindy?*

CHAPTER NINE

THERE WAS A specific reason Lucy had come all the way into the heart of the city today, but at the moment the only thing running through her head was: *Who is Mindy?*

Obviously someone important enough to capture the almighty Clarissa Stevens-Hunt's attention. For some reason it made Lucy absolutely green with envy. She had tried for years to get into that woman's good graces, but Dylan's mother could never be bothered. Maybe that was why he'd walked away so easily. His mother never approved of Lucy anyway.

"You know what? I think it was a mistake to come here." Lucy started to back away. "You have your own cases to worry about, and I really have no right to be here and—"

"No, wait." Dylan grabbed her hand and pulled her back into his office. The simple touch sent shivers down her spine. "I'm curious now. You have to tell me."

Lucy should have debated about coming here a little while longer. She probably would have talked herself out of it if she had. Now she was stuck and was going to spend the rest of the day obsessing over this Mindy woman.

Dylan took his place behind his desk and motioned for her to sit, as well. Lucy felt like the biggest hypocrite in the world. She had told him time and time again that she didn't want anything to do with him, and here she was asking him for help. She rationalized her hypocrisy as necessary to help Nora. Lucy had no one else at Open Arms to consult with on legal matters and Dylan understood these kinds of crimes better than anyone.

"I just want to get one thing straight," she began. "I know I've been kind of a jerk. I also wouldn't blame you for thinking my being here, looking for advice, makes me an even bigger jerk. But I'm not here for myself. I'm here for a client who needs your help."

"I don't think you're a jerk, Lulu. I think I did something to make you really angry with me, and you won't tell me what it was, but I don't think you're a jerk."

Opening that can of worms was not happening. "We are on opposite sides when it comes to Safe Haven, but I'm hoping you'll fight on the right side in this case." She held up Nora's file.

"Lay it on me," he said with that smile that used to set her on fire.

He listened to everything she had to say and even shared some information he had gathered over the past couple of weeks. He had precedents and loopholes he thought they could use to get Nora off on any embezzlement charges. He had done his homework even better than she had.

"Did the police get back to you about your car? Could they place this guy in the area at the time?" Dylan asked as they wrapped things up.

"Let's be real. My best shot at getting this guy put away is all in here." She patted her messenger bag as she stood up.

"Well, the sooner the better. Turn that stuff over to someone. ASAP."

His concern was endearing and disconcerting at the same time. In some ways, he was still her Dylan. Full of creative ideas for righting the wrongs of the world. But he was also another Dylan, dressed in an expensive suit, sitting behind his mahogany desk on the seventieth floor of the AON Center. One month's rent here could probably save Safe Haven and buy another property as a backup.

"Thanks for your help. I feel a lot better about where we're going with this."

"Maybe we can be friends after all." His smile was melting her frozen heart. The old Dylan was fighting for a place in her life.

"Are you going to convince your client to back off on Safe Haven?"

He shook his head. "All right, so we won't be friends. Can we at least not be enemies? We both have a job to do. I'll respect your position if you can respect mine."

There was the new Dylan. He didn't work for justice or the underdog. He got paid to keep the wealthy wealthy. She was foolish to think he would back off because he was willing to help one woman fight to get away from her abuser. She felt sorry for him. This wasn't who he had wanted to be.

"We don't have to be enemies, but I will never support selling Safe Haven to Prime Developments."

"That's fair. I've always figured your vote was solidly in the no column." He got to his feet and made his way around his desk. Lucy could smell his cologne. It was the same as she remembered. "For the record, I'm really happy we're not enemies."

"No games, and who knows—maybe we'll move up to casual acquaintances."

His laugh made her wish she was funny all the time. "Only if you're comfortable moving that fast."

She wasn't comfortable with any of this. Any relationship with Dylan was playing with fire. For some reason, she wasn't ready to blow the match out just yet.

EMMA HAD THE day off and her boyfriend obviously did not, which was why she was waiting outside Lucy's building when Lucy got home from Dylan's office.

"Did you get my text? I think my phone's broken. Charlie said he sometimes gets my texts hours after I sent them. Do you think that means my phone is broken?"

Emma followed Lucy inside. For some reason she thought Lucy knew everything about everything. Maybe it was a big sister/baby sister thing. "I have no idea, Em, but you could call your provider and find out."

"Yeah, it's probably the phone. I'm due for an upgrade soon. Well, I sent you a text asking you if you wanted to go over some of my ideas for the auction to help save Safe Haven. I have a list of businesses that have offered items for bid."

Emma was a born planner. She had amazing instincts and exceptional organizational skills. Lucy's sister was also a little bit of a dreamer, but it was the combination of those things that made Emma who she was.

"Where were you anyway?" Emma asked when they reached the second floor. Lucy stepped into her apartment and dropped her messenger bag on the floor. "I called Open Arms and they said you were working from home."

Lucy glared at Little Miss Nosy. "I was consulting with someone on a case. Do I need to show you my parking garage receipt?"

"Oh, defensive. That means you were consulting with someone you don't want me to know about." Emma plopped down on Lucy's couch, stretching out so her feet rested on one armrest and her head on the other. Emma was the tallest of the Everhart sisters at almost six feet. "Was it Dylan? I thought you hated him."

Lucy went to the kitchen for a glass so she could get some water to drink or maybe throw on her sister's head. "I don't hate him."

"Kendall said you two almost came to blows

at Simon's first basketball game. That's why you got kicked out."

An extreme feeling of defensiveness overcame her. "Dylan would *never* hit a woman."

"Ooooh, interesting." Emma sat up. "You don't hate him. How *do* you feel about him? Are you discovering some old feelings you didn't know were still there? Maybe that flame isn't completely burned out. It's not surprising. You two were the cutest couple. I used to be totally jealous."

"You can stop talking now," Lucy said, taking a seat in the oversize chair across from the couch. She kicked off her shoes and curled her legs up under her. "Which businesses offered donations and please tell me they donated some good stuff."

"Does he have a new girlfriend?"

There was a possibility Lucy was going to have to call Emma's paramedic boyfriend and have him come save her after Lucy choked her to death. Clarissa's dinner invitation echoed in her head. *Bring Mindy.* Dylan very likely had a new girlfriend. Of course he did. He was gorgeous, brilliant, rich. He had to be one of Chicago's most eligible bachelors. Mindy was probably planning their wedding. She was probably the daughter of someone equally rich and notorious in the city. Their marriage would probably be big news. Everyone who was anyone would be invited.

"Hey, are you all right?" Emma's voice cut through Lucy's ridiculous thoughts.

"Can you just tell me what I'm going to do about Safe Haven, please?"

"You know you don't have to save it by yourself."

It felt that way, though. It felt as if Lucy lost sight of the goal for a second, everything would be lost. "Then tell me who's helping me."

Emma pulled out her phone and began reading off the list of supporters she had rallied. She had found many generous donors, but none of their donations were extravagant enough to attract attention.

"We need big-ticket items," Lucy said, feeling discouraged. "Things people will want to throw lots of money at to win." Lucy had called all of her contacts and had come up empty-handed.

"Well, you're still waiting to hear from the board members, right? It's their job to find the big money. They're supposed to have all the connections."

Lucy let her head fall back and her eyes

close. She practiced the deep breathing exercises she'd learned in treatment. Concentrating on her respirations, she willed the anxiety to go away.

Emma gave her a little push and squeezed onto the chair with her sister. Her long arms wrapped around Lucy and she rested her head on Lucy's shoulder.

"Stress is not good for the body. And for someone who refuses to eat French fries, you sure like to welcome stress with open arms. You really need to stop that."

"Is that your professional opinion, Nurse Everhart?"

"It is. You don't have to save the world, Lucy. You just have to leave it a little better than you found it. You won't have any trouble accomplishing that."

Emma could be the annoying little sister, but she had a heart of pure gold. It was Emma who had sat beside her during almost all of her chemotherapy treatments. Sometimes she would read to her from trashy magazines, other times she'd simply hold her hand. Lucy was truly blessed with two of the best sisters in the world.

"I promise to take better care of myself," Lucy said, leaning into the hug.

"Good."

Lucy titled her head so she could see Emma's face. "And what do you promise to do in return?"

"Love you forever?"

Lucy gave her sister an elbow jab. "I was thinking you should promise to eat more kale."

Emma snorted. "Dream on, sister. You've got a better shot at saving the world."

EMMA DIDN'T STICK around for dinner. She never did. Too afraid Lucy would make her like healthy foods. She had plans to drop in on their parents just in time to eat with them. In fact, their mother usually made extras on Emma's days off because she always seemed to find her way there for a handout.

Lucy was fixing herself a salad when her phone beeped with a reminder. She finished chopping the cucumbers before checking it. Her to-do list was so large, she could only imagine what this was prompting her to take care of as soon as possible.

Mammogram

The word was enough to kill her appetite. Why would she set that particular reminder to go off at dinner? She was due for her yearly mammogram. It was times like this that she wished she had let the doctors take both her breasts.

A little bit of vanity had played a part in her decision to keep one. Part of her identity was tied to being beautiful. She saw the way people looked at her, the way men always gave her a good once-over before approaching her. Lucy had learned early on to be empowered by her appearance. Pretty people got special treatment. It was a sad statement on society, but it was the truth.

More than anything, though, she liked being a woman. Nothing was more womanly than having breasts. Of course, two was the optimal number. She had chosen not to have the reconstructive surgery for the opposite reason she'd had for keeping the other. Lucy's scar was a permanent reminder that she shouldn't let any man get too close. The scar was the perfect excuse to put her walls up. No one would want half a woman. Dylan wouldn't have wanted half a woman.

The cancer could come back. The cancer probably would come back. The cancer was most likely to come back within five years if it was going to rear its ugly head. That was what the oncologist who treated her had said.

Five years. If she made it to five years, there was reason to hope.

Hope could be a dangerous thing.

Lucy was still under that five-year mark. Anything was possible. All the monthly self-exams couldn't tell her what one mammogram would. Did she want to know? Of course she did. Even if it meant another fight. Cancer might kill her in the end, but she would go down swinging.

Lucy dumped her salad down the garbage disposal and grabbed her keys and jacket. Hopefully her mom had made enough to feed two daughters.

MAUREEN HAD BAKED an enormous pan of lasagna for dinner. Had Lucy and Emma not shown up, their parents would have been eating the leftovers for days.

"Can you pass the Parmesan cheese?" her dad asked.

Lucy handed it over and resisted the urge to ask her mom if the lettuce in the side salad was organic or not. It probably wasn't. What could a few pesticides accomplish before she went in for her mammogram, anyway?

"So, we're used to Emma's coincidental arrival at dinnertime. What's going on with you,

Lucy Lu?" her mom prodded from the other side of the table.

"Can't a daughter want to spend some time with her family?"

"Of course she can," her mom replied, unconvinced.

"You're welcome anytime, sweetheart," her dad added. His fork froze before reaching his mouth. His face was full of fear. "Are you here to clear out the pantry again? I'm in the best shape of my life. Don't you dare take away my cheese puffs."

Lucy patted his arm. "Your cheese puffs are safe. I would never show up to clean the pantry when you're home."

"That doesn't make me feel better."

"How's the planning for the Hope and Healing event going? Emma said you've tasked her with finding some more auction items," her mom said, passing her father the bread. Bread always made him happy.

"We need some big VIP experiences. Do you still do business with that guy who works for the Bears organization?" Lucy asked her dad, remembering she had forgotten to tap her secret asset.

"Doug? He and I had lunch the other day. I won't say where because you'll give me that look." Lucy gave him the look anyway. "That's it. I hate that look."

"Can I have his number? Maybe he can get us a tour of the locker room or a day at practice or something. That would be a big draw." She poked around her salad. "See, coming here was the best idea I've had all day."

"Her other idea involved a meeting with Dylan Hunt," Emma chimed in. Her big, fat mouth managed to take her from favorite to least favorite sister instantly.

"You met with Dylan today?" The way her mother asked led Lucy to believe Emma had already brought up this subject before Lucy arrived. "Did you need to talk to him about Safe Haven?" She played with the hair at the nape of her neck, a sure sign that her curiosity was about to kill her.

"He's consulting on a case with me. It wasn't a social call if that's what Emma told you she thinks it was."

"You know we would all back off if you weren't so close-lipped about him," Emma said. "You found out you were sick and the guy fell off the face of the earth. I never knew if I was supposed to hate him for that or not."

Lucy tried to calm herself with deep breaths, but there were too many distractions.

"Your sister doesn't have to tell us her personal business if she doesn't want to, Emma. But if she did want to tell us, we would be happy to listen." Her mom quickly added, "Without judgment."

"I think we should go back to talking about the Bears. What a game last weekend, huh?"

"I'm just saying we don't know where to stand on things when it comes to him," Emma said, refusing to let it go. "It wasn't a big deal when he wasn't around, but suddenly he's everywhere and you're running off to have secret meetings with him. You can't blame us for being curious."

Lucy could feel the heat climbing up her neck. She didn't owe anyone an explanation. She certainly didn't want her family to know she had pushed him away because she'd thought she was going to die, that she still feared she might.

"Not everyone can handle having a sick girl-friend. Let's just leave it at that, okay?" She knew it was wrong to let them think he'd deserted her in her time of need, but the truth would only make them more worried than she could handle right now. Dylan's presence in her life was temporary. As soon as she raised enough money to keep Safe Haven off the market, he'd be gone for good.

"I hate him, then," Emma said, turning her attention back to her plate. She jabbed her fork into a cherry tomato with way more force than necessary. "I hate him and you can't tell me not to hate him because I do, even if you don't."

Lucy didn't hate him. She hated herself. Hated cancer. Hated what Emma would call fate. She hated a lot of things, but she didn't hate Dylan Hunt.

CHAPTER TEN

THERE WERE MANY things Dylan needed to do to get his life on the right track. Convincing Paige Clayton that selling was her only option was one of them. Once this deal was done, Dylan would have the confidence to go to his mother and ask for a change. Taking control over his career was imperative. Open Arms was fortunate to have their shelter in such a great area. Logan Square was the perfect place for a battered woman to start over. It was clean and safe. Businesses were doing well and hiring. It was a hopeful sign for the entire city of Chicago.

Unfortunately, Open Arms didn't have the time to wait for the benefits of a slow-moving economic upswing to kick in. They needed money now. Their annual fund-raiser could help temporarily, but Lucy was kidding herself if she thought she could hang on to that property forever. Prime wasn't offering them the best price, but it was better than going into foreclosure.

Under the guise of picking up some supplies he had left behind (quite purposely), Dylan stopped by Open Arms after grabbing some lunch. He prayed Lucy wasn't there. Her unexpected visit the day prior had left him feeling a tiny bit hopeful that they could eventually be friends. If she knew he was about to help Paige see the light, that possibility would go from slim to none. She also wouldn't let Paige listen to a word he'd have to say.

Hannah smiled brightly when he stepped through the door, and she bought his excuse for being there without question. The door to Lucy's office was shut. No telling if she was here or not.

Paige exited her office. "Dylan, what a pleasant surprise."

"Eugene has been on my case to pick up these tools I forgot when we were here the other day. He's very attached to his screwdrivers."

Her laugh was quick and easy. Paige had such a sweet disposition. "I can't believe he didn't mention it when I talked to him the other day."

Dylan tried to cover his lie. "Oh, he'd never

bug you about it. It was my fault. I deserved the grief."

"Well, tell him I said hello when you see him." She started to walk away, but Dylan stopped her.

"Paige, I just want to say I hope you guys get the funding you need to continue doing all the good work you do here. I don't want you to think that because someone's interested in purchasing your house that means anyone would want you guys to be unable to provide services to the women and children who need them."

"Thanks. I appreciate that." Her smile complemented her grateful words.

"I have a feeling that with Lucy on your team, you can't lose. The good news for Open Arms is that if Prime Developments decides to build around you, your market value is going to skyrocket." Paige's body language told him he had her full attention now. "It might mean crazy property taxes, but I'm sure you'll be able to manage."

"You really think the house will appreciate enough to impact our taxes?"

"After Prime puts in some luxury condos on either side? Oh, yeah. But Lucy told me you guys shouldn't have any trouble covering the house payments. I assumed she accounted for everything, including taxes."

Worry lines creased her forehead. She motioned for him to step into her office and away from her assistant's ears. "I'm not sure she did. She calculated things based on our current valuation."

"Well, with Logan Square experiencing so much growth, everyone will benefit when the money moves in." He could see the panic in her eyes and the questions rolling through her head. "Are you worried you won't be able to cover it?" he asked, trying to sound surprised by this revelation.

"More than worried. We're barely going to be able to pay the mortgage once we hit the new year. Lucy has hung all our hopes on the annual fund-raiser. We've never come close to raising the amount she's set as our goal." The trust he had built up over the past couple of weeks was paying off. Paige was spilling all the secrets. "If we only raise as much as we did last year, we'll either miss a payment or have to cut some programs to cover it."

They were in worse shape than he had thought. "Sounds like things are more serious than Lucy's let on. If losing the house is such a possibility, I'm confused why you're not in support of selling."

"Selling means no shelter until we can buy another house. But finding something in our price range that meets our needs and is in a safe neighborhood is pretty much a pipe dream."

It was clear why Lucy had dug her heels in. She didn't want to lose such a valuable service. If Open Arms had to close Safe Haven, a lot less good could be done. With Elizabeth vying for that land, it was almost inevitable, though. Prime had the advantage. They would buy that property eventually, perhaps for more than they preferred, but they would get it in the end because they had the resources to do so.

He could see Paige was beginning to question Lucy's motives. Dylan was torn right down the middle. If he was looking out for his client's best interest, he should tell Paige she needed to consider selling to keep all their other valuable services up and running while they searched for a new shelter location. At the same time, he understood why Lucy wanted to save Safe Haven. Just like Lucy, he wanted Open Arms to protect as many women and children as possible. The Logan Square property was a fantastic asset, but one that was

going to put Open Arms at risk of losing everything by financially draining the organization.

The words that came out of his mouth
sounded worse than nails on a chalkboard.
He hated to throw Lucy under the bus. "How
much of this is about Lucy's need to win?"

Paige shook her head and sighed sadly. "I
don't know. I'm more worried than I'd like
to be. There's something very personal about
this, especially with you involved."

"If she's not taking Prime Developments's
offer seriously because of me, I will bow out.
I don't want to be the reason you guys lose
everything, Paige."

"You'd do that?"

"If that's what you need to get her to respect your opinion on this. I mean, you are
the executive director of this place. I know the
holdouts on the board are looking to you for
answers. I think you should be allowed to tell
them selling is the right thing to do. If that's
what you believe."

"Excuse me?" Lucy's voice was teem-
ing with anger. Standing in the doorway, her
cheeks were flush with that ire. "Please tell
me you two are not talking about what I think
you're talking about."

"We're having an honest discussion about

the facts. And the facts are that we aren't going to make it, Lucy," Paige said, empowered by Dylan's validation of her fear.

"An honest discussion?" She glared at Dylan. "Is that what you've been having? What happened to 'no games'?"

"He's not playing any games. He was here picking up some tools he left behind after he fixed up this place *for free*. He wished us well and actually had nothing but nice things to say about you."

Lucy clenched her jaw. He watched her bite back the nasty things she probably wanted to say. "He's playing you, Paige. This is what he does. He's gotten into your head. He knew what you wanted to hear and then he led you down a path and made you think turning left instead of right was your idea instead of his. But *all* of this was his idea."

Her completely accurate description of his actions was enough to make Dylan sick to his stomach. He had orchestrated everything perfectly, but that didn't mean he had led Paige to a conclusion that wasn't one hundred percent correct.

"At least he's not making this personal!" Paige shouted. "You can't separate your feelings for him, for the company he represents, from the facts that are staring us in the face."

The hurt on Lucy's face created a horrible ache in Dylan's chest. "Is that what you think? That I'm not being objective because someone I used to date years ago is the attorney for some real estate developer? Is that really how little faith you have in me?"

"I have all the faith in the world in you, but you haven't been thinking clearly since he walked in the door. You've been unreasonable and rude. Obviously, I know you are usually very reasonable. Perhaps a bit blunt, but not outright rude. What else is it if it's not your personal conflict?"

"Unbelievable." Lucy's head fell back and she closed her eyes. When she opened them back up, they could have set Dylan aflame. "Are you happy? Is this what's going to get you some of Mommy's attention?"

Dylan's shoulders tensed. His plan hadn't been to undermine her or drive a wedge between Lucy and Paige, but that was the way it was going down. "This doesn't have anything to do with me. This is between you and Paige."

"According to Paige, this has everything to do with you. She's so worried my judgment is clouded because of some leftover feelings she thinks I have." Lucy took a deliberate step in his direction. "Let's be clear once and for all. I have no feelings for you, Dylan. Any feelings I did have disappeared a long time ago. That's why I broke up with you. Maybe Paige isn't aware of how it works, but usually when one person in a relationship realizes he or she isn't in love with the other person, that person walks away without any lingering feelings."

Actual confirmation of what he had believed to be true was the final twist of the knife in his chest. "You've always made that crystal clear."

"Good, then it's just Paige who's confused." She switched her attention back to Paige. "I want to save Safe Haven because it's the right thing to do. I'm advocating for the women and children living there now and the women who haven't mustered up the courage to call yet but who will need a safe place to come to when they do."

"Your heart is in the right place, Lucy. Don't think I don't know that."

Lucy clasped her hands together. "Give me until after the fund-raiser. Let me prove to you that we can do this."

It was as if both women had forgotten Dylan was in the room. Lucy had given Paige pause for thought. He wasn't sure whom he wanted the executive director to side with in the end. His bitter side wished it would be him, but the little bit of idealism he had left leaned in favor of Lucy.

"I won't say anything to the board members until after the fund-raiser," Paige relented. "If by some miracle we raise more money than we ever have, I'll support fighting to keep Safe Haven."

Lucy celebrated with a fist pump. "We're going to fight and win. Don't underestimate what we can do." She hugged Paige, providing Dylan with the perfect excuse to leave the two of them alone.

"I'm just going to…" he said, pointing at the door.

"I'll walk you out," Lucy insisted.

"Lucy," Paige warned.

"I won't push him into traffic, I promise."

Dylan wasn't so sure. He swiftly exited the building and headed toward his car. Lucy wasn't about to let him get away that easily. She placed herself between him and his escape.

"You said no games. You said you would respect our decision not to sell."

"We agreed to disagree. Plus, I didn't do anything. Paige voiced her fears. What was

I supposed to do?" He played dumb, but he could tell she knew better.

"You could have kept your opinions to yourself. You could have waited to play your games until we were sitting at the negotiation table. What you pulled with Paige is exactly the kind of thing you used to loathe."

"I don't know what you think I was doing, but you should look at your real motivations here. Are you trying to hang on to Safe Haven because that's what's best for Open Arms, or because it means you win and I lose?" She had nothing to say to that. "I really need to get back to work, so if you could..." He motioned for her to get out of his way.

Lucy held her ground for a couple of seconds, then stepped aside. "Paige appreciates all you've done to fix this place up, but don't come back here. Until we have a reason to do business with you, assume you have *no* business here."

He truly hoped he never had a reason to come back. In a perfect world, they'd find a way to secure the funds they needed. Elizabeth and Prime Developments would sell those other properties for a profit and build somewhere else. She didn't need Safe Haven the way Open Arms did. But the world was far from perfect.

"Understood," he replied, climbing into his car. Lucy stood and watched him pull out of his spot and into traffic. He'd always wanted to be her white knight. Unfortunately, he was the villain in this story and she wanted nothing to do with him. She had cast him aside long ago with no intentions of ever letting him return.

As he headed back to the office, he did a little self-reflection, as well. He had such promise when he'd graduated. He'd taken his place in his family's firm, believing he was going to make it better by winning his mother's approval and convincing her to let him do things differently.

When Lucy left him, he shut down. The only way out of it was to re-create himself. Be someone new—not better, just new. With his self-confidence shaken, he became more focused on pleasing his mother by winning all the cases she put him on than on convincing her he should pursue his own passions.

Now he wanted to feel good about what he did every day. He longed to make a positive contribution to the world. So far, all he had done was help a lot of wealthy people stay wealthy. If he intended to find a woman with the same character and drive as Lucy and have that family he wanted, he needed to be the kind of man that kind of woman wanted. He needed to be happy in his own skin. Finding happiness was harder than he ever thought. At least being someone so reprehensible made Lucy's rejection seem more reasonable. She would never want someone who protected the privileged at the expense of everyone else.

Dylan had no plans to ever go back to Open Arms if he could help it. The only time he wanted to see anyone from there was when they were signing the contract to sell Safe Haven to Prime. It wasn't until he was in the elevator that he realized that in his rush to get out of there, he had left Eugene's tools back at Open Arms. His chin dropped to his chest.

Great.

CHAPTER ELEVEN

LUCY WANTED TO kick herself for trusting Dylan. She should have known better. Working for Stevens and Ellis, it only made sense that he'd see the line between right and wrong as a little fuzzy. At least that was what she told herself so she didn't have to focus on what he had said to her. Was she putting her need to win ahead of what Open Arms needed? She wanted to believe that wasn't the case. She only had Open Arms's best interests at heart.

Maybe Paige wasn't the only one who was influenced by Dylan's mind games. It had been a fluke that she had even shown up to overhear his conversation with Paige. Lucy had spent the morning at Safe Haven, running a support group and meeting with Nora. Stopping by Open Arms had been a last-minute decision. She intended to share a few ideas with Paige before heading out to meet her mother so they could try to convince some donors to provide extravagant giveaways for the auction.

When she had seen Dylan's car parked on the street near the office, she'd foolishly been excited to see him. She had moved forward with some of the suggestions he had given her for Nora's case and had thanks to pass on from her extremely grateful client. Of course, instead of thanking him, she'd basically banned him from the premises.

"Please tell me you weren't too hard on him. I wasn't lying when I said he had nothing but good things to say about you," Paige said when Lucy returned to the office.

Lucy was flustered by Paige's refusal to see Dylan for what he was. "Why do you like him so much?"

"Why do you hate him so much?" It was a fair question, but the answer was much too complicated. She didn't hate him. Maybe she hated what he'd become since they had broken up, but she could never hate him.

"Can we talk about the Hope and Healing auction instead?"

"Doesn't this place look great?" Paige continued, waving her arms around. The facelift Dylan and Eugene had given the office was remarkable. "He didn't have to do that. He certainly didn't have to do the work himself. Maybe he was trying to get in my good graces, but he could have just hired Eugene. I think Dylan helped out because it made him feel good to do it."

Lucy wasn't in the mood to grant him that much credit, even though it was strange that he had gotten his hands dirty. "I'm meeting with some possible donors today. Can we *please* talk about who hasn't RSVP'd yet? I think we should extend personal invites to the ones who have supported us in the past."

Paige sighed, a sign she was done arguing. "Fine. I'll make some calls after my meeting with the event coordinator in an hour."

"I'll forward you the names via email."

"Fine."

"I'm also going to call my contact at the *Tribune* and see how soon she can get us some free press."

"Fine." Paige's "fines" sounded less and less fine as the conversation continued.

"Okay, well, I probably won't be back here until tomorrow. So if you need me, just call."

"Fine."

Lucy took a deep breath and bit her tongue. Paige usually had the patience of a saint. She always put up with Lucy's less than pleasant moods. Today, for some reason, Paige could forgive Dylan's manipulation but not Lucy's desire not to talk about him.

"If it was a story worth telling, I would tell you," Lucy conceded. "What happened between me and Dylan isn't anything I want to rehash, and the reasons I have for being frustrated and angry with him are mine. All I can say is that I am not letting those feelings get in the way of what I'm trying to accomplish here."

Paige's face softened. "I'm sorry for pushing. I guess I just see a man who doesn't even realize that he's looking for some redemption and that you're the only one who can give it to him."

That seemed pretty unlikely, considering what he had tried to pull today. "He doesn't want anything from me except Safe Haven."

Paige put a hand on Lucy's shoulder. "He doesn't want Safe Haven, his client does. I think he'd like to see us keep it, but he can't say that."

Where Paige's faith in him came from Lucy would never know. Just like when they had broken up, Dylan's words and actions weren't lining up. He had told her he couldn't live without her, but then he'd walked away. Now he swore this wasn't a game when clearly that was exactly what it was. Lucy couldn't believe anything he said.

"We'll have to agree to disagree," Lucy said, patting Paige's hand. "I'll email you a list of people to call for the fund-raiser."

"Fine," she replied with a wry smile.

LUCY'S PHONE BUZZED with the reminder she had been avoiding all day. That mammogram needed to be scheduled. She considered holding off until after the Hope and Healing fund-raiser was over. Waiting for the results would be torture and not something she could have taking up space in her brain while she attempted to get the gala to go off without a hitch.

Still, she decided to stop procrastinating and make the call. She could always schedule her appointment for a date after the fund-raiser. Maybe booking it would help get it off her mind. A busy-sounding receptionist rattled off some appointment slots that were far enough in the future they wouldn't compete with her responsibilities to Open Arms.

She hung up with the hospital just as she pulled up in front of her parents' house. Her mom was already outside, busy pulling the last of the fall weeds from the mulch beds that bordered the porch. The woman never wasted a minute of her time. Three fat pumpkins and two baskets of mums sat in front of the hay bale Lucy's dad had purchased during their trip to a suburban pumpkin patch with the grandkids back in October.

Lucy watched her mom work for a minute or so. Her mother was her hero, a symbol of strength and compassion. After her battle with cancer, she had dedicated her time to helping other women going through the same fight. Maureen still spent countless hours volunteering at the hospital she had retired from a couple of years ago.

When she finally noticed Lucy sitting in the car, she pulled off her gardening gloves and tossed them on the porch. Maureen was built like Emma, long and lean. Lucy still remembered how scary it was to see her mother after a couple of months of chemotherapy. Her collarbones had jutted out so far Lucy had feared she would break if she touched her. All the nasty side effects of treatment had left her vibrant and colorful mother pale and skeletal.

Lucy herself had dropped almost seven pounds the first month of her treatment. It had made all the doctors nervous and led to meetings with a dietician. Cancer made everything hard, even something as simple as eating. The dread of possibly having to deal with that again momentarily overwhelmed her.

"Why didn't you honk at me?" Maureen asked as she settled in the passenger's seat, unaware of the dark thoughts in her daughter's head.

"You looked like you were having so much fun, I didn't want to interrupt you. Plus, the last time I honked when Dad was outside, he told me I almost gave him a heart attack. I love you too much to kill you, Mama."

"Oh, well, then, thank you for not killing me."

"You're welcome. You can pay me back by helping me talk these people into giving away some good stuff." Emma had sent Lucy a well-researched list of people she believed could come up with some desirable auction items. With her mother's help, Lucy hoped to convince them all to participate. Maureen had helped organize auctions to raise money for breast cancer research for the past three years.

"Where to first?"

Theo Franklin was a member of one of the wealthiest families in Chicago. He dabbled in filmmaking but was better known for his philanthropy. Lucy was hoping for a cash donation as well as something for the auction. Emma had heard he was planning to shoot a movie with some big-name Hollywood star in the city this spring. Offering someone the opportunity to be on the set could draw lots of bids.

They didn't get any farther than the receptionist at his production office. "I'm sorry. Mr. Franklin apologizes and said you could leave any promotional information with me."

"We really wanted to speak to him about a fund-raiser we're putting together for Open Arms, a local women's shelter. We know he's been so supportive of similar charities in the past."

"He also wanted you to know that all of the money he plans to donate is already accounted for this year. Maybe next year," the receptionist said with an apologetic smile.

Lucy wasn't ready to give up. "Oh, we aren't exclusively looking for cash donations—that's why we're here to meet with him. We're having an auction and were hoping he'd consider donating something like an experience on a movie set, something that wouldn't really cost him anything."

"I'm sure he'd love to help, but he was very

clear that there was nothing he could do for you this year."

This became the common theme to everyone else's refusals. No one could help them *this* year. Maybe next time. The only person who came through was her father's friend, the one who worked for the Chicago Bears organization.

Paige texted that her phone calls to previous supporters weren't going much better. She was hearing a lot of the same. This year they had chosen to donate to other causes, but Open Arms would be on the top of their list next year.

Frustrated, Lucy took her mom home. It was as if the whole city was turning its back on Open Arms.

"You want to come in for some cookies?" her mom offered. "I made oatmeal raisin with organic oats and sweetened with applesauce instead of refined sugar—just for you. I was hoping we'd be celebrating, but I guess we'll have to settle for them being comfort food."

Lucy shut off the car. She appreciated that her mom always put forth the extra effort to make something Lucy would feel good about eating. No reason to let some perfectly good cookies go to waste. She knew her dad would take one bite and toss the rest.

Inside her parents' house, Lucy felt transported back in time. The wallpaper in the kitchen hadn't been changed since Kendall graduated from high school almost fifteen years ago. Their mom had insisted they freshen the place up before all the family came to town for the big graduation party. Kendall had been mortified that they had chosen to wallpaper instead of paint. She'd offered many times since to update the look for them, but their mom loved the fruit border and matching wall covering.

All three sisters' senior pictures hung in a row in the hallway that led to the family room. Lucy's hair had been as long as Kendall's back then, reaching halfway down her back. The girl in the photo had believed nothing could stop her. Back then, Lucy had thought the combination of her looks and smarts would get her wherever she wanted to go. She had started out in college as a political science major, decided she wanted to go to law school and imagined becoming a political activist who made history.

There were no limits back then, nothing to stop her from having a house full of kids and a long list of professional accomplishments. She had been on the verge of having it all, too.

"So, that was discouraging," her mom said as she opened the container full of cookies. The smell of cinnamon and apples wafted through the air.

"I'll have to get more creative. I've got only a couple of weeks left to make this year bigger and better. The event committee is tired of hearing from me. They thought they had everything under control and then I threw this auction at them."

"You'll figure something out. You always do."

That was true. She usually did. The answer was going to come to her eventually. Lucy ate her cookie, which tasted pretty good for not having any sugar in it. Sometimes she missed eating whatever she wanted. She used to think of food as her friend instead of something that could kill her. Her cancer hadn't been caused by something she ate or drank, but what she put in her body became something she could at least control. She couldn't change her genes, which were the biggest risk factor.

"I'm a little worried about you, though," her mom added. "You look like you've been burning the candle at both ends."

"I'm fine, Mom."

Maureen grabbed them each a napkin. "You say that, but I know you."

As much as it annoyed her that her mother always read her like a book, Lucy had always imagined being just like her when she had her own children. It seemed like a superpower that only moms could possess.

"I'd be fine if these people who want to buy Safe Haven would just back off."

"Does 'these people' include Dylan Hunt?"

This was a good example of why the superpower was annoying. "He's one of them."

"Since we're on the subject of Dylan, I was wondering about something you said at dinner the other night." She was a master of leading conversations where she wanted them to go.

"What is there left to say? I think I made it clear why I don't want anything to do with him."

"That's what I wanted to ask you about. See, I have this weird feeling that there's more to this story than he didn't want to deal with a sick girlfriend. He was there for you when I was sick. In fact, he was there for *me* when I was sick. He stopped by the house several times to check on me or bring me flowers."

Lucy had forgotten that he had done that.

She remembered how much it had made her love him, though. Not that it mattered now. "It's a little different when it's your girlfriend rather than her mom who's sick."

"This is true," Maureen agreed. "Of course, Dylan's a very intelligent man. He does his homework. I think he would have known what a huge factor family history played in your chances of getting breast cancer. I think he knew the risks."

Lucy could feel the heat of her shame climbing up her chest. She shouldn't have told her family he'd walked away knowing she was sick. "Mom, I really don't want to talk about this."

"Did you know that Dylan sends me flowers every Thanksgiving? The note always says, 'Thankful for your health.' That seems like a strange thing for a guy who couldn't handle being there for my daughter to say, don't you think?"

Lucy had no idea he did that. "Why didn't you tell me?"

"I didn't want to bring up a sensitive subject those first two years. You didn't want to talk about what happened and I wasn't about to push you when you were using everything you had to fight for your life."

"Why are you telling me now?"

"Because I don't think he knew. I don't think he knows to this day, does he?" The disappointment in her tone was enough to make Lucy cry.

She blinked back the tears. "He would have left eventually. I figured cutting him loose would save us both a lot of heartache down the road."

"Oh, Lucy." Even though her mother had guessed correctly, hearing Lucy confirm it seemed to break her heart. She rose from the table and pulled Lucy up and into her arms. "I didn't want it to be true. He loved you, sweetheart. He would have been there to support you."

Lucy felt the tears rolling down her cheeks. "You don't understand. He didn't love me as much as you think. When I told him we were over, he just left. If he had loved me, he would have fought for me. He would have acted like it bothered him. I think he was relieved. He probably did know I was destined to get cancer and was glad that I let him go."

Maureen laughed through her own tears. She pulled back to look at her daughter. "You have no idea what it's like to go up against someone as strong-willed as you are, Lucy.

Arguing with you is the definition of a losing battle."

"You can't say anything—not to him, not to anyone. I don't want Kendall and Emma to find out."

"You're fine with your sisters thinking the worst of a man whose only mistake was accepting your breakup?"

What she wanted to avoid was having to talk about this anymore. Lucy dropped her head. She had buried these feelings so deep that it was excruciating to have them yanked out. "Please, let me handle it."

Maureen held her daughter's face between her hands, forcing her to make eye contact. "Being honest with the people who love you isn't easy, but it's almost always the right thing to do. Unless your sister asks you if her jeans make her look fat."

Lucy let out a breathy laugh. "If I don't tell her, who will?"

Her mom kissed her forehead. "Don't be so afraid."

Lucy's throat tightened before she could promise she wouldn't. She thrived on the fear. The fear was what kept her sharp, stopped her from taking things for granted. If she didn't embrace the fear, life was sure to knock her over the head with something that would scare her to death.

CHAPTER TWELVE

DYLAN THOUGHT ABOUT asking Bridgette to stop by Open Arms and retrieve the tools he had now accidentally left behind. She would do it if he asked. She would do anything he asked her to do. That's what her job was all about. He asked for things and she got them. Sometimes she got them for him before he even noticed he needed them. She was very good at her job.

He was a coward. He was afraid of having to face any of the women at Open Arms. By now, Lucy would have convinced Paige and Hannah that Dylan was a horrible person. There would be no smiles when he walked in the door or thank-yous for his hard work.

"Your father is here," Bridgette announced after knocking lightly on the open door.

William Hunt stepped through before Dylan had a chance to say, "send him in." Physically, he wasn't a very big man, but Dylan's father had a larger-than-life presence. He was ex-tremely knowledgeable in more than just economic matters. He was also very perceptive and patient. Dylan often wondered if he'd inherited his ability to get inside someone's head from his father.

"Hey there," William said. His blue eyes were one shade darker than Dylan's. They looked like sapphires.

"Dad." Dylan got up from his seat to give his father a firm handshake. "What brings you over here?"

His dad walked over to the floor-to-ceiling windows. The city lights glowed bright and lit up the lake's shoreline. "Your mother sure wanted you to know she's happy you're working here. I hope you appreciate this view." He turned back toward his son and answered his original question. "I'm here to take your mother to dinner. If I don't come and get her, she usually forgets she's allowed to leave."

"That sounds like Mom."

"How are things going? I hear you're working hard."

Dylan wondered where he had heard that, or if he was just saying it to make conversation. "Things are going all right. This place keeps me busy."

"I bet. I don't know how you do it. I mean, I work hard, but if your mother's schedule is any indication of what it takes to be a successful lawyer, I think I'm glad to be in finance."

His mother's schedule was anything but typical. She billed more than everyone at the firm. "I don't put in nearly as many hours as she does. I would go crazy."

"We wouldn't want that," his dad said with a laugh.

"If I could go back in time, I'm not sure I would choose this profession."

"Really? Why's that?" William took a seat, making himself comfortable.

Dylan regretted opening his mouth. All of this would get back to his mother and then he'd hear how he wasn't dedicated enough. "I don't know," he said, trying to play it off. "Don't listen to me—it's been a long day."

"I worry about you, you know." His father may not have been there for him as much as Dylan had wanted growing up, but he had always felt as if his dad cared. When his dad had missed something important, he'd asked for the details. Maybe it was just his thirst for knowledge, but it had always come across as genuine interest and concern.

"Don't worry about me. I'm good, I promise."

His dad leaned back, staring as though he

was trying to see inside Dylan's head. "Well, you didn't say 'fine,' which makes me happy because no one is ever really fine when they say they are. But I'm not sure *good* is any better."

Dylan decided to be honest. Something he hadn't been earlier in the day. "Good means I'm surviving."

"So, not happy, only alive?"

Dylan shrugged. "I haven't been happy for a very long time. I'm not even sure what it feels like anymore."

His father seemed to let that sink in. He raked his hand through his salt-and-pepper hair. Every time Dylan saw his father, he realized how much he had aged over the past couple of years. He was ten years older than Dylan's mother. Retirement had to be in his near future, but Dylan wasn't sure if the man had a vacation mode, let alone the ability to slow down permanently.

"I'm sorry to hear that, son. If there's one thing I've hoped for you in this life it's to find some happiness. It's the only thing money can't buy."

Well, it was one thing money couldn't buy. The other was love. Real love.

"Who knows—maybe I'll figure it out one

of these days. Like I said, don't worry about me, Dad."

William didn't appear convinced, but he didn't push. "Have dinner with me and your mother. We have reservations at Mon Ami, but I'm sure we could find a way to get them to accommodate three instead of two."

Dylan wasn't a big fan of French food, but the invitation was tempting, if only because it was so rare to spend an entire hour in the same room with both of his parents. "That would be really nice."

His dad smiled as if he were truly pleased. He checked his watch. "Great. I'm going to go bug her next, which means you have at least fifteen minutes to finish up whatever you need to do before she's ready to go."

"I'll meet you guys by her office in fifteen, then."

CLARISSA WAS READY to leave about half an hour later. She spent the entire ten minutes it took the restaurant to find them a table on her phone, either barking orders at people or sending emails. She most certainly did *not* have a vacation mode.

"Your mother told me you ran into Lucy Everhart recently. That was a blast from the past, huh?" his father asked once they were seated.

Dylan set his menu down. Lucy was not a topic he'd expected to discuss at this dinner. He also hadn't realized how much his parents talked about him. Whenever he saw the two of them together, which was not very often, they barely spoke. When they did, it was to iron out household details like whether one of them had called the gardener or when they should schedule the delivery of the new furniture for the living room.

"I've run into her quite a few times recently. Her nephew plays basketball with my neighbor's grandson."

"Huh. Is she married?" his father asked.

"No," Dylan and his mother answered at the same time.

Dylan was startled a bit by her response. He couldn't believe she was paying attention to the conversation and was shocked that she knew anything about Lucy, since she barely remembered her name a couple of weeks ago.

"I thought for sure she was the girl you were going to marry," his dad said.

Dylan picked his menu back up and used it to shield his face. He could feel his face getting warm and was embarrassed by the way simply talking about what could have been made him feel. "Well, she didn't want to marry someone like me."

"What's that supposed to mean?" his mother asked, sounding a tad annoyed. "What's wrong with someone like you?"

He was someone who could easily forget what was important to him—that was what was wrong with him. He was more like his mother than he had ever imagined.

"Nothing. That's not what I meant."

She pushed his menu aside so she could see his face. "What did you mean, then?"

"I don't know," he replied, flustered. "I don't know why we didn't work out. We just didn't."

"That's a shame. You seemed happy when you were with her," his dad said from behind his own menu.

He had been, but he'd blown it. He'd never know exactly how. She'd never tell him.

Thankfully, there was no more talk of Lucy. The waiter came to take their order and his mother went back to her phone.

Mon Ami was a quaint bistro. The dark woodwork was a nice contrast to the textured walls that appeared almost gold thanks to the choice of lighting. Dylan found himself taking mental note of some of the design elements and wondering how he could work them into his next project. He planned to redo his master bedroom once the kitchen was finished.

The wine arrived and was poured. Dylan's father raised his glass. "I have an announcement. I'm glad you could be here to hear it, Dylan." Clarissa glanced up from her phone with a furrowed brow. "I turned in my official notification of retirement today. As of January first, I will no longer be a member of the workforce."

Shocked but not surprised, Dylan tapped his glass to his father's. "Congratulations, Dad. That's great. Good for you."

"When exactly did you decide this?" Clarissa wasn't as excited about the news. Her glass of wine stayed right where the waiter had placed it.

"I've been thinking about it for a while now, but I wasn't sure until about a week ago."

"And you weren't going to discuss it with me first?"

"I didn't realize you would have an opinion."

This was another first. His parents didn't usually argue. They weren't around one another long enough to get angry.

His mother tugged on one of her diamond

earrings. "You're making a decision that impacts our lifestyle. Of course I have an opinion."

"I didn't realize my retirement would affect how you live your life," he replied calmly.

"What in the world will you do if you don't work? Sit around the house, bored out of your mind?" Clarissa's voice rose enough to get the attention of the people at another table.

"Maybe I'll travel. Maybe I'll do some charity work. Maybe I'll learn how to paint."

"Don't be ridiculous," she scoffed. "The right side of your brain hasn't been put to use in so long, it wouldn't know what to do with a paintbrush. And who are you going to travel with when I need to be here working?"

"Maybe I'll travel by myself, or maybe I'll invite our son."

Dylan choked on his wine. Retiring was one thing, becoming Dylan's travel companion was another.

His mother laughed. "In case you haven't noticed, our son also works."

"I'm sure his boss will give him some time off if he asks nicely." William smirked and gave Dylan a wink.

This had officially become the most interesting dinner Dylan had ever had with his parents. His mom was not finding it as entertaining as he was.

"I'm going to go make a phone call. I assume you informed them that you'll be presenting your own retirement package for their review." Without waiting for him to answer, she left the table.

"I think she's excited about this next phase in my life," his dad joked.

Dylan snorted and finished off his drink. "Yeah, I'm not so sure that was the vibe she was giving off."

"You never have read your mother very well."

"Not sure what other way there is to read her on this one." His mother wasn't hard to understand because she had no qualms about stating exactly how she felt about things. Dylan never had any trouble telling when his mom was annoyed or disappointed.

"Okay, she's not excited, but she's not as angry as she seems, either, which is what you think she's feeling." His dad adjusted the napkin on his lap. "She's afraid. She's worried that my retirement means she'll have to slow down or possibly retire, as well. Your mother has no idea how to slow down."

"I really don't see her ever retiring, Dad.

She'll probably close deals from her death-bed." Dylan's mother would never choose to stop. Her work was the most important thing in the world to her.

"Maybe she won't retire. I'm not going to make her stop working. Working makes your mother feel competent. She's very good at what she does. The things your mother doesn't know how to do, she simply avoids. It doesn't mean she doesn't want to do them or doesn't wish she knew how. There are a lot of things she's afraid she won't be any good at, and if there's one thing your mother can't stand, it's failing."

Clarissa Stevens-Hunt was the toughest woman Dylan had ever known. She wasn't afraid of anything and her confidence knew no bounds. What could possibly intimidate her?

"I don't know that I'd call it fear. I think she has her priorities and work is number one. Always will be."

His father shook his head and set both elbows on the table. "Why do you think she's always wanted you to work for Stevens and Ellis?"

Dylan could think of a lot of reasons. The most likely reason was to control him. She wanted him to be like her. It was the family firm. Her grandfather hired her father, who hired her. It made sense that she wanted her only son to work there, as well. It was expected.

"Working there was always my destiny, right?"

William frowned. "Clarissa loves you more than you'll ever know, but being your mother terrifies her. Being your boss is a dream come true because she gets do what she's good at and have you close."

Dylan needed time to process his father's explanation. Mind-blowing didn't come close to describing this information. His mother returned to the table and Dylan found himself looking at her in a different light. Did she really micromanage him because she wanted to be near him? Were all those phone calls checking up on cases just her way of showing she cared? Expectations were her terms of endearment?

"I did not make a mention of a retirement package," his father said to her once she sat back down. "I was hoping you could help me with that."

She placed her hand on his, a tiny but significant sign of affection. "I'll draft something and have it for you to review before the end of the day tomorrow."

"Thank you, sweetheart."

Just like that, their argument over his retirement was over. He had found a way to make her feel useful, allowing her to relax and accept his decision to stop working. His father was more brilliant than Dylan already thought he was.

"We should meet tomorrow and discuss what's happening with the Freemont case you're working on," his mother suggested after she sipped her water.

For the first time in four years, Dylan didn't see that as a threat but as her way of asking to spend time with him. This put a completely different spin on their relationship. As crazy as it all seemed, it made perfect sense.

"I'll have Bridgette clear my schedule whenever you can fit me in."

She nodded and flashed him a smile. Dylan caught his father grinning, as well. Suddenly, everything he thought he knew about his parents was turned on its head. It was strangely comforting, even though it meant he had misinterpreted everything his mother had ever said and done his entire life. The thought that his mother loved him in her own weird way made him feel something he hadn't felt in a very long time...*happy.*

CHAPTER THIRTEEN

AFTER A DISASTROUS day filled with Dylan's manipulation and the crushing blow of hearing the word no over and over again while seeking donations for the auction, Lucy wasn't sure what today would have in store. She hoped for the best and planned for the worst.

The only thing on her agenda was to prepare for the fund-raiser that was only a few days away. A small group of generous women had gathered at board member Sharon Langston's house. Sharon was the head of the fund-raiser committee and had donated all the auction baskets and containers. She had also provided all the materials to make centerpieces for the gala.

Lucy brought Emma along, since she had the day off. Lucy's baby sister had been helping their mother with St. Joe's breast cancer awareness fund-raiser for years. She was used to being in charge, and Sharon's way of doing things was not cutting it in Emma's book. An epic battle for control quickly began.

"What if we do this?" Emma asked, attaching a lavender paper heart to the glitter-covered branch sticking out of the vase full of purple stones that made up the centerpiece. "We could attach an item number like this and break up one of the baskets to make each centerpiece a biddable item."

"Oh, I like that idea," one of the ladies replied.

Sharon quietly seethed, then said, "We reuse the vases every year."

"But Emma's right—if we auction them off, we can bring in more money than we would by selling one basket," Lucy said in defense of her sister's idea.

"We didn't plan for the centerpieces to be auctioned off. It's too late to add another prize," Sharon insisted.

"You wouldn't have to change anything," Emma said. "Just tag each centerpiece with these hearts we were going to set on the tables anyway. I'll print up a sheet for each table so people can write down their bids, and we'll just run around at the midpoint and collect all the sheets. The only extra work you'll have to do is announce the winners."

Sharon glowered at Emma but agreed. It wasn't long before Emma offered up another suggestion and Sharon found a reason why it wouldn't work. Eventually, Lucy had to convince Sharon to run to Party City and buy every purple candy in the place just to separate the two of them.

With Emma now steering the ship, the rest of the volunteers got their work done much faster. Baskets and bins were filled and tagged. Centerpieces were glittered and also tagged. Everything was moving along nicely.

Lucy sat, working on her laptop. The responsibility of creating a slideshow for the live auction fell to her. She was typing up the description for a day with the Chicago Bears when her phone rang.

"This is Lucy," she said, holding one finger in her ear to block out the chatter coming from the other room.

"I think I'm being followed." The panic in Nora's voice sent a chill up Lucy's spine. "I was heading back to Safe Haven, but I don't think I should. What if it's Wade?"

"Where are you?" Lucy walked farther from the noise so she could focus on Nora.

She rattled off street names and Lucy told her to hang on. She quickly used her computer to search for the nearest police station to Nora's location.

"If you think he's following you, I need you to get in a cab and tell the driver to take you to the police station on Halsted. When you get there, tell the sergeant at the desk that you fear for your safety. Tell him you were being followed to Safe Haven by your abusive husband. They'll ask you if you want an escort, and you tell them you are waiting for me. I'll be there in a few minutes, okay?"

"Okay." Nora's voice was still shaky.

Lucy hung up and shouted for her sister. If Wade Young wanted to play games, Lucy had a fun little game of cat and mouse to play with him.

Lucy dropped off Emma a block away and told her to go straight into the station and wait. After a few minutes passed, Lucy parked nearby and exited her car. She pretended to be on her phone and paced outside the station for a minute or so to make sure that if Wade was watching, he saw her.

When Lucy got inside, she found Emma and Nora waiting as she had asked. Quickly, she had the two of them switch jackets while she explained the plan.

"Emma and I will leave first. Once we're gone, we'll have an officer take Nora to Safe

Haven. All I ask is that you make sure the hood of this jacket is up at all times. Can you do that?" she asked Nora, whose face was pale with fear.

She nodded but still seemed unsure. "What if he figures it out? What if he follows me?"

"He's not going to figure it out. He's going to follow me because he's smart enough to wait you out but not smart enough to know I'm smarter than he'll ever be," Lucy reassured her.

Nora swallowed hard and thanked Emma for her help. Lucy made sure the patrolman who would drive Nora to Safe Haven had all Lucy's information so he could contact her if there were any concerns the location of the shelter was compromised.

Emma wrapped Lucy's scarf around her head to cover her face, since Nora's dark gray peacoat had no hood. "Since when is your job so dangerous?" she asked as they stepped outside.

"This is nothing."

Emma glanced around even though she had no idea whom she was looking for. "You better hope my car comes out of this okay. I wouldn't have driven you around today if I knew we were going to be luring the guy who destroyed yours to come after us."

"Your car will be fine. Stop worrying and hunch over a little. You're too tall." Lucy scanned the cars along the street in the lot across from the station. He had to be around here somewhere. Hopefully, he would be fooled by the switcheroo.

The two sisters got in the car. Emma sank down in the seat. The only part of her face showing were her eyes, and they were constantly surveilling the area. "Charlie is never going to believe you talked me into this." She pulled out her phone and began texting.

Lucy's focus was on the road. She pulled into traffic and checked the rearview mirror to see if someone else pulled out, as well. Her heart was beating a mile a minute. She knew she shouldn't be worried. Once Wade found out he had lost Nora, he would retreat back to his house to start plotting again.

He wasn't going to have very long to come up with a new scheme because Lucy's plan to put him behind bars had already been put into action. Step one was getting the money that he had embezzled under Nora's name, so they could return it to the company it came from. Step two was to turn over the documents showing the rest of the money that was either hidden in some offshore accounts or dumped in a shell company he'd set up in Texas.

"Charlie says he's not too happy with you putting his woman in danger." Emma laughed and typed something back.

The two of them were perfect for each other. They were both the youngest in their families and had this childlike quality that was not something Lucy would change but could get annoying when they were in the middle of a serious situation.

"Tell him to get back to work and not to worry."

The sound of Emma giggling did help ease the tension. "I told him you know karate and would save me. He said he's going to call you Kung Fu Lu." Her phone beeped with another text. "Oh, my gosh, he just said try not to get killed because then he'd have to take the ring back. Did you hear that? Do you think he's messing with me?" She typed something out. "He better not be messing with me. Did he just propose to me in a text message?"

Lucy laughed at her sister's ridiculousness. "He didn't propose—he hinted that he might be thinking about it. Relax."

Emma exchanged a dozen more texts with

Charlie before putting her phone away. She reached over and squeezed her sister's leg. "He's seriously going to propose. I'm freaking out a little bit."

Of course he was going to propose. They'd been together for almost a year and a half. He treated her like a princess, and she was completely smitten by every goofy thing he said and did. They were meant to be together.

"What are you so worked up about? Haven't you guys talked about getting married?"

"Yes, but this isn't talking about it. This is him making plans to actually do it. *I* make plans. Charlie lives in the moment. He could do it at any time. I'm freaking out." Emma's head fell back against the headrest. "But in the best way possible."

Lucy gave her sister a heartfelt smile. "I'm happy for you. He's a good guy and he's in love with a great girl. I'm glad that some people get it right in this world."

"I'm the lucky one. He gave me a second chance and I will forever be grateful."

Emma had almost let her fear cheat her out of the best thing that had ever happened to her. Lucy heard her mother's voice in her head, reminding her that she had pretty much done the same thing. The difference between the sisters was that Emma had found the courage to overcome that fear and was lucky enough to hang on to Mr. Right. Lucy had let the fear win, but she still believed it was the only thing she could have done to protect both her and Dylan from the pain they would have suffered later.

Lucy shook off thoughts of Dylan. She glanced in the rearview mirror for a tail. "You can take off the scarf now. We're far enough away. I want him to see you're not her."

Emma unwrapped herself and threw the scarf in the backseat. "What should I do? Stick my head out the window?"

"I'm going to drop you back at Sharon's. Tell her I'm sorry we had to take off and that I'll call her later to explain." She dug through her purse with one hand while driving. Tossing a twenty-dollar bill at her sister, she slowed down and scanned for a good place to stop. "Get a cab home and I'll bring your car to you later, okay?"

"You sure you're going to be okay?" Emma was back to being as serious as a heart attack.

"I'll be fine. I'm Kung Fu Lu, remember?"

"Is my car going to be fine?" Emma arched one brow, making Lucy laugh.

Throwing the car in Park, Lucy shooed her sister away. "Get out of here. Thanks for helping me out today—both with the fund-raiser and the secret-mission stuff."

Emma did a quick scan up and down the street before opening her door. "Anytime, sis."

Lucy waited to make sure Emma was safely inside Sharon's house before pulling away. She needed to get to Open Arms and tell Paige what was happening.

PAIGE WASN'T SURPRISED by the latest developments. This wasn't the first time an abuser had come looking for his wife or girlfriend. Nora reported getting back to Safe Haven without the eerie feeling she'd had earlier. The patrolman who drove her to the shelter promised to have someone keep an extra eye out overnight.

There was also the possibility that Nora was being paranoid. The closer they got to blowing this thing wide-open, the more nervous she became. She had her mom staying with an aunt for fear her soon-to-be-ex would go after her family. It was quite possible his ego had him believing Nora wasn't going to do anything that could get her in trouble, as well. Again, he didn't know whom he was up against. Lucy would see to it that Nora didn't suffer physically, emotionally or legally because of Wade Young.

Emma had texted that she'd stayed and helped finish up the centerpieces and baskets. Everyone had understood why Lucy had to go. With that out of the way, all Lucy had to do was finish up the slideshow for the live auction and call the counselor on staff at Safe Haven to make sure she followed up with Nora tonight.

"You know I think you are the smartest person I have ever met," Paige said from the doorway to Lucy's office. "But I'm getting nervous about how much money we need to raise and how few big donors we're getting to show up at this thing."

Lucy stopped what she was doing and stretched her arms above her head, letting out a frustrated breath. "You're *getting* nervous? You were nervous long before today."

"I want you to know I talked to a real estate agent today and asked her to get me some numbers. How much is the house worth and what are some comparable places going for in the area." Paige raised a finger so Lucy wouldn't interrupt. "I just want to be aware. I need to know what all the options are if we have to look at other options."

"We have a lot of supporters, Paige. People are going to come through for us. We're getting some press in a couple of days. I have calls in to the local news stations, too. I'm hoping they'll give us some time. Even if they put information on their website, it could help."

Lucy could see Paige losing faith. Her sigh was almost apologetic. "I love that you don't want to give up. I also don't want you to hate me for thinking about it."

"I could never hate you," Lucy assured her. "I get it. You do what you need to do and I'll do what I need to do. Hopefully, all your searching will be for naught because all my work will pay off."

"I sure hope so." Paige started to go but turned back. "By the way, you might want to shut your door or get out of here. Dylan called and he's stopping by after work to get the tools he forgot the other day when you scared him away."

Of course her day would end like this. "Thanks for the concern, but I think I can handle it."

"Oh, I'm not saying you should go for your sake. I'm more concerned for him than I am you," Paige said, cracking a smile before turning to leave.

She was probably right. In Lucy's current state of mind, she was likely to take out some of her anger at the entire male population on

Dylan. He was an easy target. There was also some fear that the talk she had had with her mother the other day would make it hard not to ask him why he still sent Maureen flowers at Thanksgiving. That conversation could lead to disastrous things—like her admitting how he made her feel and why she had broken things off.

"How long do I have before he shows up?" she shouted from her desk.

"He said he'd be by around six!"

Lucy had a good hour before she had to make herself scarce. That shouldn't have been an issue. Except that she didn't realize how easy it was for her to fall down the internet rabbit hole while looking for the perfect picture to go on a slide touting a helicopter ride around the city. Arial shots of Chicago led to a link about drones, which led to an article on privacy laws. What should have been a two-minute search turned into an hour-long time-suck.

Paige reappeared in her doorway. "Please tell me you'll be nice. He doesn't want any trouble."

Lucy checked the time. She cursed herself for being so easily distracted. She closed her laptop and started shoving everything she needed in her bag. "I'm leaving. I didn't realize how late it was."

She was out the door before Paige had a chance to wish her a good evening. She wrestled with her bags and patted her pockets for Emma's keys. She should fill her sister's car up with gas as a thank-you before returning it. Maybe she'd even get it washed. That would be an extremely thoughtful gesture.

Setting her laptop bag down beside the car, she began to rifle through her purse for the keys that were not in her pocket. Had she thrown them in there? She couldn't remember. A dog barked in the distance, causing her to glance up. The street was empty and one of the streetlights was burned out. She'd call the City in the morning. Someone needed to come fix that quickly, now that it was getting dark so much earlier in the evening.

The keys weren't in her purse. If they weren't in her pocket or her purse, they were probably still sitting on her desk. She had rushed out so fast, it wasn't surprising that she'd forgotten them. Bending over to pick up her laptop bag, another sound caught her attention.

Wade Young was a large man, tall and athletically built. His shoulders were broad and his gloved hands looked as if they could easily palm a basketball. His hair was dark like his eyes, which looked almost black in the moonlight. Long legs allowed him to cover a lot of ground in a few steps. He was beside her before she had a chance to run.

"Where is she?" he demanded. His face was red, either from the cold or from his rage.

Lucy felt her heart pounding in her chest. Every sense seemed on high alert. She could smell the cigarettes he must have been smoking while he waited for her to come outside. His breath was warm on her face and her bags suddenly felt as if they weighed a ton.

Taking a cautious step back, Lucy gave him one warning. "I suggest you get back in your car and go home, Mr. Young, before you do something that will get you in more trouble than you need."

His fist came up and Lucy's hands went up defensively. The sound of breaking glass signaled it wasn't her he had planned to hit. Emma was not going to be happy. The passenger-side window was shattered. His voice was threatening as he shouted, "Where is she?"

Lucy was about to pay him back for damaging her sister's car when out of nowhere came Dylan. He slammed into Wade and wrapped his arms around him as he tried to bring him to the ground.

Wade broke free and coldcocked Dylan with one punch. Lucy felt a rush of panic and then a wave of anger. She dropped her bags. It was one thing to break her sister's car window; it was another to break her ex-boyfriend. Wade Young wouldn't know what hit him.

CHAPTER FOURTEEN

DYLAN HAD HAD one objective. Get in, get out. *With* the tools this time, of course. That had been the plan and he had been sure he would stick to it no matter what. Lucy could have been there and that would have been fine. There had been nothing left to say, so she could make whatever provocative comments she wanted to make—he would just smile and be on his way.

It had been an excellent strategy, and it would have worked, too, if it hadn't been for the man who was trying to kill the love of his life. Dylan hadn't noticed them at first. He'd parked his car and was rehearsing how he'd tell Lucy to have a great night if she started anything when he heard the glass break.

It hadn't been until he was a few feet away that he noticed it was Lucy, standing there frozen in fear. The beast of a man standing beside her had looked as if he was ready to kill.

Killing Lucy wasn't an option, however. Not while Dylan was breathing.

Granted, fighting had never been something Dylan enjoyed. He hadn't grown up with siblings to wrestle with or gotten into any kind of physical altercations with anyone. He had once broken up a fight in college, but that was the extent of his fighting experience.

The man threatening Lucy had probably been in a few brawls in his lifetime. Tackling the guy had pretty much felt like ramming his body into a stone pillar. Fueled by the most adrenaline he'd ever had running through his body, the pain hadn't registered. Dylan had believed he could get the man on the ground and restrain him until the police could get there.

Unfortunately, that hadn't been the way things went down. One minute he had been grappling with the attacker and the next he had been on the ground seeing stars. All he could think was that he had failed. Who would save Lucy now?

While he tried to shake off the fog that was beginning to cloud his vision and the ringing in his ears, Lucy was busy saving herself. By the time Dylan could see straight, the man who had knocked him out was on the ground unconscious.

Lucy knelt down beside Dylan and put her hand on his face. "Don't move, okay? I have to call the police."

She looked like an angel. A halo of light surrounded her head and her blond hair was glowing. Dylan closed his eyes; she was too beautiful.

"Hey, stay with me, Dylan." The firmness of her tone forced him to comply. "Keep your eyes open, okay?" She had her phone pressed to her ear. He wondered who she was calling.

The ringing in his ears was too loud and one eye wouldn't stay open no matter how hard he tried. The ground was so cold. And wet. Why was the ground wet? The back of his head hurt, and all Dylan wanted to do was go home and go to bed. Sleep sounded really good right now.

"Dylan! Stay with me. I need you to stay awake, okay?"

He wanted to do what she said, but it was too hard. His left eye was sealed shut and his right one could stay open for only a couple of seconds at a time. Getting some sleep was for the best. He'd be able to look at her after a little rest.

"CAN YOU TELL me your name?" a voice asked as someone forced Dylan's right eye open and flashed a light in it.

"Dylan Hunt," he replied. His tongue felt funny in his mouth.

"Good. Do you know what today is?" The man looked familiar, but Dylan couldn't place him.

"Not my favorite day ever," Dylan said, lifting his hand to his face. It felt as if the whole left side was swollen.

The man chuckled. "I bet not, but do you know which day of the week it is? What the date is?"

Dylan answered his questions as he slowly came to. It became clear that he was in an ambulance. How he'd gotten in there was a little fuzzy.

"Where's Lucy? There's someone trying to hurt her. The guy was *huge*."

The paramedic's grin was oddly inappropriate given the seriousness of the situation. "Don't worry about Kung Fu Lu. She karate-chopped that guy into next week. He's got to be hurting even worse than you are."

Dylan felt as if he was missing something but didn't have the energy to ask any more questions. His head felt as if someone had dropped a bowling ball on it. He closed his eyes until they arrived at the hospital.

The paramedic unloaded him from the ambulance and wheeled him inside. He rattled off some information to the nurses and doctors who were there to greet them.

"Hang in there, Heartbreaker. Maybe I'll catch you at the next basketball game," the paramedic said as the hospital staff wheeled Dylan into one of the exam rooms.

Who was that guy?

"She's with him," someone said as Lucy entered the room and stood out of the doctor's way.

How Dylan wished that was true. From what he could see out of the one eye he could keep open, she seemed unharmed. In fact, she was as flawless as usual. What he wouldn't give to press his lips to those cheeks. Her skin was so soft, so smooth.

There were more questions to answer, some the same, some new. What was his name? Did he know where he was? What was today's date? Did he feel nauseated?

More lights were flashed in his eyes. Were they trying to blind him? There were more tests and questions and finally some ice for his face. All the while, Lucy stood in the corner, watching silently and biting her bottom lip. It wasn't until they were finished that she stepped forward and took Dylan's hand.

"He's definitely got a concussion," the redheaded doctor said. She reminded Dylan of that one actress from that one movie. He couldn't recall the name or the title. "We could keep him overnight for observation or he could go home, but someone would have to stay with him and make sure the symptoms don't get worse."

"What do you want to do?" Lucy asked him. Both of her hands enveloped one of his.

"I want to go home." He wanted to go home *now*. The lights in this place were too bright and the smells were making him want to throw up.

"I can stay with him," Lucy said. The doctor found that acceptable and promised she'd get the paperwork together and send him on his way.

Maybe he wasn't ready to go home yet, because Dylan swore he heard Lucy say she would stay the night with him. Hallucinations had to be a bad sign. He patted his pockets, searching for his phone. "I should call Eugene."

"Paige already talked to him," Lucy said, retrieving his phone from his coat, which hung on the back of the door. "Did you want to stay with him, or is it okay if I watch out for you tonight? Do you want to call Mindy?"

"Who's Mindy?"

Lucy's cheeks turned bright pink. "You know, your friend, Mindy. Your mother couldn't wait to see her again? You should bring her to dinner?"

Oh, no. Things were worse than they thought. He'd been hit so hard he'd completely forgotten this Mindy person. It was just like that one movie with that one guy, where he's in love with that girl and she loses her memory or something and she can't remember they were married. What if he was *married* to Mindy?

"Do you remember when I came to your office?" Lucy asked as he began to panic.

He nodded, clearly remembering her showing up so unexpectedly.

"Do you remember that your mom was there?"

His mom had come to talk to him about something. Probably the Prime deal. At the time, he had no idea that was her strange way of bonding with him. He nodded again.

"Do you remember when your mom said, 'You should bring Mindy to the house for dinner. We'd love to see her?' That Mindy. Do you want to call her?"

It all came back, and the memory made Dylan burst into a fit of laughter. The left side of his face ached, but he couldn't stop. He dried the eye that wasn't swollen shut. Maybe Dylan's mother really did care more than she was capable of showing.

"What's so funny?" Lucy asked. The little space between her eyes creased. She was adorable when she was confused.

"I'm pretty sure my mother was trying to make you jealous." Saying it out loud initiated another round of the giggles.

AFTER ALL THE paperwork was finished, Dylan was released into Lucy's care. Her sister Emma showed up and drove them back to Dylan's place. It all seemed so surreal, he kept waiting to wake up and find out this was some sort of dream.

It was freezing in the car, even though Emma had the heat cranked up all the way. The busted passenger-side window didn't help. Dylan's teeth were chattering as they pulled up to his greystone.

Lucy apologized to her sister for the hundredth time. "I'm sorry about your car."

"I'm just glad you're all right. I can get my car window fixed. You, on the other hand, are irreplaceable," Emma said, giving Lucy a hug. She glared over her shoulder at Dylan. "Remember, ten minutes ice on, ten minutes off. And be nice to my sister. *Some* people show compassion when someone is hurt or sick."

"Emma, cool it," Lucy snapped, helping him out of the car. Dylan wasn't really sure why her sister hated him all of a sudden, but he didn't have the energy to care at the moment.

Lucy unlatched the gate and offered to open the door, holding out her hand for the keys. Dylan preferred not to be any more emasculated than he already had been. He insisted he could open the door. Being punched in the face hadn't totally incapacitated him.

He led her up the stairs and unlocked the door to his loft. Pushing the door open, he waved her in. "Ladies first."

Lucy stepped in and he followed behind, quickly flipping on the light. Her sister had brought her a small overnight bag, which she set on the floor. He couldn't wrap his head around the fact that she wanted to spend the night here taking care of him. He thought for sure she'd pawn him off on Eugene.

Dylan moved farther into the loft, turning

on lights and shedding his jacket. He went right for the refrigerator and pulled out a can of pop. He hoped the caffeine would help fight off what was left of his headache. "Want one?"

Lucy shook her head. "Do you know how many chemicals are in that one twelve-ounce can?"

"Can't hurt me any worse than that guy's right hook did." Dylan took one more long swig and poured the rest down the drain. "Well, this is my place. Sorry for the mess. I wasn't expecting guests."

Her smile was shy and sweet. "It's amazing. Are you finishing the kitchen yourself?"

"Eugene has helped me with a lot of it. We hung the cabinets the other night, but I'll probably put on the doors myself."

Her gaze drifted around the loft, taking it all in. "You really have taken to this handyman stuff. Where did that come from?"

"A need to keep myself busy." *So I didn't think about you.* Fixing things made him feel better about not being able to fix himself. He couldn't repair his broken heart, but he could learn how to rehabilitate places like this one. "I put in the floors, did all the trim and molding, refurbished the fireplace."

"Wow." Lucy sounded genuinely impressed. "You definitely have been busy."

Dylan sat down on the couch and held the hospital ice pack to his face. He was going to have one heck of a black eye.

Lucy came over and sat on the other end of the couch, so close but so far away. She cringed when he groaned. "Does it hurt as bad as it looks?"

Dylan barked a laugh. "I look that terrible, huh?"

"You have no idea how sorry I am that you got messed up in my problem tonight."

"I thought I was coming to your rescue and ended up needing to be saved myself. I should probably apologize for getting in the way."

Lucy moved a little closer. "You didn't get in the way. I appreciate that you were trying to help me. That guy was crazy."

That was what had Dylan so confused. How did someone like Lucy take down a homicidal maniac? "I should have known you didn't need it. The paramedic called you Kung Fu Lu."

She rolled her eyes. "Charlie thinks he's so funny."

Mystery solved: the paramedic was Emma's boyfriend. Dylan knew he had seen that guy before. The basketball game comment made way more sense now.

"Seriously, though. How in the world did you take that guy down?"

"You kept busy the last five years learning how to be a carpenter. I kept busy earning my brown belt in jujitsu."

"For real?" Dylan knew she was tough, but he had no idea she was that tough.

"Someone suggested I do yoga—" she paused as if she had to be careful about what she said "—to help me keep a clear head, but it didn't really do much for me. Jujitsu is much more useful for redirecting anger."

"Why so angry, Lulu?"

She stared down at her hands in her lap and shrugged. She didn't look like a brown-belt warrior. She looked fragile. "Lots of reasons, I guess."

He was surprised by that answer. She seemed to have so many reasons to be happy. She was doing what she loved, had her amazing family close and was still the smartest, most beautiful woman Dylan had ever known. He was surprised she wasn't married yet. What were the single men of Chicago waiting for? Someone more perfect than her? There wasn't anyone who could compete.

"So, you break my heart, learn how to kill a man with your bare hands and go to work for a domestic violence agency. I feel like I'm missing something. Did I do something to make you hate men?" The question just tumbled out of his mouth. His concussion was disrupting his filter.

Lucy was silent for a beat. When she lifted her head, the regret in her green eyes was clear. "Why do you send my mother flowers every Thanksgiving?"

Once again, she made him feel more dazed than the hit that knocked him out. "I didn't know you knew about that."

"I only found out recently," she admitted.

"Your mom was always so good to me. She was also important to you. When she got sick and you were so scared of losing her, I guess she became important to me, too." That was the only way he could explain it. It was probably inappropriate to send your ex-girlfriend's mother flowers once a year, but he did it because even though Lucy didn't love him anymore, he was thankful she still had her mother in her life.

"Why did you let me go?" she asked, sliding even closer.

"Why did you go?" That was the real question. They had been happy. There was no way she could deny that. He felt it and he knew it was real because for the past five years, that feeling had evaded him.

"It was best for both of us."

Dylan tossed the ice pack on the coffee table. Turning his body in her direction, he grasped her hand. "It wasn't what was best for me."

Lucy brought their joined hands up to her cheek. Her skin was as soft as he remembered. "You didn't say that back then."

"You had shut down on me. I didn't know what was wrong, but I figured you'd tell me when you were ready. I thought maybe it was your mom, that she was sick again. When that wasn't it, I wondered if you just needed some space. We were practically joined at the hip when we weren't working. I figured I was suffocating you. It killed me to feel you slipping away."

There had been so many questions at the end. He had been afraid to ask when she began putting distance between them. He had rationalized it a million different ways. None of the reasons he'd come up with for why she needed space were supposed to end in their breakup, though. Unfortunately, that was exactly what she wanted.

"Why did you let me?"

"Because you asked me to. Don't you remember?" Holding her face in his hands, he spoke from the heart. "When the love of your life asks you to do something because she needs you to, you just do it. I thought that was what you wanted."

Lucy's mouth twisted as the tears that had welled up rolled down her cheeks. She placed her hand on his uninjured cheek. "I'm sorry I hurt you. I didn't want to hurt you."

Dylan leaned forward, gently touching his lips to hers. The fear that coursed through his veins told him not to push her too far or she'd run for the hills. She didn't run, though. She kissed him back. She slipped her hand behind his neck and pulled him closer. In that moment, he realized every beat of his heart was for her. He could never love anyone the way he loved her.

His entire body relaxed as she planted featherlight kisses across his bruised face. He ran his fingers through her hair and breathed her in. Even her smell was intoxicating. She pulled herself up on her knees and smiled down at him before kissing his lips with the same reverence he saw in her eyes.

A loud knock on the door broke the spell they were under. Lucy scurried back to the far end of the couch, rubbing her lips as if to confirm they were still there and not attached to his.

"Dylan?" Eugene's voice was full of worry. Dylan started to get up, but Lucy told him to stay put and went to let his neighbor in.

He wasn't sure what had just happened, but he was terrified it would never happen again. That was what happiness felt like. That was love.

CHAPTER FIFTEEN

THE WAY LUCY's heart was thumping in her chest, she was sure she was having a panic attack. She had been so foolish, so thoughtless. If she had continued to let herself get carried away, there was no saying what would have happened. It could have ended with her telling Dylan the horrible truth. Imagining his reaction to her secret sucked the air out of the room.

Lucy needed to get out of there and get out fast. Eugene couldn't have shown up at a better time. She yanked open the door and showed great restraint by not bolting past him.

"Hi. We're here to check on Dylan and see if there's anything we can do to help." Eugene's grandson fidgeted behind him. Jeremy reminded Lucy of Simon, adorable but self-conscious.

"I'm fine." Dylan wasn't a very good listener. He got up from the couch and joined them by the door. "I think everyone is more worried about me than they need to be."

Eugene inspected the damage like a concerned parent. "Yeah, you'll live. It probably doesn't hurt as bad as it looks, huh?"

"Sheesh, you guys are going to give me a complex. It is really that bad?"

"It's so…puffy," Jeremy said, squinting up at his neighbor.

"Puffy? Oh, man. Thanks a lot, Jer." Dylan mussed the kid's hair.

"We won't stay," Eugene said, already backing out the door. "We just wanted to make sure you were okay and remind you that we're just a phone call away if you need us."

"I appreciate that, guys."

Lucy's only shot at escape was quickly fading away. Offering to stay with Dylan had been a mistake. She had let her guilt put her in a situation that was way too risky. He had stripped away her defenses so easily and anything could happen in this vulnerable state she'd found herself in.

"Can I ask you a big favor?" Lucy said as they were saying their goodbyes. "Can you check on him a few more times tonight? Just to make sure he's not feeling sick or that the symptoms get worse? I have to go and it would really make me feel better if I knew someone was checking."

"You have to go?" Dylan's dismay tightened the viselike grip the panic had on Lucy's chest.

She took a deep breath, trying to fight off the anxiety that consumed her. "I have to go. I'm really sorry." *For so many things.*

Eugene threw his arm around Jeremy's shoulders. "We'll keep a close eye on him. Dylan's family. We've got this."

His reply eased the guilt she couldn't shake completely. Snatching up her bag and jacket, she couldn't bear to look anyone in the eye. She slunk out like the coward she was.

"Hey," Dylan said, chasing her down the stairs. "Stop, please. If this is about what happened before they showed up, I'm sorry I got carried away. I don't want you to go unless that's really what you want."

Without turning around, Lucy forced herself to stay strong. "I need to go."

"Is this when I'm supposed to ask you to stay?" She could hear him take a couple more steps in pursuit. "Do I need to beg so you'll come back up and give me some more answers? Tell me what I'm supposed to do, Lulu." His voice was so raw with emotion, it took everything Lucy had to keep moving down the stairs.

"Let me go, Dylan. Please."

Outside, the sting of the cold air filling her lungs was almost a welcome relief. She set out to find a cab and wasn't surprised to find Dylan had given up his chase. Not surprised, but still disappointed. Maybe her mom was right; maybe she bullied the fight right out of him. He always gave her what she wanted, even when what she said she wanted was never really what she longed for.

BACK AT HOME, Lucy found no comfort in her retreat. Her apartment had never seemed lonelier than it did tonight. Not even Elmer the cat could fill the hole. She had to remind herself that this was what she wanted.

Hope was a dangerous thing. When she had kissed Dylan, she had felt that hope spreading like a cancer through her body. It was made up of a poisonous combination of what-ifs and maybes.

What if he still loved her?

Maybe he would understand.

What if she could be enough?

Maybe being alone wasn't the only answer.

Those thoughts were more destructive than

any disease because they could only lead to heartbreaking disappointment. She could only be let down. It was so much safer to shut him out than to risk letting him in.

Lucy walked into the bathroom and began undressing for bed. Standing in front of the mirror, she took a good, hard look at herself. Mastectomy bras weren't what she would consider sexy. The pink one she wore today wasn't horrible—it had a little lace, apparently to make her feel feminine. It was all part of the ruse. It was supposed to trick people into believing she was just like every other woman out there. But she wasn't.

Lucy pulled out the breast form that filled the empty space on her left side. This was the real her. The scarred warrior. With the love and support of her family, she had survived. She didn't need to drag anyone else into her never-ending battle to stay alive. Dylan deserved someone who could give him that family he wanted. Someone who didn't have to force herself to look in the mirror.

Her phone rang as she finished getting ready for bed. Kendall's name and picture lit up the screen. No doubt she'd heard all about the day's events from Emma by now.

"Hey, K."

"Can you talk, or is Dylan right there?"

Lucy sat on the bed. It wasn't late, but the stress of the day had left her feeling exhausted. "I'm home. His neighbor is checking on him tonight."

"Oh, I thought Emma took you to his place."

"She did, but I left." Left, ran away. Kendall didn't need all the details.

That didn't mean she wouldn't try to get them. "What happened?"

"Nothing," Lucy lied. "His neighbor offered to keep an eye on him."

"Are you okay? Because I'm freaking out over what happened and it happened to you, not me."

Kendall was the sister who always felt everything so deeply. When they were little, she'd cry when Emma would get hurt or if Lucy got in trouble. "The guy did me a huge favor. He got arrested and is off the streets for the time being, at least until I can make sure he's put away for good."

"I know you can take care of yourself, but you still need to be more careful. What if he had a weapon?"

Lucy had more to fear from Dylan's lips than some crazy guy's gun. She fell back on her bed as thoughts of kissing Dylan ran through her head. The way he'd looked at her had been as if she was a waterfall in the middle of a desert. Then he had called her the love of his life. It was as if he still felt that way.

She couldn't afford to think like that. "Don't worry about me. Nobody's going to hurt me. I won't let them."

"I was worried about you before this whole attack. Mom had Simon after school today."

The only reason Kendall would mention that was if they had talked about her. "Mom wasn't supposed to say anything to you."

"She's worried about you, too."

This was why she didn't want them to know. She didn't want to deal with them trying to get in her head. She didn't want to have to answer questions about why she chose to be alone. They wouldn't understand.

Emma and Kendall would hopefully never know what it was like to have their bodies try to kill them, and their mother hadn't been diagnosed until she was married with three grown children. Her father had already committed to her in sickness and in health. Maureen had no idea what it would be like to ask someone with his entire life ahead of him to settle for someone who was basically waiting for the other shoe to drop.

"There's no reason to worry. What happened between me and Dylan is ancient history. He's moved on and so have I."

"Don't you think he deserves to know?"

Lucy put her hand on her chest like a kid pledging allegiance. Her scar was under there, and even though she shouldn't have been able to feel it, it seemed to be pushing back. Maybe he deserved to hear the truth, but that didn't make her want to tell him.

"It wouldn't change anything. All it would do is make him feel bad." She had learned tonight that she'd hurt him enough.

Kendall sighed into the phone. "Tables turned, you would be livid."

She was probably right. It still didn't matter. Dylan was better off never knowing. As soon as they raised enough money to save Safe Haven, he'd be out of her life for good.

FOR THE NEXT couple of days, Lucy spent every waking hour getting ready for the fund-raiser. When the day finally came, she was confident they were going to reach their goal. They had to, and positive thinking was all Lucy had to cling to right now.

Both Sharon and Emma were walking around with clipboards, looking important.

Sharon had put Emma in charge of the live auction. It had been Emma's idea and was the biggest wildcard of the night, since they had never done one before. Lucy found Emma in the main ballroom, getting some help with the microphone and sound system from the hotel's event coordinator.

This was the room where everyone would eat, dance and bid on the live auction items. They also had a salon set up next door for the silent auction. The room was exploding with all things purple, the color for domestic violence awareness. The centerpieces were all tagged and ready to be auctioned off with all the other items. At the front of the room, a huge thank-you card from the women and children Open Arms was currently helping was displayed for guests to read. Some of the kids had drawn sweet pictures while their mothers had written heartfelt notes of gratitude.

"Check, check, check," Emma said into the microphone. The speakers did their job and projected the sound all the way to the back. Emma thanked the woman assisting her.

"All set?" Lucy asked, confident Emma would have everything under control.

"We're ready to go. No worries."

"Have you seen Kendall? She said she'd be

here by now." Lucy checked the time on her phone. They had one hour before people would start arriving.

"Haven't seen her," Emma said, crossing something off her list. "I need to make sure the projector works. Maybe you should text her."

Lucy didn't want to resort to badgering, but Kendall was leaving her with no options. She started to type a text out just as Kendall and Max walked through the doors.

"I was getting worried," she said, giving her sister a hug.

"Sorry, we had a last-minute babysitting issue."

"I thought Simon was sleeping over at a friend's house."

"He was," Max said, sounding a tad annoyed. "Until your mother decided to intervene."

Kendall elbowed him in the chest and with nothing more than a look made him zip his lips.

"What does Mom have to do with this?"

"Dad's not coming tonight," Kendall said. The apology was in her eyes. "He's the backup babysitter for Simon. There wasn't enough time to drive him out to Max's mom's house, where we left Darcy. He's really sorry, but he wants you to know that you have his full support. He gave Mom the checkbook and told her to go crazy."

If Lucy didn't know how uncomfortable these kinds of things made her dad, she would have been more upset. She couldn't hold it against him that he was helping with Simon so the rest of them could all attend.

"Got the banner up, Kung Fu Lu. Do you need me to hang anything else?" Charlie's six feet four inches came in handy for reaching up high. "Special K! Big Poppa." Emma's boyfriend greeted the rest of the family. Max and Charlie were best friends, which meant the two couples did lots of things together. It only made Lucy a little bit jealous. At least that was what she told herself.

"That's it, but you might want to check with Emma and see if she needs anything."

Max and Charlie went to see what they could do for Emma, leaving the two sisters alone. Kendall fidgeted with her clutch.

"I thought Simon was staying at a friend's house tonight. Did the parents flake on you last-minute?"

"Something like that," Kendall said, avoiding eye contact.

"What does that mean?"

"We actually knew he wasn't going to be

home. It was his babysitter who had to cancel." Kendall opened her clutch and pulled out some gum. She was a nervous chewer. She could wreak havoc on a pencil back in her school days.

Something fishy was going on and the last thing Lucy needed was a surprise. "If you took Simon to Mom and Dad's, how come you didn't bring Mom with you?"

Kendall's eyebrows pinched together as she tried to come up with an excuse. "She's coming on her own."

"Lucy, can you come here a second?" Sharon popped into the ballroom with her clipboard pressed to her chest and a slightly aggravated expression.

There was trouble with the temperature controls in the salon. It was significantly warmer in there than throughout the rest of the hotel. Sharon was worried people wouldn't want to spend much time looking around and making bids if the room made them sweat. Lucy went to find the event coordinator but ran into her mother first.

It was obvious the moment Lucy saw her why Kendall was stressing out and why her father was watching Simon and his friend, who was most likely Jeremy. Paige and Eugene were talking to Maureen, and they were all laughing as if they didn't have a care in the world. It wasn't the fact that Eugene had his hand resting on Paige's lower back, a clear sign that they were here together, that sent Lucy reeling. It was the man standing next to her mother.

Dylan's black suit had to have been custom-made. His face was no longer swollen, but the bruise had turned yellow and purple. It matched his purple tie perfectly. He turned his head and caught sight of her. Those eyes that made her knees weak sent her heart into overdrive.

How could her mother think inviting him to this event was a good idea? Having Dylan here meant nothing but trouble for Lucy. She tried to regain her composure as her mom realized Dylan was staring at her daughter.

"Everything looks amazing, honey." Maureen took Lucy in her arms and whispered, "Don't be mad."

Lucy let out a puff of derisive laughter. It was a ridiculous request. She was going to be mad whether her mom wanted her to be or not. "You are in big trouble."

Paige was also full of compliments. Eugene was polite and soft-spoken as usual.

"Your dad had to watch the boys," her mom said. "I assume Kendall already told you."

"She left out other important details, but she told me Dad wasn't coming."

Maureen was unfazed. "I figured you wouldn't mind if I filled the spot at our table with someone else. My new date's pockets are much deeper than your father's."

Everyone chuckled except for Lucy and Dylan. His gaze had remained fixed on her, bringing back memories of kissing him on his couch. The silent auction room would have felt like an icebox compared to the heat creeping up her neck.

"I need to find someone," she said, using the only excuse she had. "You guys have fun."

She was going to read her mother the riot act for this. The only way she would let the woman off the hook was if Dylan donated enough money to save Safe Haven. Wouldn't that be ironic?

CHAPTER SIXTEEN

THIS WAS PERHAPS the worst idea anyone had ever had in the history of ideas. The horrified expression on Lucy's face when she had seen him almost had Dylan skipping out on the lovely Mrs. Everhart. He wasn't sure what Maureen was thinking. It was quite obvious Lucy wanted nothing to do with him.

"Don't worry," Maureen said as if she was reading his mind. "She's not good with surprises, good or bad. Let's go sit."

They were early. People were still scrambling to get things in place, but it seemed as if the event was coming together just as it should. He wouldn't expect anything less from Lucy. She had so much riding on this night. He hoped she wouldn't be let down if the evening didn't turn out as she hoped.

Kendall and her husband were sitting at one of the tables, along with the paramedic who had ridden in the ambulance with Dylan earlier in the week. Charlie was the first one on his feet.

"Mama Everhart, you look beautiful tonight," he said, pulling the chair out for Maureen. Charlie seemed to be a decent guy. He and Emma must have been dating long enough for him to be comfortable with the rest of the family. He held out a hand to Dylan. "Well, if it isn't Heartbreaker. The eye's healing up nicely."

Dylan wondered what he had done to earn that particular nickname. He didn't recall breaking anyone's heart. Lucy had been the one to deal the fatal blow to their relationship.

"I'm sorry I didn't recognize you that night. I hope the concussion is enough of an excuse," Dylan said, shaking Charlie's hand.

"Don't worry about it."

Emma stormed over to the table. "What is *he* doing here?" she asked her mother with a nod in Dylan's direction.

Emma was a teenager when Lucy and Dylan had first started dating. She was a very driven young lady but always very sweet. At the last basketball game they had both been at, she'd been all for them going out for ice cream together—much to Lucy's dismay. This new negative attitude didn't make much sense unless she hadn't known Prime had hired him to negotiate the deal for Open Arms's house.

"He's my guest," Maureen replied. "Watch you manners, Emma Elaine."

"After what he did?" she scoffed. "Why in the world would you want anything to do with someone who would do that to your daughter?"

"Em," Kendall said, shaking her head as if to warn her to stop.

Clearly stunned that her sister was supporting their mother, Emma turned on Kendall. "Are you really okay with him sitting with us, socializing like nothing happened?"

If Dylan hadn't already been questioning his sanity for coming, now he was sure he was completely nuts. He racked his brain for what he could have done that was so offensive, but he kept coming up blank.

Kendall rose from her seat and pulled her sister away for a more private conversation. Charlie jumped up to follow them while the rest of the group, including Eugene, stared at Dylan. He felt as if he should apologize, but Maureen beat him to it.

"I'm sorry. I didn't expect her to act that way. She doesn't know what she's saying."

"Did I do something?"

"You didn't do anything," she assured him. "Emma has some bad information, that's all."

The way Emma's mouth was now hanging open, it appeared that Kendall had set her straight. Emma covered her face, which was now red with what Dylan hoped was embarrassment instead of rage. When she dropped her hands, she began searching the room until Lucy was in her sights. She charged in Lucy's direction, but Kendall stopped her. The two sisters argued a bit until Charlie said something to Emma that seemed to calm her down.

None of this was making any sense to Dylan. When they returned to the table, Emma's regretful expression was a relief. She placed a hand on his shoulder. "I'm sorry for acting crazy and I'm sorry my sister is a lying—"

"Emma!" Her mother stopped her.

"I'm done. I'm done." Emma raised her hands in surrender. "I have things to do. But if you see Lucy before I do, you might want to warn her that I am *not* happy."

Eugene leaned in toward Dylan. "Am I missing something?"

"Only the same thing I am."

Eugene straightened back up and offered to get Paige and the other ladies a drink. Max was quick to offer his help. Paige suggested she should check to see if they needed her help before things got started.

Maureen and Kendall exchanged looks but said nothing. Kendall was obviously waiting for her mother to speak.

"Is someone going to tell me what the problem is?" Dylan finally asked.

"There's no problem. I brought you here for the reason I've already shared. I think you and Lucy need to talk. You deserve some answers that only she can give you."

Kendall shook her head.

"You don't think so?" he asked her.

Kendall sighed sadly. "I think the three of us know Lucy better than anyone. Putting her on the defensive is never a good plan. To her, the best defense is a good offense."

Dylan wanted answers, but he certainly wasn't looking for a fight. "Maybe I should go. Your husband can come, and I'll watch the kids."

Maureen placed her hand on his arm. "My husband is happy he didn't have to come to this. Big social events make the man a little anxious. We aren't forcing Lucy to do anything. I just want her to see you for the man I know you are and not the person she's created in her head because of this business issue."

Dylan would have loved to pick Maureen's brain more about the man she thought he was. He felt very much like the man Lucy probably saw. He decided to stay in hopes he'd find out who he really was.

The room began to fill. Open Arms was a well-respected agency in the community. It was good to see so many people come out and show their support. Everyone was encouraged to check out the silent auction items and to buy raffle tickets.

Dylan followed Maureen around, munching on hearty hors d'oeuvres and sipping his drink. She seemed to know many of the guests. Some were from the hospital she had worked at when he first met her. Others were longtime supporters of Open Arms. Dylan didn't see Lucy again until it was time for her to introduce the night's emcee, a local news personality.

Dylan couldn't focus on anything that was being said. His thoughts were too distracting as he watched Lucy standing off to the side. Had she even been fazed by what had happened between them the other night? That was one question he wanted answered. Why was Emma so mad at her? What had she lied about? Something that had to do with him— he was sure about that much.

She was so beautiful. That was usually the first thing people noticed about Lucy, and he was definitely not blind to it. It wasn't why he had fallen in love with her, though. It was that mind of hers. That brain that never rested and was always surprising him. It was her ability to care so much about someone other than herself. Lucy's compassion for all living things made him feel guilty for loving cheese-burgers so much.

There was something so remarkable about her. She wasn't afraid of anything, and she would take on the world if someone in need asked her to. Dylan admired the way she loved. How he wished she loved him half as much as he had thought she did all those years ago.

After the emcee finished acknowledging a few people for their work at Open Arms, there was a little break before the live auction. Everyone was encouraged to get their bids in for the silent auction items. Dylan snuck away to that room to write his name on a few of the prizes. Jeremy would love the giant basket full of superhero stuff. Maybe he could share some of it with Simon. He bid on a romantic brunch and hot air balloon ride that he'd seen Eugene looking at earlier. Maybe he could convince the older man to ask Paige out on a real date.

"Trying to win the perfect date?" Lucy appeared out of nowhere.

One side of Dylan's mouth quirked upward. "Are you jealous?"

"Maybe I would be if Mindy was real."

"Guess not, then."

She moved through the crowd and he followed. She stopped in front of the superhero basket and checked to see what his bid was. It was generous and over double the previous bid.

"Maybe I should be worried that you're trying to steal my mother away."

He should have guessed that was coming next. "Your mother is a lovely lady, but she's very devoted to your father. I'm not a home-wrecker, either."

"Good to know." She continued out of the salon and into the hallway, which was much less crowded. "Why are you here?" she asked, glancing at him over her shoulder.

"Your mom asked me to come."

Lucy spun around, folding her arms in front of her. "What has my mother told you?"

"Told me about what?" The Everhart women

were all speaking to him as if he knew what they were talking about.

She watched him, perhaps trying to figure out what he did or didn't know. "We should talk about what happened the other day, but not here."

"Does your mom know what happened the other day?" He was desperate to make sense of everything that had been said tonight.

"No one knows what happened the other day."

No one but the two of them. He took a step toward her. She was all he had been able to think about for days. "I can't stop thinking about it, Lulu. I can't stop thinking about you."

His words seemed to cause her pain. "Dylan, we can't do this."

"Too late. We already did it. I came tonight because I know you feel it, too. The way you looked at me, the way you kissed me—"

"Stop," she begged. "I have too much to deal with tonight. I can't talk about this right now." Turning, she took off for the ballroom.

At least she hadn't denied what he said. She had felt it.

"Dylan Hunt?" a voice said behind him.

Dylan turned to find Quinn Denton, who appeared shocked to see him there. Quinn worked for a company that had hired Stevens and Ellis to defend them in a dispute with their union.

The two men caught up, and Quinn introduced Dylan to his wife. She quickly excused herself to say hello to Sharon Langston. "I'm surprised to see you here. Wait—" he lowered his voice "—are you here to report back?"

Dylan wasn't following. "Report back to who?"

Quinn glanced around to see who was listening and continued to whisper. "Are you here to see who showed up?"

"I'm here because I was invited."

"Right," Quinn said as if he was playing along. "Just so you know, I'm only here because my wife is friends with someone on the board. I don't want any trouble with the Kerringtons. Please don't say anything about us being here. I don't want Elizabeth messing with my kid's acceptance into Parker."

The blood drained from Dylan's face. The accusation was horrifying. Was he really doing business with someone who would sabotage a fund-raiser just to ensure purchase of a property? Was he working for someone who would prevent a child from going to a private school because of the charity her parents supported?

It appeared Quinn not only thought he was but believed Dylan would help Elizabeth catch those who dared to defy her.

"I can't believe she'd stoop so low as to hire you to report back to her about who was here. It was already pretty gutsy of her to put it out there that people should withhold their support this year. Elizabeth is ruthless. But we're good, right?"

"Yeah, you're good," Dylan said, still reeling. Quinn went back into the salon to find his wife and discourage her from putting their names on anything.

"I can't believe you!" Dylan hadn't realized Lucy was standing just a few feet away. "Are you seriously here to report back to Elizabeth Kerrington?"

"No, no, no." He wanted to explain, but Lucy wasn't listening. She was pulling him out of the hallway and through a service door.

"I can't believe you. Is this what you've become? Someone who would help sabotage a fund-raiser that takes care of and protects women who are abused?"

"I'm not. I didn't do anything to help anyone sabotage this night. Come on, Lulu, you know me."

"Do I?" she asked with eyes blazing. "Because the Dylan I knew swore he'd never work for people like Elizabeth Kerrington. Yet here you are."

"I'm here because I was hoping you would talk to me and explain what it is that you're hiding. I know you're hiding something."

"Oh, don't you dare try to turn this on me. I don't owe you anything." She was livid and Dylan feared there was nothing he could say that would calm her down.

"I didn't say you did. Your mother was the one who invited me here because *she* thinks you owe me some answers."

Lucy's hands were balled into fists. "Stay away from me. Stay away from my mother. I'm sorry I kissed you the other night. I felt bad that you got hurt and I got caught up in the memories we were talking about, but I am really clear where we stand now. I want nothing to do with someone who would help Elizabeth Kerrington take from women who have already been victimized enough."

He tried to stop her from leaving, but as soon as he put his hand on her, she attacked, twisting his arm behind his back and pinning him against the wall. "Don't touch me," she warned.

Letting him go, she disappeared out the door

that led back to the event. Dylan punched the wall in frustration. If there was any hope of reuniting, it had just evaporated into thin air.

CHAPTER SEVENTEEN

THE REST OF the night went by in a blur of anger and regret. Months of planning, hours upon hours of preparation—all for nothing. Elizabeth Kerrington had seen to it that the people with the power to do the most good in this community would withhold their support until it was too late for Safe Haven.

The live auction was well received but didn't generate nearly enough money to meet the goal they'd set. Lucy didn't need to wait for the final numbers; she had already accepted her defeat. She had let everyone down.

She felt sick to her stomach. If she continued to fight to keep Safe Haven open, other valuable services would have to be cut. It was tough to win against someone who not only didn't play by the rules, but also didn't care that there were rules in the first place.

Dylan hadn't stuck around for the live auction. Once she had outed him for being the lowlife that he was, he had no reason to stay. How could she have been so blind? She couldn't trust him. She knew that, and yet it still hurt to know it was true. Thankfully, she hadn't trusted him with her heart. She had been right to hide the truth, to run as far from him as possible. She didn't care what her mother or sisters thought. Dylan Hunt was officially no good.

"You need a lift home?" Kendall asked when the ballroom was cleared out except for the hotel staff there to clean up.

"I'm fine. I'll grab a cab."

"Everything was awesome, sis. I think you definitely raised more than last year."

It was nice of Kendall to be so optimistic, but there was no ray of hope. Lucy was stuck under a permanent rain cloud. "It wasn't enough."

"You don't know that until all the numbers are crunched."

Lucy shook her head. "I don't need to wait for the numbers to come back. I know what we needed those live auction items to go for and we didn't come close."

"I still think you did a lot of good here tonight. Even if you have to find a plan B for Safe Haven, tonight was still a success for Open Arms as a whole."

It was hard to look at it that way. Safe Haven

was the reason Lucy had dedicated so much time to this event. Maybe it was more about winning than she had wanted to admit. "Get Mom home safe."

"Any chance you know why Dylan took off?" Kendall asked cautiously.

"Because he's a horrible person who finally had a crisis of conscience?"

Kendall cocked her head to the side. "I'm never going to understand why you are so angry with him, am I?"

"Probably not." Explaining how he was a phenomenal disappointment wouldn't begin to cover all the reasons why she was so infuriated with him. "Thank you for coming and thank you for giving to the cause."

Kendall hugged her sister tightly. Lucy hadn't realized how much she needed that embrace until she was in Kendall's arms. She felt like such a failure tonight and a little comfort was welcome.

"You'll figure it out, Lucy. You always do."

That wasn't so easy to believe. Not when she didn't have a clue where to start to make this better.

Their mother returned from saying her goodbyes to some old friends from the hospital. "Good night, sweetheart." She swept Lucy up in her arms once Kendall let her go. "You did great. Everything was executed perfectly."

Lucy didn't want to argue. Emma, on the other hand, was ready to pick a fight.

"We're leaving," she said, holding Charlie's hand and glaring at Lucy as she had most of the night.

"Is there something you need to say to me?" Lucy asked, ready for whatever it was that Emma needed to complain about.

"I don't know. I'm worried that if I ask you a question, all I'll get are lies."

"What's that supposed to mean?"

"You let me believe Dylan knew about the cancer and ran. You let this anger fester inside me when that's not what happened, is it?"

Lucy glanced at Kendall, who quickly defended herself. "She was about to kick the guy out for leaving you when you were sick. I had to set the record straight. Did you want Dylan to hear the truth that way?"

She didn't want Dylan to hear it any way. Better to deal with Emma's wrath than his.

"I don't know what reasons you have for lying to him. I'm not sure how you could rationalize something like that, but what really makes me mad is that you couldn't be honest with your family about it. Maybe you were scared we'd try to talk you out of it, but that's what family is for. We're supposed to tell you when you're screwing up so you can stop." Emma's anger turned to sadness. "You're making some really bad choices, Lucy. Stop."

"You don't understand." Lying was wrong when done for selfish reasons, but if Emma knew everything, she might see why Lucy had done it in this case.

"You're right, I don't understand. You should still stop lying. You should be honest with Dylan, with us and most important with yourself." That was all she had to say on the subject. She kissed her mother goodbye, said good-night to the rest of them and left with Charlie.

Lucy could add being a good big sister to her list of failures for the night. She shouldn't have let Emma believe Dylan had left fully aware what they would have had to face together. That didn't mean she felt bad for not telling him. He had proven tonight that he wasn't the man she wanted him to be—needed him to be—if she was going to trust him to be there for the long run.

Paige came over to steal Lucy away. Some of the board members and the rest of the event committee were still there counting the receipts. Tanya Robbards, one of the board members who had been in favor of selling from the get-go, wore a smug expression.

"Lots of money was raised tonight, ladies. We should all feel good about what we accomplished here," Tanya said before shifting gears. "With that being said, we didn't raise enough to meet our target. So, I suggest we start putting some thought into the offer Mrs. Kerrington and Prime Developments made us."

"We should meet soon to talk about it," Paige replied while Lucy bit her lip. Lucy couldn't say anything. Tonight's losses had taken all the fight out of her.

"Are you changing your position on selling Safe Haven?" Sharon asked Paige. If Paige gave up, so would everyone else.

"I've been considering our options. Perhaps we should meet next week to talk about what those are."

The other options weren't very promising, but Lucy knew they didn't have any choice but to explore them. She'd still fight tooth and nail not to sell the house to Prime. That was an option she was willing to do anything to stop.

MONDAY MORNINGS WERE the days Lucy spent at Safe Haven doing art therapy with the women staying there. She wasn't as talented with a paintbrush as Kendall was, but she knew enough to help the women express their feelings using some paints and a canvas.

Today's project was to create a future self-portrait. The objective was for the women to imagine themselves a month, a year or whatever future date they chose from now. They were supposed to think about who and where they wanted to be and draw that person.

"The idea is to use this as a way to jump-start your path to becoming who you want to be," Lucy explained. "Don't be afraid to be someone you don't recognize."

Everyone got started. Some used paints, some used oil crayons. Lucy walked around, asking questions and offering encouragement. Nora was painting an ocean scene.

"North Avenue Beach?"

"No way!" Nora laughed. "This is how I imagine the Atlantic. I've never seen the ocean, but I want to go down to Miami and watch the sun rise from the beach."

"That sounds like heaven, especially on a day like today. I nearly froze to death on my way in this morning," Lucy said, feeling chilled just thinking about it.

Nora's face fell. "I'm so sorry about what

happened to your car, what happened to your sister's car. You've had to put up with so much because I asked for your help."

"Don't do that. Don't apologize for things Wade did. You are not responsible for his actions." That was rule number one at Safe Haven. "My car will get fixed. Wade is going to jail. And you are planning a trip to Miami."

Nora's smile made getting her car smashed up more than worth it. Lucy moved on to the next painter, impressed by the talent some of the women were displaying.

When art therapy ended, Lucy cleaned up and put the room back in order. Safe Haven's social worker had a kids' group in here after school today. Hiding all traces of the art supplies was a must, or things could get seriously messy.

Lucy was almost done when Nora reappeared. She seemed nervous, as she had the day she showed up to Open Arms with all the evidence against her husband.

"Are you okay?" Lucy asked, tossing the paper towel she had used to wipe down the table into the garbage.

"Can I talk to you for a second? Up in my room?"

Lucy agreed and followed her upstairs. Safe

Haven was an enormous house that had been remodeled to fit their needs as a shelter. The first floor was all common area, made up of the kitchen, the group room, a library and a great room, which functioned much like a traditional family room. The second floor had three bedrooms and two bathrooms, while the third floor had four bedrooms and two bathrooms. The second floor rooms were slightly larger to accommodate women with children. Women like Nora, who were here by themselves, tended to stay on the third.

Nora offered the desk chair to Lucy and went to sit on the bed. Lucy wasn't sure if she was up there to act as Nora's lawyer or as a counselor. She waited for Nora to speak.

"I know you said it's not my fault what happened, and I know that's true, but I still feel like I owe you for being there for me and helping me through this whole ordeal."

"That's my job, Nora. You hired me as your attorney. It was my job to help you."

"To help me, not risk your life."

"My life was never in danger. I can take care of myself, I swear."

"Physically, maybe." Nora slid off the bed and dropped to her knees. She bent all the way down and pulled a suitcase out from under the bed. "But I heard that Open Arms was looking for some financial help. Some of the girls here were talking about how there might not be a Safe Haven if you guys don't get the money you need to pay the bills."

"You don't need to worry about that," Lucy assured her. "We're doing everything we can to make ends meet. It might mean we have to relocate, but we're going to make sure women have a safe place to stay while they get back on their feet. You don't have to leave."

Nora pushed the suitcase toward Lucy. "I want you to have this."

Lucy stared at the suitcase for a second, wondering what the gesture could mean. Maybe she wanted to donate her things to the cause? "We don't need you to do without anything, Nora. Seriously, keep your things."

"No, it's not filled with my stuff. It's filled with money."

Lucy's eyes probably popped out of her head. "What money?"

"Once I knew Wade was locked up, I thought maybe I should take off and start somewhere new, somewhere he could never find me once he got out." Somewhere like Miami, maybe. "I emptied all those accounts that were in my name. I know you said I needed to turn that money back over to the company, but it was so tempting to run away with it."

"Nora, you can't—"

"Please, you can use it to save this place. We can turn in the records that show Wade stole all that other money and you can use this fifty thousand to keep things going. Open Arms needs this money more than Wade's company does."

"Nora," Lucy started. As sweet as she was for wanting to help, this was wrong. So wrong but so tempting at the same time. Nora was right—they could easily turn over the documents that showed how Wade had laundered millions without revealing the bank accounts he had set up in Nora's name. It would come out eventually, though. Lucy had to remind herself of that before she did something crazy like accept this money.

"Think of all the good it would do," Nora pleaded.

That was what Lucy was thinking about. Unfortunately, fifty thousand would still leave them out of reach of their target. It would still get them significantly closer and would make up for whatever Elizabeth Kerrington had done to keep people from supporting Open Arms. But it would also put Lucy in jail eventually.

"We have to give the money back to the people it belongs to. I appreciate what you're trying to do. I really do. But the right thing is always the right thing to do, even when breaking the rules seems like it's for the greater good."

Nora's sigh was resigned. "I get it. Can you do me a favor, though?"

Lucy stood up. "Sure."

"Can you take it with you so I don't run away with it before we have a chance to give it back?"

It was an honest concern. Lucy smiled and grabbed the handle. "I'll go lock it up until our meeting with Wade's partners tomorrow. I'm sure those guys are going to love us showing up with fifty thousand in cash."

Lucy lugged the suitcase down the stairs. She needed to lock this thing up quick before she changed her mind and considered trying her hand at being Robin Hood.

CHAPTER EIGHTEEN

JUST WHEN DYLAN didn't think things could get any worse than the disaster Saturday night had proven to be, he received a lovely email from Elizabeth Monday morning. She was asking him to draft a letter to Open Arms's board of directors reminding them that their thirty days were quickly coming to an end and if Prime didn't hear from them by Friday, the "generous" offer was off the table.

Dylan could picture the look of disgust that would surely be on Lucy's face when she saw his name at the bottom of a letter that sought to kick them when they were down. Elizabeth had won. There was no way Open Arms could have made enough money at their fundraiser to allow them to hold on to Safe Haven and keep all their other programs funded. Not with the interference from Elizabeth. Either the house was going to go into foreclosure or they were going to have to sell, and he'd set it up so Paige would sell to Prime. He wished he hadn't.

Bridgette came in with the mail as Dylan stared at the blinking cursor on his blank computer screen. The words refused to be written. "Your mother's assistant called. She's wondering if you're available for lunch at noon. Your schedule is open, but I wasn't sure what you wanted me to say."

He couldn't pull his eyes away from the screen. "Whatever she wants. I don't care."

"I'll let her know. Is there anything else I can do for you?" The concern in her voice made him close his laptop.

"Can you erase the last month from my memory?" One month would at least resolve his guilt over Open Arms. "No, wait. How about the past five years?" Going back to the only happy time in his life seemed like the lone solution for this complete self-loathing.

"Sorry." Bridgette was good at a lot of things, but memory erasure was not one of them. "I'd ask you if you want to talk about it, but I know better."

"Can you grab everything we have regarding the Prime deal with Open Arms? I have to throw in the towel and ask my mother if she'd let me delegate the responsibility of the deal to someone else."

"Sure," she said with a sharp nod.

There was no way he could be a part of the negotiations anyway. Dylan would have to explain to his mother that the negative emotions between him and their legal counsel were too great and would hurt Elizabeth's chances of getting the best deal. He'd leave out the part about knowing Lucy would eat any lawyer in their firm for breakfast and Prime Developments would definitely get the worst possible deal. It was the best Dylan could do, even though it wasn't nearly enough.

The only way he could win Lucy's approval was by doing something incredible. He had considered selling his car and signing the check over to Open Arms. Just as he'd considered clearing out his bank accounts and showing up with huge sacks of money to save the day.

It might work, but then there was the chance Lucy would refuse to take a dime from him out of sheer stubbornness. She had made her feelings about him as clear as she could. He was working for the devil and was unredeemable. She had no faith in him. And why should she? He didn't even believe in himself. The only thing Dylan could do for Lucy was to stay far away.

NOON ROLLED AROUND faster than Dylan thought it would. He was caught off guard when his mother waltzed into his office.

"Do you want to walk a couple blocks or have my driver take us?" She was dressed appropriately for a stroll outside in the late fall. Her black wool-and-cashmere Caban coat had been a gift from Dylan last Christmas. Had he used that money to give a new winter coat to needy kids in the city, more than a couple of dozen would have been warm last winter. He could guess what Lucy would think of that. Their wealth made him feel so ashamed.

"Let's walk. I need some fresh air." He offered her his arm and she smiled as she took it. At least he had discovered this new side of his mother. For so long, he'd thought she felt very little for him, but the more time he spent with her, the more he realized how far from the truth that really was.

They walked east along Randolph to a steakhouse Clarissa suggested. As they headed toward Field Boulevard, passing Daley Plaza, Dylan glanced across the street. The Cancer

Survivors Garden entrance was marked by two giant columns from the demolished Chicago Federal Building and a wrought-iron pergola. Dylan had brought Lucy there when her mother was in treatment, hoping it would provide her with some solace, or at least a beautiful distraction. Even though it was located in the Loop, it was a rather secluded spot. Tourists didn't bother to venture that far from Millennium Park very often.

The memory of Lucy kissing him under the pergola left him momentarily breathless. That kiss had been so much like the one from the other night. She had held his face after he had confessed to going there to pray not only for her mother to be well but so that Lucy would never suffer the same fate. He had admitted he couldn't imagine life without her. He had sworn he'd be lost if she wasn't there beside him. She had promised that she planned to live a very long life. She had kissed him and vowed he would never have to know what it was like to be without her.

Funny how quickly things could change. A year and a half after that kiss, instead of getting married in those gardens, Dylan had walked them alone, wondering why she didn't love him anymore. He had been the only honest one back then. He was very much lost without her.

At lunch, his mother was busy with her phone. Her mind was always in at least two different places. When she finished answering the last of her emails, she turned her attention to her son. "So, what's the latest with the Prime deal?"

For once, he was glad she brought it up. "I wanted to talk to you about that, actually. Things have gone from bad to worse with Lucy Everhart. I present a huge risk to Elizabeth and Prime getting what they want. I was thinking of handing the case over to Henry. I can brief him on the details and have him up to speed in no time."

"Wait." Confusion colored her features. "Why have things gone from bad to worse? I don't understand this woman. You risk your life trying to help her when she's attacked by a madman. Then you go to her fund-raiser and still she has this chip on her shoulder?"

"How did you know I went to her fund-raiser?" Dylan didn't remember telling her he had gone.

"I know a lot of people in this city, son," she reminded him.

"Of course." He wondered how many other

things she knew about him that they never talked about. "Well, I'm not sure how to explain other than that she has a very strong dislike for my association with Prime Developments— or maybe just with Elizabeth Kerrington. Did you hear that Elizabeth encouraged people not to support Open Arms this year so she could have the advantage in buying the house from them? Who does that? She's making life harder for women who have had a hard enough life as it is."

"Elizabeth is ruthless. That's why she's so successful. People may disagree with her tactics, but she gets things done."

Dylan didn't like that attitude one bit. "That's what's wrong with the world. Too many people accept bad behavior because it gets results. But what kind of results is she really getting? Her condos will house a few people for an obscene amount of money in comparison to Safe Haven, which keeps over a dozen women and children out of harm's way at any given time. Why don't more people value that?"

"Certain people value it greatly. Elizabeth and the rest of her pals in the one percent choose not to think about it."

"What about you?" Dylan asked. He was

curious what she thought, since she hadn't lumped herself in with Elizabeth's elite. "You call her ruthless, but do you agree she crossed a line? Do you get why Open Arms is valuable?"

Clarissa folded her hands in her lap and took a moment to think about it. "I understand there is a need for a place like that. I'm also sure if I was in Elizabeth's position, I would do the same thing," she said.

He was disappointed in that answer. "So, you'd be fine with taking sanctuary away from abuse victims?"

"Don't be so overdramatic, Dylan. It's not as personal as you're making it out to be. It's business. This isn't about the people Open Arms services, it's about a piece of property they own. Prime isn't stealing the house from them, they are offering money for it. Open Arms will find somewhere else to shelter those women."

"It is about those women to Lucy. If they lose this house, the alternatives are limited. They may be able to open another shelter, but it won't be in as nice of a neighborhood. It won't have all the amenities this house has. They will have to sacrifice things. For what? So Prime Developments can make some money? That's a shame."

"This is why I've always worried about you. You feel things so deeply." She said it as if it was a bad thing. Maybe it was. If Dylan could turn his feelings off, it would make life a little easier. "And that Everhart woman only exasperates things."

"Lucy doesn't make me feel things." At least not in the way his mother meant. "She lives her life following her functioning moral compass and she isn't afraid to challenge those who don't."

"You don't have a working moral compass?"

Dylan shrugged. "Sometimes I wonder. Lucy has decided I don't because I associate with the likes of Elizabeth Kerrington, whose moral compass is definitely broken."

"You're sitting here asking me to remove you from a deal you feel is unjust. That speaks to your character."

That was true, but that wouldn't change Lucy's opinion of him. She had already made up her mind. She had lumped him in with the Elizabeths of the world, and there was nothing he could do about it. Regardless of Lucy's feelings for him, he wasn't going to compromise his morals any longer.

"Does that mean you'll let me put Henry on it?"

Clarissa picked up her water and glanced down at her phone for the first time since their conversation started. That had to be a record. "If you can get him up to speed before the end of the day, that's fine by me."

"Thank you." It was a relief to know he was going to be done with Prime Developments. It wouldn't put him back in Lucy's good graces, but at least he wouldn't have to face her again.

"Tell me one thing," Clarissa said, straightening her napkin. "What would it take to make everyone happy? Elizabeth, Lucy, Prime, Open Arms...*you*?"

That was an impossible question. How could you give everyone what they wanted when they were all vying for the same thing or, in the case of Dylan and Lucy, such very different things that there was no middle ground?

"You'd need to be a miracle worker, Mother. Honestly, the only one I care to see happy is Lucy. She works so hard to make a difference, and even though she hates my guts, I still love her." He couldn't believe he'd said it out loud, but it was true. "I'd do anything to give her what she wants, but getting Elizabeth to back off is never going to happen. At this point, I'm ready to give up my own place so they have somewhere to go. But that's not reason-able, either."

Clarissa had no response, choosing to go back to her phone. She surely saw there was no solving this problem. The only winner was Prime Developments. The rich would get richer and those in need would make due with less. The waiter delivered their lunch and Dylan found he didn't have much of an appe-tite. He pushed his food around his plate.

"You're a good man, Dylan. If Lucy Ever-hart doesn't see it, that's her problem. Not yours."

"What if I don't see it, either? To be a good person, you have to do good things, not just regret the bad things you've done."

Clarissa set her fork down. "What would make you feel like you were doing good?" She leaned forward, giving a clear impression that she truly wanted to know.

Dylan wasn't sure if he should tell her that what would make him feel better would be working for anyone other than her. They had just started figuring out this mother-son rela-tionship, but it was highly tied to their roles as boss and employee.

"I'd be doing work that mattered to more than the one percent," he answered.

"Like what? How could we make it work at Stevens and Ellis?"

Was she serious? Dylan dove in, telling her he'd like to use his environmental law background. The tricky part was not creating any conflicts of interest for the firm. They couldn't take on cases that put them on the opposing side of some longtime clients. Dylan understood he couldn't overhaul Stevens and Ellis's image all at once.

Clarissa listened and asked questions when they arose. The two of them ate and discussed the possibility of generating some new business with a focus on improving the community at large. It turned out she wasn't completely opposed to Dylan doing some pro bono work.

"Can I be honest with you?" he asked her on the way back to the office.

"I would hope so," she said, thumbing through the messages she had missed on her phone while they had been talking.

"I didn't think you would listen to anything I had to say."

"Why?" She looked up at him with genuine surprise.

"In case you haven't noticed, you and I have a different way of looking at things sometimes."

Clarissa shook her head and waved a dismissive hand. "I can't be afraid of new ideas. Change can lead to progress. I certainly don't run the firm the way my father did, nor did he choose to practice law exactly the same way as his father. Stevens and Ellis is your legacy, son. For it to be successful, you have to believe in its mission. If your vision is different than mine, it's time for us to work toward finding some common ground. Don't you think?"

He did. For the first time in his life, he actually felt as if his family's law firm could become *his* law firm.

CHAPTER NINETEEN

CHY FINANCIAL'S PARTNERS were extremely interested in what Lucy had to say as she presented the documents proving Wade Young had been taking money from them and their clients for years. They were also slightly flabbergasted when she set the suitcase of money on the table.

"We understand that you need to take all of this information to your own lawyer and I strongly suggest speaking with an accountant before deciding what you want to do. We are here to return the money that was being held in accounts with my client's name on them. I want to be clear, though. This is not an admission of guilt on her part, and we will not sign anything that states she had anything to do with taking the money."

The man seated across from her, Dan Hillard, absently rubbed his fingers against his bearded jawline, deep in thought. He glanced at the man to his right, who had scratched his head more than once as he waded through all the evidence.

"How can we be sure you haven't manipulated this information?" Thad Collins reminded Lucy of Wade Young. It wasn't surprising they had gone into business together. She loved the way he still wanted to defend the man who had robbed them blind.

"That's why I suggested you have your accountants do their own thorough audit. I believe they will find the same things when they look at all of your records."

"It's a lot to process. You didn't know he was doing this?" Hillard asked Nora, who shook her head. "We trusted him with so much. He was always so good at explaining things away. I never had the time to question anything he said."

The truth was sinking in. "We ask that you sign this, acknowledging that you have received this money from Mrs. Young," Lucy said, sliding the document across the table. Protecting Nora was her number one objective. The rest of this mess was theirs to sort out.

"We need our lawyer to look at that before we sign anything," Thad said, pushing it back.

Dan grabbed the piece of paper. "She returned the money. She gave us everything we need to send Wade where he belongs. The woman's hiding in a shelter, for heaven's sake. You and I both know what kind of man Wade is. I'm not burying my head in the sand anymore." He scribbled his name on the line at the bottom and gave it back to Lucy. "I'm sorry, Nora. For shutting my mouth when you showed up to work with bruises, for letting Wade believe I thought he was telling the truth when he called you clumsy. I should have helped you." He stood up. "I won't support coming after Nora. Wade's head is the only one I want on the chopping block."

Nora thanked him. Dan might not have helped her when he should have, but Lucy could respect that he was trying to do right by her now. Thad, on the other hand, wasn't convinced.

"I'll wait until I talk to our lawyer. There are always two sides to every story," he sneered.

"You're right, Mr. Collins. And yet you never really asked Nora what her side was, did you? The bruises, the absences from work, the verbal and mental abuse you witnessed right here in this office—you only listened to Wade's side of those stories, right? She deserved to be shouted at. She was such a klutz. She sure knew how to push his buttons. That's

Wade's side. The other is that Wade Young is a controlling, wife-abusing embezzler who stole millions from right under your nose. I sure do hope you'll consider that side. It would be a shame for Wade to get away with all that money you could be spending on yourself."

Lucy rose to her feet. She was done here. Nora followed her outside and waited quietly while Lucy hailed them a cab. In the back of the taxi, Nora's eyes filled with tears.

"What's wrong?"

"I wish I was as strong as you are. Thank you for standing up for me. I don't know what I would have done if you hadn't taken my case."

Lucy threw an arm around Nora's shoulders. "You are brave. You are strong. You stood up for yourself and said you had had enough. All I did was come along for the ride."

"Thad scares me as much as Wade and you just put him in his place. You're my hero."

Lucy couldn't help but chuckle. The look on Thad's face when she stuck it to him was pretty priceless. "Men like that thrive on control. Nothing brings them to their knees faster than when you point out they weren't as in control as they thought."

"You're fearless, Lucy. I hope I can be like that someday."

"If that's what you want to be, you will be," Lucy said, giving Nora a squeeze.

"I decided to go stay with my brother in Ohio. Now that we've turned over the money, I want to get out of Chicago for a while."

"Not Florida, huh?"

Nora smiled. "No, not yet. Someday, hopefully. My brother offered me a place to stay and has a friend who's a dentist and needs a new receptionist. It's not my dream job, but it's a job."

"Good for you."

"I hope Dan and Thad press charges against Wade so he goes to prison. I feel like I'm going to spend my life looking over my shoulder."

"It's okay to be vigilant, but don't let him stop you from living."

"I'll try," she said, staring down at that empty ring finger. "I leave Saturday, but you have my number and I have yours. You'll keep me posted on how things are going?"

"I will keep you in the loop. I promise."

"Thank you. I know you don't want to take any credit, but I believe you saved my life."

It was kind of her to say that, but Lucy truly felt no one could save anyone who didn't want to be saved. Nora had to do her part or none of this would have been possible. Just as they got back to Safe Haven, Lucy's phone chimed with a reminder.

Mammogram 2:00

Fearless was the last thing Lucy felt. Not everything could be put in its place with a snide comment and thinking positive didn't always come so easily. Nora wasn't the only one who understood that believing was usually harder than doing.

LUCY OFTEN WONDERED how her sister could work in a hospital. There was nothing about hospitals that Lucy liked. No matter how comfortable they tried to make the waiting rooms or how they attempted to dress things up with plants or holiday cheer, it was still a place where people came because something was wrong. Except for the people in the maternity ward, no one was here to celebrate some joyous occasion.

She checked in at the desk and was directed to one of the changing rooms to put on her gown and prepare to give up a little bit more of her dignity. Even the kindest nurses made that face when they saw Lucy's scar. There was this overwhelming sympathy in their expressions. They knew she had fought the battle and was likely to fight it again. It was the "I'm sorry" in their eyes that made Lucy want to scream.

In the dressing room, she pulled her sweater over her head and folded it neatly on the chair. She unhooked her bra and placed it on top of the sweater. Lucy looked at herself in the mirror. Her scar seemed to be redder today, angry maybe that they were back to see if they were in for another fight.

Had she had the surgeons take both breasts last time, she wouldn't have to go through this yearly trauma. She'd have two big scars on her chest, no breasts, but peace of mind. Maybe. Would she ever believe she was safe from cancer? Probably not.

Cancer was her Wade. Even when she banished it from her body, she worried it might come back, find a new way to take her out. It didn't care that she hated it and wanted it gone. It wouldn't let her go without a fight.

She slipped into her gown and exited the dressing room. All her things went into a locker and she sat down to wait. She could page through one of the many magazines sitting on the end tables, but there was no point.

She'd only be going through the motions. Her head was too full of what-ifs again.

What if she had missed something when she did her self-exams?

What if it was back?

What if they had missed something a year ago and now it was too far along this time?

What if it killed her this time?

The panic began to build and controlling her breathing became more of a challenge. Good thing they didn't need to take her blood pressure; it was sure to be off the charts.

"Lucy Everhart?" the tech called.

Rising to her feet, Lucy squared her shoulders. It didn't matter what happened in there. As she'd done with Wade, she would kick cancer's butt if it came back. Believing was half the battle.

THERE WAS AN urgent text from Paige when Lucy finished and retrieved her things. When she called, all Paige would say was that she needed to come to Open Arms immediately.

Hannah had a strange look on her face when Lucy walked in. "Is everything okay? What happened?"

"There's someone here who wants to meet

with you and Paige. She's in there with Paige now."

Lucy's stomach dropped. "Elizabeth Kerrington?"

Hannah shook her head. Lucy's curiosity was piqued. She knocked before entering Paige's office.

"Come in," Paige said from the other side.

As soon as Lucy saw Clarissa Stevens-Hunt sitting across from Paige, she understood why everyone was freaking out. Had Dylan turned over negotiations to his mother? Negotiating a house sale seemed a little beneath her.

"Good, you're here," Paige said, jumping up and motioning for Lucy to take a seat next to Clarissa.

"To say I'm surprised to see you here, Mrs. Stevens-Hunt, would be an understatement. To what do we owe the pleasure?" This was likely to be anything but pleasurable.

"As I was telling Ms. Clayton, I am here with an offer."

"Well, as I am sure your son has told you, we have heard all of Prime Developments's offers and we are considering all of our options. We really don't appreciate the unnecessary pressure that Mrs. Kerrington feels she needs to place on us. Our property is not on the market." The frustration began to seep into her tone. "We may be interested in selling someday, but we are not going to be bullied into doing it until we're ready. There are women living there who have no other place to go. There are children there who need to know that they are safe and that no one is going to make them leave until their mom is ready."

"Lucy," Paige said with warning in her eyes.

"No, I'm not going to bite my tongue. I don't care who she is."

Clarissa appeared completely unfazed by Lucy's tirade. In fact, she seemed a bit impressed. "I'm not here on behalf of Mrs. Kerrington or Prime Developments. I am here because I, personally, have an offer for you."

Lucy sat back and crossed her arms over her chest. "I apologize. I'm listening."

Clarissa handed Lucy a folder. "There is one property in Logan Square and one right here in Lincoln Park. Both would need some work to meet your needs. All of that would be handled by me, of course, before you took possession."

"Possession?" Lucy paged through the folder. Inside, there were real estate listings and photographs of each property."

"I want to donate a new shelter to Open Arms. I think if you take a look, these properties offer things your current location doesn't provide. Both are close to parks. This one," she pointed to the building in Lincoln Park, "we could easily redesign so there would be almost fifteen separate residences. They'd only be studio apartments, but still much more than a bedroom."

Lucy's brain exploded. That could be the only reason why she couldn't put together one single coherent sentence. Clarissa Stevens-Hunt was offering them a dream.

"I'm not sure we even know what to say," Paige admitted as she flipped through her own folder.

"Well, I don't expect you to choose without looking at both properties." She handed Paige a business card. "This is my real estate agent. She will set up the showings and take you through both of them, answer any questions you might have. I can also send my contractor at the same time. He could give you an idea of how much time it would take to complete the remodel."

"This would be contingent on selling Safe Haven to Prime Developments?" Lucy figured this was Clarissa's strange way of getting Elizabeth's offer signed, sealed and delivered. It was an expensive bribe.

"I don't care what you do with your other shelter house. Sell it to whomever you want. I would strongly suggest that you consider Prime's offer—it bodes well for you to keep your relationship with them positive. Mrs. Kerrington has many connections in this city."

"So we've learned," Paige said with a sigh.

"I'm doing this because my son told me it would make you happy. I happen to believe that if you are happy, my son will also be happy. There is nothing I want more in the world than to see my son happy. So, consider my motives selfish if you must."

As if the offer of donating a multi-million dollar property to Open Arms wasn't mind-boggling enough, Clarissa's reason for doing so caused Lucy's head to spin.

"This is incredibly generous. We have never received a donation of this magnitude. I'm not even sure what we would need to do to make this happen." Paige was freaking out, as well. She was giddy, giggling as she read through the proposal.

"Miss Everhart is the best of the best, I'm told. I am sure she will figure it out. If you have any concerns or questions, you can call me directly. My number is in there. I do ask that you name the property after my mother.

She would never admit to being a battered woman, but we all know that there are things that happen behind closed doors. You should have seen what my mother could do with makeup. The woman could have worked for a movie studio." Clarissa stood up and started to leave. She stopped when she reached the door. "No child should have to go to bed afraid for her mother's safety. What you do here is worthwhile. I'll be waiting to hear from you."

Lucy and Paige sat dumbstruck. There were no words for what had just happened.

"Am I dreaming? Because if I'm dreaming, I never want to wake up," Paige said, looking to Lucy for some confirmation that all this was real.

"You're not dreaming. That just happened. Dylan's mother just offered us our choice of properties to build a bigger, better women's shelter. Can you imagine what we can do with something like this?"

"In addition to the money we could get for selling Safe Haven? Lucy, we'd have money to do things I have only fantasized about."

Dylan's mother had given a gift that could never be repaid, and all because she wanted her son to be happy. Somehow, that happiness was contingent on Lucy. No pressure.

CHAPTER TWENTY

NO LONGER HAVING the black cloud of Prime Developments hanging over him, Dylan felt as if an enormous burden had been lifted off his shoulders. It might have also had something to do with the possibility of taking on new clients who didn't fit the classic Stevens and Ellis profile.

Once he had prepped Henry to take over Prime, Dylan had spent the whole next day calling up some old contacts. It was amazing what doing something that felt worthwhile did to improve his morale at work.

For the first time in years, he smiled on his way out of the office. Even Bridgette mentioned how much she was enjoying his mood. He drove home, excited about what tomorrow would bring. He wasn't changing the world yet, but everyone had to start somewhere, and Dylan was ready to begin.

He parked in the garage and walked around to the front of his building, hopeful that Eugene and Jeremy were home. He felt like going out for a nice dinner and needed someone to join him.

Sitting on his front porch wearing that pink hat and blowing into her hands to keep them warm was the only person who could put a damper on this great day. He wasn't sure why she was here. Maybe she had to pick up Simon. It was possible her being there had absolutely nothing to do with him at all. If it did, it couldn't be good. Ever the glutton for punishment, he sort of hoped she was there to see him.

"Hi," she said, getting to her feet as he came up the walkway.

"Hey there. It's a little cold to be sitting outside. Are you waiting for Simon?" He decided to lead with the least confrontational reason for her to be here.

"I'm waiting for you, actually."

His heart skipped a beat but quickly began to race as the panic set in. She was probably here to remind him how angry she was with him. Henry had probably drafted the letter Elizabeth had requested the day before. Lucy probably wanted to tell him to his face that they would never sell to Prime because she hated Elizabeth and she hated him.

She didn't look as if she hated him, though. She almost appeared remorseful. But he'd been wrong too many times to assume he could tell how she was feeling. He invited her inside and upstairs.

"Can I take your coat or is this going to be quick?" he asked once they were in his loft.

She took off her jacket and handed it to him. So, she planned to let him have it for more than a minute or so.

"Do you want some coffee? You look cold." He snapped his fingers. "Let me make you some hot tea. I bet you don't drink coffee. Too many bad things in there, right?"

"Right." One side of her mouth quirked up. "Tea would be nice."

Nice. That wasn't a word he'd thought she'd ever use around him again. He filled up the kettle and lit the burner on the stove.

"You got the doors on the cabinets. It's really nice," she said, taking a seat on one of the bar stools by the breakfast counter.

There was that word again. "Thanks. Eugene came over Sunday and helped me get it done. We make a good team."

"Eugene is so nice. I see why you and Paige like him so much."

Nice had become the only adjective in her

vocabulary. Something was up and he braced himself for the bomb she was sure to drop.

"Eugene is the best friend I've ever had, but I'm guessing you didn't come over here to talk about Eugene."

Lucy's gaze dropped to the counter. Her finger lightly traced one of the dark veins in the quartz. "No, that's not why I came."

The silence that followed was almost enough to kill him. Dylan just wanted her to get it over with so he could go on with his life. The kettle whistled before she spoke again. Dylan shut off the burner and poured the boiling water into two mugs. He pulled out the tea he had on hand and let her choose.

"I talked to your mom today," she said as she dropped a tea bag into her mug.

Dylan's eyes went wide. "Why were you talking to my mom?"

Lucy's bottom lip was clamped between her teeth. She bobbed the tea bag up and down in the water.

"Lucy," he said, losing patience. "What's going on?"

She looked up at him. "Did you tell her that you wanted me to be happy?"

Dylan suddenly felt like a humiliated teenager. Had his mother really gone to discuss him with Lucy? This was mortifying. "What in the world were you and my mother talking about?"

"She's donating two million dollars to Open Arms so we can relocate Safe Haven. She found a couple of properties that are incredible, and she's given us complete control over how they'll be remodeled. Paige and I have spent the past few days trying to figure out which programs to cut so we could hold off selling until the last minute, and your mom just made it possible for us to think bigger instead of smaller."

Dylan needed to sit. The shock made it hard to hold himself up. He walked over to the couch and plopped down. She'd done it. His mother had done exactly what he said would solve the problem and make Lucy happy.

"Did you tell her to do that? Did you tell her to do it because you wanted me to be happy?" she asked, sitting next to him.

"I kind of did." His mother had become a complete anomaly. She really had been listening during their entire lunch yesterday. "I didn't think she would actually do it. I thought we were just speaking in hypotheticals."

"So, you didn't ask her to make me happy?"

Dylan's head snapped in her direction. "Not exactly." He tried to remember exactly what he'd said. Clarissa had asked him what would make everyone happy, and he'd admitted Lucy's happiness was all that really mattered. "I told her I wanted you to be happy. I didn't ask her to make it happen."

"Why would you care if I'm happy?"

Was she really going to act this dense? "Because I'm in love with you, Lulu."

Lucy blinked and blinked again. "After everything that's happened? After I accused you of coming to the fund-raiser to spy for Elizabeth? You're still in love with me?"

"I'm not going to stop loving you because you're mad at me. That's not how it works."

"Well, you need to stop, Dylan." She stood up and went back to her tea.

"That's all you have to say? I tell you that I'm in love with you after everything we've been through and your only response is, 'stop it'?"

"I can't deal with this right now."

"Deal with what? I'm not chasing you around town begging for another chance. I didn't send my mother to Open Arms with her checkbook to guilt you into loving me back if that's what you think."

She made everything so difficult. She acted as if being loved was some huge burden. He wasn't asking for anything in return. He simply couldn't turn off his feelings just because she didn't reciprocate them.

"I don't think that." Lucy rubbed her temples with the heels of her hands. "You deserve better than someone who can't love you back. I want you to be happy. Let me go so you can be."

"Then give me closure," he said, joining her in the kitchen. With his elbows on the counter, he leaned forward and ducked his head so she had to meet his eyes. "What happened five years ago? What did I do wrong? Help me understand so I can move on."

Lucy groaned quietly. Was it such a difficult question? "Dylan, I... There's nothing you did. It was me."

"No, don't pull the 'it was me, not you' card. I don't believe it. We were in love. We were talking about getting married and starting a family. Something happened to make you not want those things with me. What did I do? Did you wake up one morning and realize you couldn't handle being married to a guy who likes two sugars and no cream in his coffee? I did or said something. Just tell me. It can't be worse than the things you've said to me over the past few weeks."

She hid behind her hands. Her head shook back and forth.

"A couple of days ago, you thought I was the devil. Did you think that about me five years ago? Tell me."

Lucy dropped her hands. "Fine. You feel too much. You loved me too much. You needed me too much. It was more than I could handle. I felt like I was destined to let you down. So, it was me and you. We were both the reason I didn't think we could make it."

He'd loved her too much. That he could believe. Hadn't his mother said the same thing the other day, that he felt too much? It worried his mother and it had scared Lucy away. He let out a long sigh.

"Okay. Well, thank you for telling me. I guess I need to dial it back. I'm sure my future wife will appreciate you giving me the heads-up."

"Why did you come to the Hope and Healing fund-raiser this weekend? Be honest. Were you there for Elizabeth?"

"Do you think someone in love with you would show up to your fund-raiser to spy for your mortal enemy?"

"You worked for her. Loving me didn't stop

you from showing up at Open Arms to negotiate a deal for our house."

"I took her on before I had any clue you were involved in the deal. Had I known, I would have asked someone else to take it." That was a lie. He would have taken it to see her. He loved her too much after all.

"So why did you come, then, if it wasn't for Elizabeth?"

"Your mother invited me. I told her it was a bad idea and she said, and I quote, 'You're reading her all wrong. She's got secrets that need spilling.' How could I resist with that kind of bait?"

"My mom doesn't know what she's talking about. I'm sorry she did that to you."

Dylan couldn't blame Maureen. "Your mom will always be one of my favorite people in the world. Every time I go by the Cancer Survivors Garden, I say a little prayer for her."

Tears brimmed in Lucy's eyes. She blinked them back and swallowed down whatever emotion had overcome her.

"What? What did I say?"

Lucy grabbed his face and kissed him as if she meant it. "I lied," she said when she stopped. "I'm a liar. That's why you should stop loving me."

She spun in her seat and started for her coat. Dylan ran around the counter and grabbed her arm, reminding him of Saturday night when she'd nearly broken his arm off for doing the same. This time, she didn't fight back. Instead, she fell against him and cried against his shoulder.

Another memory hit him. The one of her crying in his arms when she learned her mother was sick. He stroked her hair and kissed the top of her head. "Is it your mom? Please, Lucy, talk to me."

"It's not my mom. It's me." Dylan didn't understand. He tried to hold her tighter, not wanting to ever let her go, but she pulled away. "It was *my* cancer that caused all the problems."

Suddenly, it was as if she was speaking another language. Dylan needed to ask her to repeat herself but he didn't want to hear those words come out of her mouth again. "That doesn't make sense. When did you have cancer?"

Lucy wiped her face with the back of her hand. He knew how much she hated crying. Cancer was a good reason to cry, though. "About five years ago."

Dylan shook his head. That couldn't be right. She had been so healthy back then.

She ate right, exercised, didn't smoke, didn't drink. She had been so careful. So worried. So scared it was going to get her. She had made a big deal about getting a mammogram. Made sure her sisters got one, too. She had gotten tested…and then she shut down on him.

It all began to make sense. A sickening feeling came over him. She'd had cancer and chose not to tell him. She had asked him to leave when she had needed him the most.

"Why would you do that? Why didn't you tell me?"

"I truly did feel overwhelmed by how much you loved me," she answered. "How many times did you tell me you wouldn't be able to handle it if anything ever happened to me? Well, something was happening to me and there was a chance I wasn't going to make it."

"Oh, come on!" Confusion quickly gave way to anger. "I said that because I wanted you to know how much you meant to me. I didn't literally mean I couldn't handle it. I would have handled it! I would have been there for you." He began to pace. His head was swimming. Looking back on everything with this information changed so many things. "No wonder Emma thought I was some kind of slimeball.

Did you tell your family that I knew and left you anyway?"

"I didn't tell them anything at the time. Recently, I may have let Emma believe you knew. My mother didn't believe it and got the truth out of me. She blabbed to Kendall, who set Emma straight. No one thinks you're the bad guy. They're all mad at me for keeping it from you for this long."

"Good." That was some consolation, at least. "Did you have breast cancer?" Lucy nodded. "Was it bad? What kind of treatment did you have? Did you have to have surgery like your mom?" All these questions came tumbling out. He felt as if he had missed so much. As horrible as it all must have been, he was still angry at her for denying him the chance to be there for her while she had to suffer.

"It was Stage II. It was in my left breast. It spread to my lymph nodes. I had chemotherapy, radiation and a left-side mastectomy. It was not pleasant, but I survived."

As soon as she said she had had a mastectomy, he couldn't help but look at her a little closer. She didn't appear to be missing any parts. There was no evidence that anything was different.

Recognizing that she was being inspected,

Lucy explained, "I wear special undergarments that make it look like everything is still there, but it's not. I am not the same woman I was. I have a scar that runs from here to here." She pointed to her chest. The scar was long. Dylan couldn't imagine what she'd been through. "I am at risk for reoccurrence because I didn't opt to have them remove both of my breasts. I am not the woman you want to be in love with. I let you go so none of this would be your burden or your worry."

Dylan let out a frustrated snort and dug his fingers through his hair. "How dare you? That wasn't your call to make, Lulu. That should have been my decision." He pointed at his own chest, his anger making his hand shake. "I should have been given the chance to choose."

"Well, what if I told you the truth and you walked away because you couldn't handle it? Or what if you chose to stand by me, but it all proved to be too much for you? What if you stood by me and I died? None of those outcomes appealed to me, and I was the one who had to get in the mind-set to fight. I was the one who needed to find the will to live."

"What if?" She was unbelievable. "What if you had died? What if I had read in the paper that you died from breast cancer a year after

we broke up? You think it would have been any easier for me because you let me go a year earlier? And hey, thanks for having some faith in me, some faith in what I felt for you. I loved you. I would never have walked away from you because you were sick."

"I agonized over that decision!" The edge in Lucy's tone matched his. "I didn't leave you because I wanted to hurt you. At the time, I did what I thought was best. For me. For you. For both of us. Maybe I chose wrong. I can't go back."

"No, you can't." Dylan wasn't sure what else to say. There were so many questions, so many feelings. Lucy and his mother were right; he did feel things too deeply. This news had sent him into a tailspin.

"I'm sorry for not being honest. I truly am." Her regret was genuine. The lie had been misguided but not malicious.

"I believe you."

"I think I need to go home." She went for her jacket again and this time he didn't stop her. "We can finish this conversation after we both let the dust settle."

He didn't want her to go, though. "I have a million more questions."

"I'm sure you do, but it has been one heck

of a day and I need to get my head on straight so I can answer those questions the way you deserve."

That seemed fair enough. "We'll talk soon, then."

"Simon and Jeremy have a game tomorrow. Maybe we can talk after that," she offered.

"Perfect." He helped her with her jacket. As he watched her go down the stairs, Dylan couldn't shake the feeling that not all the secrets had been revealed. Whatever it was, he was going to get to the bottom of it once and for all.

CHAPTER TWENTY-ONE

LUCY COULDN'T BELIEVE the words had come out of her mouth. She hadn't gone to Dylan's to confess. Her only objective had been to find out what he had said to his mother that would make her donate millions. One look into those soulful eyes and she had been reduced to a pile of regret. His heart hadn't changed. It was still so big and soft. When he had said he continued to pray for her mother, she'd lost it.

Given his reaction, he might not forgive her for lying. She wasn't sure she wanted him to. Wasn't it better if he stayed clear of her? Had anything changed? She still wasn't right for him. It didn't matter if he loved her or that she was in love with him. She couldn't give him what he deserved—a family, the next fifty years.

Lucy grabbed a cab to Kendall's. She was the only one who would understand. Emma was angry about the lies. Their mother was too sympathetic toward Dylan. Kendall would see it Lucy's way. She would lend her support.

She knocked before walking in. "Anyone home?"

"Aunt Lulu!" Simon shouted from the family room. The nickname was particularly hard to hear tonight.

Lucy pulled off her hat and shoved it into the pocket of her coat as she made her way back to where the family was busy with some big art project.

"We're making turkeys with our hands for school." Simon held up his paper. The palm of the handprint was brown, and a bright red wattle dangled from the thumb.

"Cool," she replied, taking off her coat and draping it over the back of one of the chairs.

Kendall was attempting to trace Darcy's little hand without much success. The baby kept making a fist and crumpling the paper before her mother could get all the way around it.

"Need some help?" Lucy took a seat beside her sister and held Darcy's hand flat so Kendall could finish the job.

"Thanks."

"Want to make one, too?" Simon asked. He handed Lucy a blank piece of paper. "Trace your hand, then write what you're thankful for on each finger, which are the feathers, by the way. Then color it and write your name on the back."

"What happens if I write my name on the front?" Lucy asked, grabbing a black colored pencil off the coffee table.

"You're teaching my child that following directions isn't important," Kendall said, getting up and putting Darcy in her jungle-themed exersaucer. Darcy swatted at a plastic monkey hanging from a vine in front of her.

"Well, I think following directions is very important, so I am going to put my name on the back," Lucy conceded. "I am not a rebel."

"What's a rebel?" Simon asked without looking up from his picture.

"A rebel is someone who likes breaking the rules. Don't be a rebel, Simon. It will make your mommy very sad."

"Don't worry, Mom. I'm not a rebel."

"I'm not worried about you, man. Aunt Lucy has always been the family rebel. We need to keep an eye on her."

Simon was focused on turning each finger into a very detailed feather. The kid was so naturally artistic it was scary. It made Lucy wonder what her child would have inherited from her if she had had one.

The thought sent a sharp pain through her chest. Simon's slate blue eyes lifted from the paper. They were the same color his father's had been. Would her son's eyes have been blue like his father's? The pain that image conjured up forced her to drop her pencil and place her hand over her heart.

"Are you okay?" Kendall asked. She rubbed her back as she had when Lucy was sick after her chemo treatments. Her sisters had been there for her. Kendall had flown home more than once during that time to be a support. Her sisters and her parents were the only ones she could rely on.

Lucy nodded as she fought back the tears. It had been a very long day. From saying good-bye to Nora, to her mammogram, to Clarissa's donation, to her conversation with Dylan, the day had been one giant roller coaster of emotion. She took a deep breath and reminded herself to stay present in the moment. The past was done and the future was yet to be determined.

She picked up a green pencil and began coloring in the outline of her pinkie finger. Simon stopped her.

"You have to write what you're thankful for first, Aunt Lulu. See? Like mine."

Simon's turkey had the words *family*, *friends*, *school* and *cool cars* written on the fingers in black marker. Cool cars. Like Dylan's. The tears spilled over.

"Hey, Simon?" Kendall got his attention. "Aunt Lucy and I are going to go in the kitchen for a minute. Finish coloring, okay?"

Simon placed his hand on Lucy's. "It's going to be okay, Aunt Lulu. Don't be sad. We don't think you're a rebel because you didn't write what you're thankful for first."

He was such a sweet boy. Lucy wiped her eyes. "Thanks, bud."

Kendall grabbed the baby and the two sisters went into the kitchen. Kendall situated Darcy in the high chair with some crackers while Lucy blew her nose into a tissue. Maybe a good cry was all she needed. She sat at the kitchen table and held her head, letting the emotion take over.

After a few minutes of crying, she felt better. Some of the tension in her shoulders was gone, but her nose was running like crazy. Kendall handed her a few more tissues.

"What's the matter?" Kendall's voice was soft and comforting. "You can tell me."

"Today has been totally nuts. I don't even know where to start."

"Start at the beginning," Kendall suggested. She cracked a smile and gave Lucy's arm a pat. "That's what you'd tell me."

Lucy gave her sister a rundown of her day. Kendall was shocked to hear about the donation and even more surprised that Lucy had told Dylan the truth. What she didn't understand was why Lucy was feeling so confused.

"He knows the truth and he loves you, Lucy. That's good news. That means you don't have to be alone."

"Doesn't it? What's changed? Nothing. I'm still a ticking time bomb, K. I had my yearly mammogram today. What if they call me tomorrow and tell me it's back? What if I'm right where I was five years ago? What has really changed?"

"You aren't going to get that call tomorrow. You can't think that way."

"I have to think that way!" She didn't mean to raise her voice, but she'd lost all self-control. "I am more at risk than the average person. It could come back, and what if I can't beat it this time? Why would I ask Dylan to be a part of that?"

"I get it." Kendall let out a frustrated breath. "I do. You have to consider the worst case, and in that scenario, you don't think it's fair to ask him to waste his time with a woman who's sick. But it isn't fair of you to ask him not to care, either. People don't stop feeling because we ask them to. Let him in or don't—he still loves you. So, who does it really hurt not to let him be there for you?"

That was a valid point. Right now, it hurt Lucy. It also hurt her to let that hope in. Babies with blue eyes and a strong desire to fight for the underdog weren't a possibility no matter how much she wanted them to be.

"You can't let your fear stop you from living," Kendall said.

Lucy scrubbed her face with her hands and gave her sister a sad smile. "My fear is what keeps me alive."

TALKING TO KENDALL hadn't offered Lucy the solace she had hoped she'd find. For some reason, no one could see it Lucy's way. Maybe it was because her shoes were hard to walk in.

Wednesday morning, Lucy went to Open Arms to meet with Paige, two of the board members and Clarissa's Realtor. They were going to visit the two properties today and hopefully make a decision before Thanksgiving, which was a week away.

Without the usual burdens weighing heavy

on her mind, Paige seemed more vibrant than ever. Her smile was bright and her laugh bordered on obnoxious. Lucy could tell the wheels in her head had been spinning overtime since the donation from Clarissa had come in. All the things Paige had dreamed of doing for the community were a real possibility, and she was absolutely giddy about it.

The Lincoln Park property was Lucy's favorite. She liked Clarissa's idea of creating studio apartments. The women with children would appreciate the extra space. There was also space to have a dining hall, two counseling rooms, a play area for the kids and a basement that could be used for storage, something they were lacking in the current house.

"I know which one I want. What about you?" Paige asked as they climbed back into Sharon's SUV after the second showing.

"This one," Lucy and Sharon said at the same time.

"Me, too," Paige said, clapping her hands in excitement. "I love it. I want to move in there."

"What's your thought on selling the Safe Haven house?" Sharon asked Paige. "Aren't we close to the expiration date on Prime Developments's offer?"

"Friday," Paige replied. "We got a letter from them reminding us our time is up."

"Maybe we should take it," Sharon said.

"We should definitely take it," Tanya added. As board treasurer, she had been the most out-spoken about selling from the beginning.

Lucy still held a grudge. "Maybe we should put it on the market and let Elizabeth Kerrington worry that someone else might snap it up."

"Maybe," Paige said with a smirk. "Or maybe we simply make a counteroffer she can't refuse and be done with it."

Lucy laughed. "You are so much nicer than me."

"You're not as mean as you think you are."

Lucy would disagree. They returned to Open Arms, ready to contact the rest of the board and open up discussion about what their next move would be. Lucy didn't like the idea of Elizabeth Kerrington thinking she got away with something, but in the end, Open Arms was coming out on top.

Her phone rang as she stepped out of the car. The number wasn't one that she recognized. She put her hand over her other ear to block out the street noise. "Hello?"

"May I speak with Lucy Everhart, please?"

"You are," she answered.

"Hi, Miss Everhart? This is Sandy from Dr. Benson's office. I'm calling with the results from your mammogram yesterday. Unfortunately, there was an abnormal result and Dr. Benson would like you to come in for an additional viewing. We could schedule that right now, if you'd like."

Lucy's blood ran cold. It was her worst nightmare come true. *Abnormal result.* It was a repeat of the conversation she had had with a nurse five years ago. They had asked her to come in for an ultrasound. The ultrasound had led to a biopsy. The biopsy had confirmed the malignancy of her tumor.

Her breathing was labored and suddenly the street was silent. There was no noise except a weird buzzing in her head. She leaned against Sharon's car for support as her knees became weak.

"Miss Everhart? Are you there?"

She was dying. The cancer had come back just as she knew it would. Her body was trying to kill her and she was going to have to fight it to stay alive. All the things she had to do to get rid of it would also feel as if they were trying to end her. She hated hospitals. Hated them.

"Lucy, what's the matter?" Paige's voice broke through. Lucy blinked and her concerned friend's face came into focus. "Who is that?"

The grim reaper. The angel of death. The bearer of the worst possible news.

"I'm fine. I'm here. Can I call you back?" she asked the nurse.

The woman rattled off the number and their closing time for the day. Lucy hung up before the woman finished speaking. Paige stood in front of her with worry lines etching her face.

"Who was that?"

"No one." Lucy straightened and shook off the shock. She had to be stronger than this if she was going back to war. "I have to go home. If you need me, you can reach me on my cell."

"Is everything okay?" Paige followed her to the street where Lucy was searching for a cab. "You look like you've seen a ghost. Maybe you should come inside and have some water before you head out."

Lucy had seen a ghost, all right. She'd seen herself. Cold and white, dressed in lace and placed in a satin-lined box. She needed to go home, soak in her tub and let all this sink in. Then she needed to call the doctor and schedule another appointment. Another viewing. Another test that would tell her what she already knew. She was dying.

CHAPTER TWENTY-TWO

WEDNESDAY MORNING, Dylan went straight to his mom's office. Her assistant, Vivian, was perfect for his mother because she didn't like anyone, so it didn't bother her to be rude when she needed to be. Of course, she was also rude when she didn't need to be, like today.

"Is she in?" he asked, pointing at the door as if she didn't know to whom he was referring.

"She is, but she's busy. Can I take a message, or do you want to email her yourself like everyone else who wants to get in touch with her?"

Sometimes she made Dylan want to pull his son-of-the-boss card, but he chose to smile and knock on the door anyway. He pushed it open to find his mother on the phone. She was scowling until she noticed it was him. Waving him in, she went back to her call.

"She says I can come in," he whispered back to Vivian, who was also scowling. She really didn't like him.

Clarissa's office was twice the size of his. The corner office had views of both the lake and the city. The late November sky was gray. Winter was coming, and hopefully it wouldn't be as cold as the last, when being outside for just a few minutes could give a person frostbite.

Resting against his mother's desk was a painting of what seemed to be the Chicago skyline, but he couldn't be sure. He squinted at it, trying to figure out what he was missing. There had to be something special about it that would have made Clarissa buy it. Maybe it was painted by someone famous.

His mother ended her phone call and folded her hands on the desk. "Your father."

Dylan's face scrunched in confusion. "What about my father?"

"He painted that."

Dylan's gaze dropped back to the painting. It was atrocious. "Oh, no."

"Oh, yes. This is what he wants to do when he retires. I'm going to have to hang that up in here for people to see. And Lord knows what else he'll create for the house. I need you to think up another hobby for him. Quick," she said, making Dylan laugh. "You won't think it's so funny when you see what he's making you."

That wasn't as funny. "I'll think of something."

"Good," his mother said. "Now, why are you popping in unannounced?"

"I came to say thank you for what you did for Open Arms. When you asked me what would make everyone happy, I didn't think you were asking so you could actually make it happen. But I'm very happy you did."

Clarissa's smile made her look younger than she was. "Then I accomplished what I set out to do. Was there anything else?" She glanced at her computer screen, where there were surely dozens of emails waiting for her attention. Warm and cold. This woman couldn't decide what she wanted to be. At least Dylan was beginning to understand that she was capable of being both. That was a definite improvement.

"That was it." Dylan got up to leave her to her work.

"I hope that you found out because it made Miss Everhart happy, as well," she said, halting his retreat.

"I think she's very happy about the donation. She stopped by to tell me personally."

"Did she?" Clarissa wasn't very skilled at pretending she wasn't digging for information.

"I also learned the real reason she walked out on me. She had breast cancer."

That garnered her full attention. She closed her laptop. "She had cancer, so she broke up with you? How does that make sense?"

"It doesn't. Not to me." Dylan sat back down. He needed someone to talk to about this and his mother was better than no one. "She tried to say it was because she thought it would be better for both of us. She wanted me to move on with someone else who wasn't sick. I was the idiot who let her go without pushing for answers. If I had just stood up to her a little, made her tell me what was wrong, maybe things would have been different."

That was the thing that bothered him the most. She had asked him to leave her alone and he had. Without a fight. No wonder she thought he didn't really care about her, or that he would have run away if he'd known the truth.

"She's fine now? Healthy?" his mother asked.

"I guess. We're meeting tonight to talk."

Clarissa's expression was unreadable. "Well, don't get sucked into something you're going to regret. Maybe she was right. Maybe it was best for you two to go your separate ways. The last thing you need is to invest time into someone who doesn't have very much."

That wasn't the response he was expecting. The laptop was reopened and her focus went back to her work.

"We're all dying, Mom. There are no guarantees for anyone. I could get hit by a bus tomorrow. Should we not care about anyone because everyone dies someday?"

"There you go with the dramatics again. All I'm saying is that you should think about what you want. I imagine you want a wife, children. You need to choose wisely so you can have the things you want in life. Making decisions on temporary feelings is silly and unwise."

"Temporary feelings? You mean love?"

"Call it what you want. Love, infatuation, lust. These feelings are not permanent no matter what the fairy tales tell you, Dylan."

This was the mom he knew and knew well. Feelings scared this woman more than anything. Why was it that the emotions that were so foreign to her were the ones he felt so strongly? Maybe he had been born with his and hers.

"I can't control who I fall in love with. It's not a choice. It's a feeling, and I've been feeling it for years whether I want to or not." That was what he needed Lucy to understand, as well.

"It starts as a feeling and becomes a choice as time goes on. Don't let anyone tell you differently. You don't have to be ruled by your emotions. I would prefer it if you weren't."

Vivian buzzed on the intercom. "Your eight-thirty is here."

"I have a meeting, but I'm glad you stopped by," his mother said, dismissing him.

"I love you, Mom. No matter what you say or what you do or what you prefer," he said as he walked out. He wasn't going to be told not to feel. Not by his mother and not by Lucy. Both women were going to have to deal with his feelings whether they liked it or not.

ONE PHONE CALL from an old law school buddy and Dylan was ten minutes late getting out of work. The light snow falling on the asphalt caused traffic to move at a snail's pace. He was a good fifteen minutes late when he pulled into the parking lot of the school where Jeremy played ball.

As worried as he was about disappointing the boy by being late, Dylan was more anxious about what kind of message not being there would send to Lucy. He didn't want her to think the conversation they were going to have after the game wasn't important to him.

He pushed open the gym door and scanned the bleachers for her. He found the Everhart family, but no Lucy. What if she'd left because she thought he wasn't going to show? He cursed under his breath and climbed the steps closest to Maureen and the rest of the family.

"You made it!" Maureen's smile made him feel a little less nervous. Eugene was sitting with them and pointed at the empty spot next to him. Dylan apologized as he stepped in front of Kendall and her husband to get to Eugene.

He checked the scoreboard and waved to Jeremy, who was taking a break on the bench and definitely noticed his late arrival. Leaning forward, Dylan tried to get Kendall's attention. "Is Lucy here?"

"Nope." Kendall checked her phone. "I texted her a couple minutes ago, but she hasn't replied. Let me text her again."

Maybe she was running late as he had been. The roads were a little slick. Hopefully, she'd be here any minute. Dylan tried to concentrate on the game, but his gaze kept drifting toward the door. He checked his watch and tried to keep the negative thoughts at bay.

"Did Lucy text back?" he asked when Kendall looked at her phone.

"Not yet. I wonder why she's ignoring me." Kendall glanced over her shoulder at her mom. Maureen's concerned expression made Dylan nervous.

"Has anyone talked to her at all today?" Emma asked.

They all answered that they hadn't. "I talked to her yesterday," Kendall reported. "I texted her this morning. She replied to that one."

Emma pulled out her phone and sent off a text. Maureen took her phone out and made a call.

"She's not answering," Maureen said, hanging up without leaving a message.

Emma's phone beeped. Dylan's body relaxed, assuming it was Lucy finally responding. "Charlie says he hasn't seen her. At least we know she's not in an accident in this part of town."

The tension returned. *Where was she?* Dylan was ready to get in his car and scour the city for her when Maureen's phone rang.

"It's her!" She answered it and immediately read her daughter the riot act. "You have everyone in a panic here. Where are you?"

Dylan was relieved she was safe but began

to worry she wasn't there because she was avoiding him. She had promised him answers, and he was going to get them. Maureen stood up and swiftly made her way down the bleachers and out the gym doors. Everyone exchanged looks.

Emma and Kendall communicated silently. Max wrapped an arm around his wife and gave her a squeeze. He whispered in her ear and kissed her cheek. Her head fell on his shoulder and her teeth dug into her bottom lip. They knew something. Something bad.

"Is everything okay, you think?" he asked, hoping they'd tell him what they were so worried about.

"I'm going to check on Mom." Emma climbed over her dad and jogged down the stands.

A torturous two minutes later, Emma came back into the gym. She grabbed her mom's jacket. "We need to go," Emma told her dad.

"What's wrong?" Dylan was freaking out. They needed to tell him or he was going to lose it in the middle of an elementary school gymnasium.

"She's fine," Emma tried to reassure him. "She's upset about something. We need to go talk to her."

"*I* need to talk to her. Is it about me? Because we were supposed to meet here tonight, and you all are acting like you know something, and if it's about me, I think I have a right to hear it. Is she hiding from me?"

Kendall and Emma shared another glance. "Not exactly," Emma said.

"She's avoiding everyone at the moment," Kendall added. "It's not about you."

Mr. Everhart buttoned up his coat. "Come on, Dylan. You can follow us over there."

"Dad," Emma protested.

"What? If he cares about your sister, he should come with us. She needs to know we're all here for her, Dylan included." He bent down and gave Kendall a kiss. "Tell Simon he played well and we're sorry we had to leave before the game ended.

"I'll come by after we get the kids home," Kendall said.

This was a real family intervention. It had to be serious if they all had to go. He followed them out. Maureen was still on the phone when they found her in the hallway.

"Don't say that," she said. "You don't know that… We're coming over… Yes, we are." She smiled sadly at Dylan. "See you in a couple minutes." She hung up and gave him a hug. "Glad you're here."

He didn't understand but was happy to have her approval. Mr. Everhart tossed her the keys. "I'm going to ride with Dylan. We'll meet you two over there."

Feeling more than a little nervous. Dylan walked with Lucy's dad to his car. Unlike her mother, Lucy's father was a man of few words. He was friendly but quiet, soft-spoken.

"Is Lucy all right?" Dylan asked when they got in the car.

Mr. Everhart shrugged. "Guess it depends on what your definition of all right is."

"Did something happen to her? I'm confused why we're heading over to her place when it sounded like she didn't want that."

"I'm not sure what happened, but if Maureen thinks we need to go over there, Lucy needs her family whether she wants us or not."

That wasn't really an answer. Dylan still had no idea what they were going to do once they got to Lucy's.

"You know, when Maureen told me the doctors found cancer in her breast, my first thought was, 'not my wife. Dear God, don't take my wife.' When the doctors told us the best course of action was chemo followed by a double mastectomy, you know what I thought?"

Dylan shook his head. "No, sir."

"I thought, do whatever you got to do. All I wanted was Maureen, alive and well. That night we went to bed and I held her in my arms. She started crying. Hard. Sobbing. I thought she was scared. It had to be scary. I was scared out of my mind, and I wasn't the one who had to go through all those treatments and the surgery.

"When she finally calmed down, I told her it was going to be okay, and she looked up at me and asked me if I would still think she was pretty without any hair." Mr. Everhart let out a chuckle. "This was what the woman was worried about. Of all things. I told her if she could still love me and my bald spot, I would love her bald head, too. She still made me promise to buy her lots and lots of scarves."

Dylan laughed. When Maureen was sick, she had worn some of the most beautiful scarves on her head.

They turned down Lucy's street and Dylan found a parking space. They waited in the car for Maureen and Emma to get there.

"Maureen was terrified that I was focused on what was going to be missing once the doctors got finished with her. Thing was, as long as her heart was beating and her mind was in-

AMY VASTINE   325

tact, I didn't care what they did to the rest of
her. That's hard for a woman to believe, especially if her last name is Everhart."

Maureen and Emma had parked and were
standing outside the building. Maureen was
back on her phone. Emma pressed the button
by the door, waiting for Lucy to let them in.
It became clear, however, that Lucy was not
going to buzz them in.

"Guess it's up to me and you," Mr. Everhart said to Dylan, opening his door. "Stay
here. I'm going in. She'll talk once I get done
with her."

CHAPTER TWENTY-THREE

"THIS IS RIDICULOUS. It's freezing out here. Let us in," her mother begged.

"Please go home."

"Don't do this, Lucy."

"Mom, I don't want you guys coming in here and telling me everything is going to be okay when it's not. Just leave me alone for tonight."

"Lucy?" Her father's voice came over the line. "Buzz me in."

"Dad, I don't want to talk to anyone right now."

"Just me, sweetheart. Open the door."

It wasn't like her father to get in the mix when one of them was having a nervous breakdown. The sisters often got together for SSB (Serious Sister Business) and their mother had no problem inviting herself to an intervention, but her dad tended to stay out of it.

"Only you," she said, buzzing him in.

She opened the door just as he reached her landing. "Hey, baby."

"Hi, Daddy." That was all she could get out before dissolving into tears. Her dad closed the door behind him and pulled her into his arms. He didn't say anything, just held her while she cried.

"How bad is it?" he finally asked once her sobs turned to sniffles.

"They said it was an abnormal result. They want to get another look at it."

"They didn't order a biopsy?"

"Not yet." Even if the doctor didn't say it, Lucy knew that would be ordered next.

"So, it's wait and see," her dad said. "We'll wait and they'll see. And if it's back, we'll fight like we did last time."

Burying her face in his chest, she couldn't suppress the fresh round of tears that accompanied the thought of having to suffer through all those treatments again. She'd do it because there was no way she would give up, but she sure didn't want to.

"I'm sorry you have to do this again. It's not fair. You don't deserve this." He squeezed her tighter. "You don't even eat cheese puffs."

His attempt at humor worked. She laughed in spite of her misery. Her head felt so heavy from all the crying. She stepped back and searched for the tissues.

"Dylan's here. Well, he's downstairs, stuck outside with your mother and sister."

Lucy bristled with anger. Dylan was the last person on the planet she wanted to face right now. "I'm going to kill mom for bringing him here."

"It wasn't your mother's doing. If you're mad, be mad at me. I told him to come. The poor guy was out of his mind with worry waiting for you to show up to that game."

It had been a mistake to tell Dylan anything. Now he expected answers. He wanted her to apologize for not allowing him the chance to prove he would have stood beside her five years ago through all the ups and downs. There had been many more downs than ups, but it was easy for him to say he could have handled it when he was under the impression she had survived. To him, the threat was over. He had nothing to lose by loving her now.

Except that it wasn't over. There was a very real threat growing in her chest right this minute. History was repeating itself and Lucy needed to come up with a game plan. She had to give thought to the decisions she had made last time, figure out which choices were mistakes not to be repeated and which she had only considered mistakes because other people didn't agree with them.

"You should go. Tell them to go. I can't deal with everyone right now. I need to be alone."

"What are you so afraid of?"

Lucy let out a sharp laugh. "Where do I start? Being sick. Feeling like I got run over by a truck every morning when I wake up—if I'm even able to sleep, that is. Losing my hair again. Having doctors cut me up. Being the reason for my parents' and sisters' sorrow. *Dying.*"

Her dad listened to it all without interrupting, then hugged her like a father saying goodbye to his child before she went off to war. He cleared his throat and let go, placing his hands on her shoulders and leveling his gaze with hers. "You get to be scared. So do I. So do your mother and sisters. So will Dylan if you tell him what's going on. Stop pushing. You aren't saving him from any heartache by shutting him out."

Lucy blinked, willing the pointless tears to stop. She was tired of crying and feeling sorry for herself. She wanted to be strong and brave, but she was all tapped out. Letting Dylan in when she was this vulnerable could only lead to trouble.

"Maybe it's my heart I'm worried about. He thinks he loves me, but he's in love with who I was, not who I am. He's in love with the woman he met in law school. The one with the smart mouth and the perfect body. I'm not that girl. I'll never be her again."

"Hey, that smart mouth hasn't gone anywhere. Cancer can't touch your sarcasm," her dad pointed out.

She sighed and sank down onto her couch. "You know what I mean."

"If he only cared about what you looked like, he wouldn't have carried a torch for you all these years. The infatuation would have faded over time. Another pretty face would have captured his attention. He certainly wouldn't be sitting outside your apartment with your crazy family waiting for you to let him in. You're more than your looks, honey. I know you hung your hat on that for years, but there is so much more to you than a body."

She knew that, deep down; but for so long, she'd associated her looks with her power. People noticed her because of how she looked. She was granted favors and given the benefit of the doubt because she was a beautiful woman. Cancer made her feel anything but beautiful.

"Talk to him. I'll take your mother and sister home. You can deal with them tomorrow. But don't close the door on Dylan. If your mother hadn't let me take care of her when she was sick, I would have gone completely insane. Loving her gave me a purpose. Don't take that away from him."

Lucy held her throbbing head in her hands. It was hard to be on the other side. She knew that. She had been there for her mom. She had suffered the helplessness.

Her dad kissed the top of her head. "I love you."

"I love you, too, Dad."

He left the apartment door open a crack when he left. Elmer the cat joined Lucy on the couch and walked across her lap as if to make sure she noticed him. He let her stroke his back a couple of times before he moved on, jumping up on the chair on the other side of the room.

It would be nice to be a cat. Cats were smart. Affection was given and received on their terms. They didn't need it all the time like an obnoxious dog. Being alone didn't cause them intolerable anxiety. They needed their space, seeking companionship when the spirit moved them.

Dylan's knock on the door pushed it open. "Sorry, I didn't mean to—"

"Come on in," she said although she wasn't sure this was the best plan.

"You look terrible." His honesty caught her off guard. He tried to backpedal. "I mean, you look like someone died. Did someone die? Is that what's going on, because no one will tell me anything, and they all seem like they know what's happening and I would really like to know, too."

His endearing rambling made Lucy smile ever so slightly. He must have gone to Jeremy's game straight from work. His suit was wrinkled from sitting in the car so long. The knot of his tie was loosened and the top button of his shirt was undone. She watched his Adam's apple move up and down as he waited for her to explain.

"No one died." *Not yet.* "I got some bad news."

His eyebrows pushed together. "The whole family freaks out when you get some bad news?"

"Pretty much. That's how the Everharts handle a crisis. Everyone comes to the rescue." She would have to call her mom later and apologize for not letting her in. Some people didn't have family who cared. Lucy should have been grateful for having too much.

"What was the bad news?" he asked, almost sitting on Elmer, who wasn't too happy about sharing his seat. The cat let out an unfriendly meow and Dylan shot back up. "Holy cow! That ninja cat is going to be the death of me."

Elmer had had enough of humans and leaped down from the chair, running off to the bedroom. Lucy probably wouldn't see him again until he wanted his breakfast. Being a cat was definitely the life.

"It's safe to sit," Lucy said, trying not to laugh. "If he comes back, I'll use my Kung Fu Lu moves on him to protect you."

Dylan's crooked smile made her pulse speed up. He opted not to sit in the chair, but next to Lucy on the couch. "So, the bad news. It doesn't have anything to do with me, anyone related to me or anyone who works for anyone related to me, does it?"

Shaking her head, Lucy tucked her legs under her. "Nothing to do with you or your mother. She's still my new favorite person."

"That's a relief." He leaned back, making himself more comfortable. "So you weren't trying to avoid having this conversation with me tonight?"

She didn't bother to explain that the conversation they were about to have was not the one he had been looking forward to having. "No."

"Can I ask you some questions, then?"

"Sure." There was no harm in finding out what he wanted to know. Maybe it would make telling him about what was coming next a little easier.

"How long between your diagnosis and when you told me you didn't want to be with me anymore?"

These were painful and scary memories, given her present situation. The parallels made her chest tighten. "I got a call after a routine mammogram. They needed me to come in for an ultrasound. They wouldn't tell me anything, just that I had an abnormal result, so I didn't share it with anyone, not even my family. I had the ultrasound and they immediately ordered a biopsy, which made me a little more nervous. That meant there was definitely something there and they couldn't rule out cancer. That was when I started to pull away, and not just from you. I didn't want to scare anyone— I was already scared enough, and if everyone else freaked out, I'd lose it for sure."

"So that was when the calls stopped getting answered and the excuses about not feeling good and needing some space started."

"Pretty much." Lucy could remember wishing he would show up even though she'd told him to stay away. At the same time, she had needed him to keep his distance because she knew that if she had seen him, she would have told him everything in the first few weeks.

"How long did it take to get the results of the biopsy?"

"The longest three days of my life."

His hand rested on her knee. Those pretty eyes were so sad. "I'm so mad at you for going through that alone. I should have been there, suffering those three days alongside you."

"Your friend Brad was getting married. You had happy thoughts on your mind. I wanted it to stay that way."

"That's right." His other hand smacked his forehead. "I remember that. You were so hard to pin down. Then you were sick, you weren't going to come to the wedding. I thought you were trying to get out of going because you never liked Brad. He's the one who made me think I was suffocating you. His wedding got me thinking about our wedding and he convinced me you were trying to tell me to back off."

Lucy *didn't* like Brad. She liked him even less with this added information. "Wonder what ever happened to good ol' Brad."

"Divorced less than a year after he got married," Dylan said. "I think he moved to Colorado. Haven't heard from him since."

They sat in silence for a moment. Neither one seemed to know what to say next. His hand was still on her knee and she didn't want him to remove it. She wanted to climb onto his lap and let him hold her as he used to. He would run his fingers through her hair and kiss her slowly. Back then, they had all the time in the world.

Dylan broke through her reverie. "When you told me you didn't feel the same way I did and that's why you wanted me to let you go, that was a lie, right? You said that so I wouldn't argue."

The hurt in his tone created a lump in her throat so big she didn't think she'd be able to speak around it. She nodded.

"You were in love with me like I was in love with you?"

"Very much so," she managed to squeak out.

"You were a really good liar." His hand slipped from her knee and she felt the absence of it immediately.

"I had my first chemo treatment the day you came to pick up your stuff from my place. I think I was still in shock. I was angry at everyone and everything, so it was easy to make it look like I was mad at you."

Wasn't she doing the same thing again? Ever since the call from the doctor's office, it was as if she had tunnel vision. She couldn't focus on anything but her own anger and fear.

"I'm sorry I hurt you. You didn't deserve that. I tell myself I was trying to protect you, but the truth is I was trying to protect myself. I didn't think you could love someone who wasn't whole."

His penetrating gaze bored right through her. "You thought it would matter to me what you looked like?"

"I know what people see when they look at me. I'm not blind to where their stares travel."

"Had my arm fallen off five years ago, would you have loved me less?" he asked.

"No," she said with a sigh of regret. She knew what he was trying to prove.

"I love you. I love everything about you.

The only thing I would have been afraid of losing was what's inside your chest, not what's on top of it."

In this moment of weakness, she gave in to his impassioned words. Her lips found his and the contact her body had been craving was satisfied when he pulled her closer. One of his hands disappeared in her hair while the other wrapped around her waist. He tasted like cinnamon. Being in his arms felt like home.

He pressed his lips to her neck and she felt her pulse racing beneath them. He had a way of making her forget about time and place. She had forgotten how her worries disappeared in his embrace. Her fingers slipped under his jacket, over the soft cotton of his shirt.

"Be mine again, Lulu. Tell me you'll let me stay. Promise you won't run away."

What she wouldn't give to be able to make him promises. There were no guarantees in Lucy's life, however. She tried to catch her breath and looked deep into his eyes. His fervent gaze was almost too much.

"I need to tell you about my bad news."

Breathless, Dylan released her and sat back. "What was your bad news?"

She took a deep breath and told him the

truth he deserved. "I got a call today about the results of the mammogram I had done a couple of days ago. It came back abnormal."

"What? But you can't get it again. That's not fair." His voice was thick with emotion. "How can you have it again?"

It was the same argument she had with God earlier in the day. "Most reoccurrences happen in the first five years. It's not that uncommon. That's why many women opt to have a double mastectomy. I foolishly thought I should only do one."

Dylan's head fell back and he stared up at the ceiling. "That's why everyone was freaking out."

"I have to go in for more tests. I'm not certain that it's cancer, but we know how this story ended the last time."

He turned his gaze back on her. "But there's a chance you could be fine?"

She shrugged. "A chance. I'm not betting on it, though."

"I can't believe this." Dylan was lost in his own thoughts. Lucy wished she could climb in his head and hear what he was thinking. It was one thing to say he wanted to be there and another to be faced with the possibility of having to watch her die. The reality of it seemed to be hitting him hard.

"I'm not going to tell you what to do this time, but I'm also not going to let you jump in without taking the time to consider what this means. If the cancer is back, I'm not going to be very fun to be around for a while. There won't be romantic dates or talk of a wedding or starting a family. This won't be a normal relationship, Dylan. This will be hard. Really hard."

He wasn't quick to make false promises. There was no profession of undying love. Dylan sat, absorbing what she had said.

"This time I need you to think about it. Think about what you want. Think about *your* life, not just mine. I have an appointment the day after tomorrow. I'll be at St. Joseph's Center for Cancer Care at ten in the morning. If you come to support me, then I promise not to chase you away. If you aren't there, I'll know where we stand. There won't be any hard feelings. I want you to do what's best for you."

"Okay." He stood up and fidgeted with his tie. "I'll think about it. It's a lot to think about."

"You've got until Friday."

"Friday," he repeated. He reached up to caress her cheek. When he kissed her she wasn't sure if he was trying to tell her he'd see her soon or if he was saying goodbye. It could go either way.

CHAPTER TWENTY-FOUR

FIVE HOURS OF internet research and Dylan knew nothing more than he'd known when he walked out of Lucy's apartment. A woman with cancer in one breast had an increased risk of developing a new cancer in the other. Much more so than a woman who had never had it before. An abnormal mammogram meant that there was the possibility of cancer, but additional tests were usually required to make a diagnosis.

The facts were they wouldn't know anything for sure until the doctors got another look at what was going on. If they found something, there would be more tests to make sure it hadn't spread beyond the breast. If it had spread, that would make it a higher stage.

It took all of Dylan's self-control not to throw his computer across the room. The world was so unfair. Why did bad things happen to good people? Why did they happen over and over to the same good people? He wished cancer was something he could tear apart, stomp out, destroy by whatever means available.

The cancer was only one part of the problem, though. The other concern was the doubt running through his head. Lucy had asked him to think about what he wanted. That was easy—he wanted her. She had asked him to think about his life, not hers. That was a little tougher. When he imagined his life ten to fifteen years from now, he saw him and Lucy running off to a basketball game or dance recital. He imagined being the Tooth Fairy. He dreamed about sleeping beside Lucy every night. When he thought about his life, it always included Lucy and the family he so desperately wanted.

When he tried to picture it with someone other than Lucy, he couldn't. He was certain the only option was to show up to that doctor's appointment. There was no way it could be as bad as Lucy wanted him to believe.

He fell asleep on the couch that night. It was a fitful sleep full of nightmares. He had dreams where he was holding Lucy's hand while the cancer ate her up from the inside out. He sat there helpless while she took her last breath and he woke up in a cold sweat after dreaming about what it would be like to stand beside her grave. He would never survive it in real life.

Maybe Lucy and his mom were right. His feelings were too intense. They made him weak. How could he be any good to Lucy if he wasn't strong enough to let her go? He understood now why she had made the choice to go it alone last time. She didn't need to worry about him while she was trying to fight for her life.

He had been so sure he would have handled everything when she had already survived. The truth was, he had no idea what she had endured. He was angry that she'd left him out, denied him the opportunity to support her, but he hadn't stopped to think about what that really meant. Now Lucy was asking him to decide if he could watch her die. A choice she didn't force him to consider last time, for which he was almost grateful.

It didn't help that he also had his mother's words playing over and over in his head. *Making decisions on temporary feelings is silly and unwise.* But which feelings were temporary? His love for Lucy didn't feel very temporary. His love felt permanent. Was it the fear? Would that fade over time? Could he get over the feelings of sheer terror that overwhelmed him when he imagined seeing her take her last breath?

Clarissa had said something else that stuck with him. Love started out as a feeling but turned into a choice. If that was true, he needed to choose. Love her or leave her. It shouldn't have been so scary, but it was.

THE ONLY THING that could take Dylan's mind off the situation the following morning was working with his hands. Instead of tackling his bedroom, which was at the top of his renovation list, the master bathroom became his next victim. Nothing relieved stress like taking a sledgehammer to a wall. Dylan imagined every tile was a cancer cell and smashed it to smithereens.

Eugene wasn't too happy with him for starting demolition without having a real plan in place, but he let Dylan do what he wanted. He must have sensed this wasn't about needing a new shower.

Dylan wiped the sweat from his forehead. He was breathing heavily from the physical exertion. The shower was completely destroyed. He wouldn't be able to bathe in there until he figured out what he was going to put in its place.

"Do you want to check out some of the ideas I've worked up?" Eugene asked once the shattering and pounding had stopped. He had come upstairs to see what Dylan was doing and went right to work making a plan.

Dylan needed some water, making it a good time for a break. He followed Eugene out into the kitchen, where he had been sketching some plans. Eugene tossed his friend a water bottle from the fridge.

"That's quite a workout, huh?"

Dylan nodded before guzzling down the whole bottle all at once. Jeremy was sprawled out on the couch watching television. He giggled at something a cartoon character said. Dylan envied him. He'd give anything to be carefree.

"I hated that white tile," he said to Eugene. "I don't want any white tile in my new bathroom."

"No white tile. I'll write that down so you don't forget." Eugene pushed a rough sketch in his direction and explained why he thought that layout was the best option. "You can turn this right here into a walk-in closet. That would be nice for resale."

"You thinking about getting rid of me, neighbor?" Dylan challenged.

"I always think in terms of resale. Even if you don't plan to sell it for thirty years."

Eugene always had good ideas. This one was no exception. He changed the floor plan a little bit, made the shower wider and added the closet.

"So what do we do after I clean up in there?" Dylan asked, getting another water bottle.

"Rip up the floor, I guess."

"Good, more demolition."

"Are you okay?" Eugene asked, concern etched in his features.

"Yeah, why?"

"Well, it's a Thursday night. You didn't go to work today. I came home from picking up Jeremy from school to find you taking a sledgehammer to your bathroom with absolutely no plan. I don't know, you tell me why I might wonder if something's wrong."

"I'm fine."

"Any plans to tell me what happened after you left Jeremy's game last night?"

Dylan didn't want to think about last night anymore. He also didn't want to think about what he was going to be doing at ten o'clock tomorrow, but that was all he could think about now that he was finished destroying the bathroom.

Dylan and Eugene rarely spoke about Gwen. Occasionally, Eugene would share a memory or muse about what she would think about something that was going on in the world. He rarely brought up the years when she was sick, and he never spoke about the day she died.

"How do you do it?"

"Do what?"

"Keep going after losing Gwen?"

Eugene clearly wasn't expecting that question. He took a seat at the breakfast bar. "I don't really have a choice. I'm alive and she isn't. That's just the way it is."

"Does it stop hurting or does it feel the same and you become kind of numb to it?" The thought of feeling that much sadness for the rest of his life was unimaginable.

"Why are you thinking about this stuff?"

Dylan glanced over at Jeremy, who wasn't paying their conversation any mind. He lowered his voice anyway. "Lucy had breast cancer five years ago and there's a chance it's back."

Eugene's shoulders slumped forward. "Oh, Dylan. I'm so sorry. Paige said something about her missing work today. I didn't realize it was that serious."

It was serious, all right. "She has an appointment tomorrow to find out for sure. I have to decide if I want to hold her hand through all this or not."

"Is that really a question? Why wouldn't you?"

"What if I'm not...man enough?"

"Man enough to hold her hand?"

"Man enough to watch her die." Saying it out loud didn't make it any less scary.

Eugene's gaze fell back on Jeremy. "That kid over there has dealt with more loss in his eight short years than most people do in a lifetime. His dad walked away, his mother chose a needle over being his mom and then he had to watch his grandma fade away. He's amazingly resilient because he needs to be. If he can be man enough, don't you think you should?"

Dylan felt guilty for forgetting he was the only one in the room who hadn't dealt with real tragedy. "I should. I want to be. I need to know if the pain lessens. I need to know that I'm not going to be miserable the rest of my life."

"That's up to you," Eugene said, pointing a finger at Dylan's chest. "If you want to spend the rest of your life miserable, you will. Does the pain go away? Never. Does it fade a little? Sure. I still wake up every morning and realize Gwen's not here anymore. And it hurts, but I get up and I make Jeremy some breakfast. I drop him off at school and I grocery shop. I watch the Cubs lose and I play cards with the guys over at Willie's. I find reasons to keep living because I figure I was given more time than she was for a reason. Maybe it was to take care of Jer. Maybe it was to make sure my neighbor didn't bust open a pipe and flood our place when he was in the middle of a nervous breakdown. Whatever the reason, it's better to man up than stay in bed missing someone who isn't here."

Dylan could hear his mother now. *Stop being so overdramatic, Dylan.* Eugene seemed to be telling him the same thing.

"I need to get over myself, is that what you're saying?"

Eugene let out a little laugh. "Yeah, sort of."

That seemed like solid advice. Dylan gave his friend a pat on the back. "I'll work on it."

"Good." Eugene twisted his wedding ring around his finger. "For what it's worth, I think you were asking me the wrong question. You should have asked me if I would have given up even one second I had with Gwen before she died."

Dylan knew the answer, but asked anyway. "Would you have given up one second?"

"Not for anything. Every second was a gift, even the ones that ripped my heart out."

Dylan didn't need to decide if he could survive without Lucy. He needed to decide if there was a good reason to give up any of the time they had left. He couldn't think of a single one.

CHAPTER TWENTY-FIVE

LUCY HAD TO tell her mother three times that she didn't need to come to the hospital with her. She had to tell Kendall twice. Emma was working, so she had an excuse for being in the building, but there was no reason she should show her face in the Center for Cancer Care. Emma had to be told only once.

There was only one face Lucy wanted to see in the waiting room today, but there were no guarantees he was going to show. Asking someone to enter into a relationship with no promise of a tomorrow was a lot to ask. There were billions of women in the world. There were so many women who had so much more to offer if Dylan made the decision to move on.

The hospital was already dressed up for Christmas. It didn't seem to matter to the powers-that-be that Thanksgiving was still six days away. They were skipping right over it. Maybe it was a better idea to focus on Christmas cheer rather than asking sick people to think about what they were grateful for.

She pulled her phone out as she walked through the main hall. If Dylan wasn't going to show, the least he could do was call or text her. A little warning would be nice. It was ten minutes to ten. She was supposed to be here fifteen minutes before her appointment, but it had been difficult to pull herself out of bed this morning. Every ache and pain had to be cancer. She had lain awake for hours last night, sure that the twinge in her side was stomach cancer. It had to be.

She glanced around the waiting room when she arrived at the radiology check-in. There were no blond heads in the room. Not a lot of men, period. She tried not to let the disappointment overwhelm her. He was going to go on and have the life she had hoped for him the first time she went through this. She should be happy for him.

The woman behind the desk needed so many different cards and signatures to check a patient in that they should have asked her to come fifteen *hours* before her scheduled time. After dealing with the mountains of paperwork from her cancer treatments, Lucy had considered spending the rest of her life taking on the medical insurance and health care system. It was even more inefficient than the legal system, which was a pretty amazing accomplishment.

Once Lucy had signed away her life and paid her co-pay, she took a seat and prepared herself for the wait ahead. Best-case scenario, they would have the results by Wednesday. The results would make for either the best or the worst Thanksgiving.

She began to wonder how mad her mom would be if she just skipped the holidays this year. Rationally, it was just another day. Eating turkey wasn't some super special event. People did it all the time. Although, if more people knew how turkeys were treated and how inhumane it was to raise those poor, helpless birds with that much meat on them, they would all boycott Thanksgiving.

It was five after ten when she checked her phone again. Seeing the numbers on the screen made it impossible for her to deny that Dylan wasn't coming. There was no way he would show up late to something like this. Late had to mean not coming. He'd made his choice and she had to accept it. She had promised him no hard feelings.

She laughed out loud at herself, earning her

a strange look from the woman seated across from her. Lucy had been so foolish to believe she could have no hard feelings. Dylan was proving what she had believed all along. He couldn't handle this. He didn't love her enough to want to deal with her being sick. This was why she had made the choice for him five years ago. At least then she could pretend he might have stuck with her. Now she had to accept that she wasn't worth the fight.

Out of the corner of her eye, Lucy saw the woman in the corner of the waiting area drop her newspaper for a second before quickly hiding behind it again. Lucy's shoulders fell. She should have figured at least one of them would have ignored her request. The sound of quiet whispering between the woman with the paper and the person sitting back-to-back with her made it clear two of them were bad listeners.

"Text her that you're thinking positive thoughts so she thinks you're at home," Kendall whispered to their mother.

"I can't hold the paper and text at the same time. You text her that we're having breakfast together and thinking about her but can be there in a heartbeat if she needs us."

"Or maybe you should text me how sorry you are for purposely ignoring my request to stay away," Lucy said as she pushed the paper down.

Caught red-handed, Kendall and their mother smiled sweetly up at her. Maureen folded up the paper and set it on her lap. "We're sorry. We just wanted to make sure you weren't alone this time. Don't be mad. We love you."

Kendall sent a text to someone, but just as she hit Send, Emma came in dressed in her hospital scrubs.

"I thought you guys were hiding." Her phone buzzed, and she nodded when she read the message. "Ah, you were busted."

Lucy closed her eyes and prayed for some patience. "What was the plan? Wait to see if Dylan showed, and send in Emma when he didn't, hoping that if I let her be here, I'd invite you all to come?"

Maureen shrugged apologetically. "Sort of."

"I really can't stay," Emma said, giving her a hug. "I was coming to tell you that I love you and I believe it's going to be okay. And if it's not, we're here for you whenever you need us."

"Or whenever I don't need you, apparently."

"You always need us. Don't lie." Emma let go and headed back to the ER.

Lucy sat down next to her mom just as another woman's name was called. Lucy wondered what she was here for. Maybe she was getting her yearly checkup, no big deal. Or maybe she was like Lucy, here because of an abnormal result. Was she feeling as panicked as Lucy? Had she spent an hour last night doing a self-exam, trying to find the lump so she could tell how big it was and self-diagnose what stage she was in?

Clearly, Lucy had not gotten enough sleep. She rested her head on her mom's shoulder. She may have asked her not to come, but since she was here she might as well take advantage. Maureen patted her on the leg.

"Whatever happens, we'll see it through together."

Lucy rubbed her eyes and picked her phone back up. She considered texting Dylan and letting him know she was cool with him not showing. She would wish him well and tell him she hoped he would find a wife and have fifty-one kids. That would show him how not-hard her feelings were. She had her family and they would never desert her.

"Is this seat taken?" Dylan's voice was like something out of her dreams. It took a minute for it to register as the real thing. He was dressed in jeans and a bright blue sweater that matched his eyes. In his hands, he carried two cups and a brown paper bag that smelled like the most delicious cinnamon apples.

Lucy couldn't speak, but her mother had no problem. She jumped up. "Dylan! Here, let me help you."

He handed her one of the drinks and sat down. "I didn't realize the whole gang would be here."

"We aren't staying," Kendall said, getting to her feet.

"Right." Maureen grabbed her purse. "We leave you in good hands, sweetheart," she said, giving Lucy the drink Dylan had brought her. "Positive thoughts."

The family spies gathered their things and scurried out of the waiting room. Dylan watched them go with a curious look. "I didn't scare them away, did I?"

Lucy shook her head. "They weren't supposed to be here in the first place."

"Sorry I was late. I stopped at this café in Logan Square that's known for being organic and was going to buy you tea and a bagel in case you hadn't eaten anything, which if you're like me, you didn't because you were too anxious about how things were going to go. But then I smelled this apple fritter and I was like, she is not going to care if she eats dessert for breakfast on a day like today because carpe diem, right?"

Big, fat tears rolled down her cheeks as he fumbled with his drink and the food. He was here and he'd brought food. He was telling her that he loved her by showing her instead of just saying some empty words. She quickly swiped the tears away as he glanced up and held out a plastic fork.

"We need to eat this while it's hot."

Lucy leaned over and planted a kiss on his lips, which were still cold from being outside. "Thank you, thank you, thank you."

"It's only tea and fritters. No biggie."

She wasn't thanking him for the food, but she could tell he knew that. They ate the apple fritter and drank their tea and Lucy almost forgot she was sitting in the Center for Cancer Care waiting room until the woman called her name. Dylan quickly took her trash and threw it away. As the nurse led them back to the room where they would do the testing, he reached for her hand and threaded their fingers together. He made her feel strong by doing things that were so small.

She was given a gown and directed to a small changing room. Dylan waited patiently for her to return. She felt horribly self-conscious, since he had never seen her without her mastectomy bra insert in. Lying in the hospital bed with nothing but a thin gown covering her, she felt so exposed.

Dylan's gaze stayed firmly fixed on her eyes. He took her hand and placed a couple of kisses on her knuckles. She tried to focus on him and not the reason she was there.

"Nervous?" he asked when she closed her eyes and did a few deep-breathing exercises.

"A little," she lied. "Okay, a lot."

"Me, too. You're going to have to teach me that breathing thing. I probably need to learn that."

Making her laugh did more to relax her than any deep-breathing exercise. The ultrasound technician entered the room and introduced herself. Lucy's stomach began to hurt so badly that she considered asking the woman to rub that wand over her belly to check for stomach cancer, too.

"Whatever happens, I think you're brave and beautiful," Dylan whispered. "I love you."

The ultrasound was a completely painless procedure. The images on the screen only made sense to the technician. Maybe there were cancer cells in there. Maybe not. If the technician knew, she gave no indication. Lucy would have to wait. Thankfully, Dylan was there and he loved her. In the end, that was all that mattered.

"WHERE TO NEXT, Miss Everhart?" Dylan asked, holding her hand as they walked out of the hospital.

She didn't want to be a downer, but she had neglected all of her responsibilities the day before to wallow. She had planned to go to Open Arms.

"I need to go to work."

Dylan didn't seem to like that idea. "I'm pretty sure Paige will understand if you need another day off. Don't make me play hooky by myself."

He was a bad influence, but irresistible when he looked at her with those puppy-dog eyes. "How do you propose we spend the day?"

"Let's go to all the tourist traps and pretend to be from…Nebraska," Dylan suggested. "We'll take selfies and pretend to post them to our Facebook page to make all our friends back in Omaha jealous."

He was crazy, but maybe being silly was exactly what she needed to keep her mind off all things cancer. "Can we be here visiting your eccentric aunt for Thanksgiving?"

"Aunt Philomena? Who else would we be here to see?"

Lucy laughed at his choice of name. "I can't imagine spending Thanksgiving with anyone else. Where to first?"

"The top of the Willis Tower, of course." He pulled her close as they walked out front to grab a cab. Lucy was happy wherever they went as long as they were together.

The two of them hit all of the Chicago highlights. They stood in the glass skybox hanging off the side of the Willis Tower. They ate lunch at the Billy Goat Tavern. Dylan said she couldn't be a vegetarian if they were from Nebraska, so she ordered a cheeseburger. They took pictures with the sea lions at the aquarium and with the stone lions outside the Art Institute.

The last stop before it got dark was Millennium Park and the Bean. Dylan made her pose in front of the giant stainless-steel legume-shaped sculpture with her arms spread wide. It was quite possibly the best visit she had ever had to her hometown.

They walked through Daley Plaza and Maggie Daley Park, heading toward Randolph Street to catch a cab to somewhere warm. Lucy didn't realize where they were until she spotted the first black metal plaque. She led Dylan over to it.

Make a commitment to do everything in your power to help yourself fight the disease.

Lucy read it twice. They had ended up in the Cancer Survivors Garden. Inspirational quotes were posted all around. She remembered when Dylan had brought her there years ago when her mom was fighting the disease.

"I forgot this was over here." She let go of his hand to find the next quote and the next.

Dylan came up behind her and wrapped his arms around her waist. He placed a kiss on one shoulder. "'Have plans for pleasant things to do and goals to accomplish,'" he read off the sign.

"That's good advice." *Keep living. Keep planning. Don't think of this as the end.* She turned to face him and put her arms around his neck. "I plan to be with you."

"That sounds very pleasant," he said with a teasing smile.

"I'm not going to give up. If the cancer is back, then I'll fight and I'll win. That will be my goal."

"No, survival isn't the goal—it's the only outcome we're going to accept. Your goal should be to continue to do pleasant things with me. Daily." He kissed her. "Nightly." He kissed her again.

That was definitely worth fighting for.

CHAPTER TWENTY-SIX

THANKSGIVING AT THE Everharts' was always a huge production. Dylan was overjoyed to be included in their festivities once again. He had missed the raucous laughter and the fabulous home-cooked meal. Lucy joked that her mother thought she was Julia Child on Thanksgiving. She described how the woman brought out things like a potato ricer that never saw the light of day any other time of the year. This year, Maureen had promised something even more extravagant because Dylan's spot at the table was going to be filled once again.

"Can you help your sister by setting the kids' table?" Maureen asked Lucy the moment they walked into the kitchen.

"Well, hello and happy Thanksgiving to you, too, Mom."

"Sorry," she said, giving her daughter a kiss on the cheek. "Hello, happy Thanksgiving. Set the kids' table. Good to see you. I've been up since four in the morning. Don't give me a hard time."

"It smells wonderful in here, Maureen," Dylan said, his arms full of flowers and pumpkin pie.

"Dylan!" Lucy scowled as he got the royal treatment. Maureen stopped everything she was doing to take the flowers from him and thank him for his thoughtfulness. He was quick to give Lucy full credit for baking the pie. It was organic and sugar-free, and he didn't want anyone to think he had anything to do with making it if it turned out to taste terrible.

Emma came into the kitchen carrying a giant fruit bowl. She shooed Lucy out of the way so she could get into the refrigerator. "No one touch this fruit. It's for the Fletchers." Like Dylan and Lucy, who were due at his parents' house for dinner later, Emma and Charlie were splitting the holiday this year. Lucy said her mom didn't mind splitting. Last year, Emma and Charlie were in Colorado and that had made their mother a little depressed.

"You're bringing them a fruit bowl? What did you bring for us?" Maureen asked.

"You told me you had it all under control.

Why would I bring something when you told me you had everything?"

"You could have been creative and brought something no one would expect," her mother suggested as she opened the oven to baste the turkey.

Emma rolled her eyes. "Watch out, Mom. Your crazy is showing. You might want to cover that up in front of Dylan."

Maureen shot her a glare that sent Emma running for the safety of the family room, where the men were all watching football.

"Is there anything I can do to help?" Dylan offered. He wanted her to know how much he appreciated being there.

"No, no. You go watch the game while Lucy helps her sister set the kids' table." Her voice rose with every word until she was practically shouting.

Her mother earned herself another eye roll. Lucy took the turkey paper plates into the dining room, where Kendall was setting the adult table. Dylan followed her anyway. He still felt a little out of place.

"Hey, happy Thanksgiving," Kendall said, giving her big sister a hug. Lucy plopped the two paper plates on the small card table. Simon and Max's son, Aidan, had the table to themselves, since Kendall's daughter was still in a high chair. Dylan couldn't help but picture a couple blue- or green-eyed towheads sitting around the tiny card table someday.

"Done," Lucy announced. "That was tough. I'd better go sit down. I don't want to over-exert myself."

The third eye roll of the day came from Kendall. "Thanks so much for the help."

"Let me finish this up," Dylan suggested. "Do you want to help in the kitchen? Your mom looks like she has her hands full and I barely know how to boil water. I think I'm better off helping with the forks and spoons."

Kendall shook her head. "I can't go in the kitchen. The smells are getting to me." Dylan noticed her place a hand on her stomach. *Interesting.* "I have this under control. Don't worry."

"Let's go say hello to everyone else," Lucy said, pullig him into the family room. She seemed all too happy to escape any work.

The men and children were all watching football, but welcomed the new guests. Max sat on the floor with his son on one side, Simon on the other and the baby on his lap. He was teaching the boys about the game of football and they managed to pay attention for about two minutes before they asked if they could go down to the basement, where their grandma kept all the toys.

"Where's Jeremy having Thanksgiving?" Simon asked as they got to their feet.

"Your aunt Lulu's friend Ms. Clayton invited Jeremy and his grandpa over for some turkey this year," Dylan replied. Eugene and Paige continued to test the waters. Their friendship had great potential, but they had been taking it slow. Spending a holiday together was a big step for them. "I usually eat at Jer's house, so it's a good thing your grandma let me come over here."

"Maybe next year we can all have Thanksgiving together," Simon suggested.

"The more the merrier," Lucy said with a smile. She was in such a good mood today. It looked good on her.

There was a big play in the football game. Mr. Everhart nearly jumped out of his chair. Charlie tried to look as if he was following the game but his mind was obviously somewhere else. He kept checking the time on his phone and patted his pants pocket at least a dozen times as if he was making sure something was still there. *Very interesting.*

"Lucy, can you grab some water bottles out of the garage?" her mother called from the kitchen.

She grabbed Dylan's hand and shouted that they'd take care of it. As soon as she got him in the garage, she planted a kiss on his lips. He wrapped his arms around her waist.

"What was that for?"

"I like having you here. Thank you for coming." Her eyes sparkled and her lips curled in the sweetest smile.

"Thank you for inviting me. I missed spending the holidays with your family."

"We're going to make sure you spend all of them with us, then." She threw her arms around his neck and kissed his cheek.

Dylan hugged her tight. "I like that idea. I'm never letting you go, Lulu."

"Good," she said even though she slipped away and hoisted a case of water bottles off the floor.

"Let me help you with that." He reached for the water.

"I got it. It's not like I'm helpless or with child or something. You can open the door for me."

Dylan obliged. There was no arguing with her. "Speaking of being with child…" He lowered his voice. "Twenty bucks says Kendall's expecting."

Lucy's eyes went wide. "No way."

"Way."

"No way. She would have told me."

Dylan shrugged. He was sure he was right. "I think Charlie's going to pop the question, too."

"Shut up." Lucy was not buying any of this.

"He's got a ring. Front right pocket."

"You were in the same room as him for less than five minutes."

"Take the bet, then."

"You're on," she said, shoving the case of water into his arms and heading back inside the house. This was going to be the easiest twenty dollars he ever made.

Maureen planned lunch to fall perfectly during halftime. Everyone gathered around the table. The adults passed the food around while Kendall and Max helped the kids get settled. Before everyone could dig in, Maureen raised a glass. Dylan noticed that everyone at the table had been poured a glass of wine except for Kendall.

"I want you all to know that your dad and I are so thankful that everyone could be here today. We love you all so very much."

Kendall tipped her glass in her mother's direction. "I want to thank Mom for this wonderful meal. You really outdid yourself this year."

Everyone raised their glass to that and Maureen got a little misty-eyed. Dylan nudged Lucy under the table and nodded toward Kendall's water, raising his eyebrows. She shook her head. Still unwilling to admit he was right.

"We also have a little announcement to make while we have everyone here," Kendall continued. Dylan could see Lucy accept her defeat.

"Max and I are expecting again."

Maureen shrieked and all the women got up to hug Kendall and Max. Dylan could tell this might not have been a planned pregnancy but was a welcome surprise for both expectant parents. Max beamed with pride as he accepted hugs from his sisters-in-law.

"I have something I want to say before we eat, too," Charlie said, pushing his chair back and rising to his feet.

Dylan covered his mouth with his fist and whispered to Lucy, "I win."

Lucy scowled.

"I just want to thank you guys for welcoming me into your family the way you have. I am so fortunate that not only did I find the most amazing woman in the world, but I have been blessed with some pretty amazing future in-laws. At least, I hope you'll be my in-laws."

With that, Charlie dropped to one knee, causing Emma to gasp. There was no way this had been part of her plan for the day. He presented her with a ring box, opening it and making her cry at the same time.

"Nightingale, I want to spend all my todays, tomorrows and forevers with you. You are my best friend. My true love. You ready to marry me?"

Emma didn't have to think about it. She screamed yes and proceeded to jump on her giant of a fiancé, knocking him back and sending the kids' table toppling over.

Green beans scattered across the wood floor. Mashed potatoes and stuffing splattered. Gravy was everywhere. The little boys thought it was hilarious. The Everharts' dog couldn't get enough. Kendall argued that Emma should have to clean it up.

"I just got engaged! I can't get my new ring dirty." Emma let Charlie slide the engagement ring onto her finger. It was likely she would spend the entire day staring at that thing.

"Lucy, help your sister clean up the mess, please," Maureen said, rising to give Emma and Charlie a hug.

"I didn't knock the table over," Lucy complained.

"I'll help," Dylan and Max said at the same time.

"I got it," their dad said as he lifted the table back into place. Luckily, the little turkey plates didn't hold that much food.

Dylan and Max cleaned up the mess while the women all congratulated Emma and Charlie. The sisters were genuinely happy for them. Lucy always spoke highly of Charlie—not so much of his nicknames for everyone, but of his character and his love for her sister.

"Well, since we're making announcements," Lucy said once everyone sat back down. "I have one."

Even Dylan was curious. Had she bet him that she had a secret to share, he would have lost. It was just like her to be the one person whose mind he couldn't read.

"I got a call yesterday from the doctor." The entire room went dead silent. Even the baby quieted down. All eyes were on Lucy, all ears were waiting to hear the results. Dylan grabbed her hand under the table, his heart in his throat. "Turns out the shadow they saw was nothing. I'm fine. There's no lump, no cancer."

Maureen's hands covered her mouth as a

new batch of joyful tears glistened in her eyes. Everyone else let out a cheer. Dylan nearly fell out of his chair.

No cancer. It was the best news he'd heard in his entire life.

"Why didn't you tell me?" he asked her. He'd figured they were going to have to wait until after the holiday weekend for some news. He was trying to be optimistic, but the longer they waited, the more worried he got.

"I wanted to tell everyone I loved at the same time," she answered simply. He could handle being lumped into that group.

The sisters all had another round of hugging. The food was going to be cold by the time they ate it, but it didn't seem that anyone would care. Not with the kind of news being shared.

Lucy wasn't finished with her surprises. "I've decided I'm going to go ahead and have surgery, though. I don't want to go through this anymore. I don't think I can handle the worrying and the wondering."

She glanced around the room, but her gaze landed on Dylan. She seemed to be checking for a reaction. Maybe she was still nervous about how he would feel about it. She was worrying for nothing.

He leaned over and kissed her. "I think that's a great idea. The safer you are, the better."

Mr. Everhart stood up and cleared his throat. There was one more toast to be had before they could eat.

"I thank God for this food. I thank God for this family. We have all suffered our share of tribulations. But as I look around this room and I listen to the news you've all had to share, my heart swells because we are truly blessed."

He held his glass up high as did the rest of the family. Dylan relished being a part of the big, crazy family. Someday it would be them making the announcement that they were engaged or pregnant. Dylan felt that was a real possibility now. Even better, he was sure Lucy believed they could have it, as well.

* * * * *

LARGER-PRINT BOOKS!

GET 2 FREE
LARGER-PRINT NOVELS
PLUS 2 FREE
MYSTERY GIFTS

Love Inspired®

Larger-print novels are now available...

YES! Please send me 2 FREE LARGER-PRINT Love Inspired® novels and my 2 FREE mystery gifts (gifts are worth about $10). After receiving them, if I don't wish to receive any more books, I can return the shipping statement marked "cancel." If I don't cancel, I will receive 6 brand-new novels every month and be billed just $5.49 per book in the U.S. or $5.99 per book in Canada. That's a savings of at least 19% off the cover price. It's quite a bargain! Shipping and handling is just 50¢ per book in the U.S. and 75¢ per book in Canada.* I understand that accepting the 2 free books and gifts places me under no obligation to buy anything. I can always return a shipment and cancel at any time. Even if I never buy another book, the two free books and gifts are mine to keep forever.

122/322 IDN GH6D

Name	(PLEASE PRINT)

Address		Apt. #

City	State/Prov.	Zip/Postal Code

Signature (if under 18, a parent or guardian must sign)

Mail to the **Reader Service:**
IN U.S.A.: P.O. Box 1867, Buffalo, NY 14240-1867
IN CANADA: P.O. Box 609, Fort Erie, Ontario L2A 5X3

**Are you a current subscriber to Love Inspired® books
and want to receive the larger-print edition?
Call 1-800-873-8635 or visit www.ReaderService.com.**

* Terms and prices subject to change without notice. Prices do not include applicable taxes. Sales tax applicable in N.Y. Canadian residents will be charged applicable taxes. Offer not valid in Quebec. This offer is limited to one order per household. Not valid to current subscribers to Love Inspired Larger-Print books. All orders subject to credit approval. Credit or debit balances in a customer's account(s) may be offset by any other outstanding balance owed by or to the customer. Please allow 4 to 6 weeks for delivery. Offer available while quantities last.

Your Privacy—The Reader Service is committed to protecting your privacy. Our Privacy Policy is available online at www.ReaderService.com or upon request from the Reader Service.

We make a portion of our mailing list available to reputable third parties that offer products we believe may interest you. If you prefer that we not exchange your name with third parties, or if you wish to clarify or modify your communication preferences, please visit us at www.ReaderService.com/consumerchoice or write to us at Reader Service Preference Service, P.O. Box 9062, Buffalo, NY 14240-9062. Include your complete name and address.

LILP15

LARGER-PRINT BOOKS!

GET 2 FREE
LARGER-PRINT NOVELS
PLUS 2 FREE
MYSTERY GIFTS

Love Inspired®

SUSPENSE
RIVETING INSPIRATIONAL ROMANCE

Larger-print novels are now available...

YES! Please send me **The Montana Mavericks Collection** in Larger Print. This collection begins with 3 FREE books and 2 FREE gifts (gifts valued at approx. $20.00 retail) in the first shipment, along with the other first 4 books from the collection! If I do not cancel, I will receive 8 monthly shipments until I have the entire 51-book Montana Mavericks collection. I will receive 2 or 3 FREE books in each shipment and I will pay just $4.99 US/ $5.89 CDN for each of the other four books in each shipment, plus $2.99 for shipping and handling per shipment.*If I decide to keep the entire collection, I'll have paid for only 32 books, because 19 books are FREE! I understand that accepting the 3 free books and gifts places me under no obligation to buy anything. I can always return a shipment and cancel at any time. My free books and gifts are mine to keep no matter what I decide.

263 HCN 2404   463 HCN 2404

Name	(PLEASE PRINT)	
Address		Apt. #
City	State/Prov.	Zip/Postal Code
Signature (if under 18, a parent or guardian must sign)		

Mail to the **Reader Service:**

IN U.S.A.: P.O. Box 1867, Buffalo, NY 14240-1867
IN CANADA: P.O. Box 609, Fort Erie, Ontario L2A 5X3

* Terms and prices subject to change without notice. Prices do not include applicable taxes. Sales tax applicable in N.Y. Canadian residents will be charged applicable taxes. This offer is limited to one order per household. All orders subject to approval. Credit or debit balances in a customer's account(s) may be offset by any other outstanding balance owed by or to the customer. Please allow 4 to 6 weeks for delivery. Offer available while quantities last. Offer not available to Quebec residents.

Your Privacy—The Reader Service is committed to protecting your privacy. Our Privacy Policy is available online at www.ReaderService.com or upon request from the Reader Service.

We make a portion of our mailing list available to reputable third parties that offer products we believe may interest you. If you prefer that we not exchange your name with third parties, or if you wish to clarify or modify your communication preferences, please visit us at www.ReaderService.com/consumerschoice or write to us at Reader Service Preference Service, P.O. Box 9062, Buffalo, NY 14269. Include your complete name and address.

READERSERVICE.COM

Manage your account online!

- Review your order history
- Manage your payments
- Update your address

We've designed the Reader Service website just for you.

Enjoy all the features!

- Discover new series available to you, and read excerpts from any series.
- Respond to mailings and special monthly offers.
- Connect with favorite authors at the blog.
- Browse the Bonus Bucks catalog and online-only exculsives.
- Share your feedback.

Visit us at:

ReaderService.com

LARGER-PRINT BOOKS!
GET 2 FREE LARGER-PRINT NOVELS PLUS
2 FREE GIFTS!

HARLEQUIN®

super romance®

More Story...More Romance